THE GIRL I LEFT BEHIND

A GRIPPING PSYCHOLOGICAL THRILLER

LE HILL

TIDE END PRESS

PROLOGUE

Every day, since it happened, I have talked to you in my head as I went about my day. I couldn't imagine not telling you what I'd had for breakfast or how I was thinking about colouring my hair and what shade did you think suited me best?

When I was working at the hospital it was easy to find a quiet moment where I would sit with my coffee in the stuffy staffroom and tell you about what had been happening. Do you remember crazy Mrs Peters in ward four with the extremely handsome son? And the actor who caught his nether regions in the door (or so he said). I knew you would have loved to hear the silly work gossip and I would sit there smiling as I told you. Then someone would come in and shatter the peace by scraping the chairs and banging the cupboards as they looked for teabags or biscuits.

I loved walking through the park on the way home, watching the birds and the changing seasons and colours, and thinking about you and how much you were missing. I remember how much you always loved my stories Julie, even when you were little, and everyone always said I had a great imagination. For a long time, I didn't need anything or anyone else. I went to work and came home and didn't see anyone else. And I was happy with that because I knew you were always there for me.

Then I met Elliot and for a while I just wanted to take a break from you Julie. It wasn't that I stopped loving you or anything like that. You'll always be my sister. I just wanted the chance to do something different and to try to be normal. I enjoyed being part of a couple and having a boyfriend who treated me nicely and took me to the cinema and for romantic walks along the beach. I didn't want to share that time with anyone, not even you. For a while I just wanted to forget. Because if I'm honest, until then I had been so very lonely.

Then I fell pregnant and I watched in amazement at my belly swelling more and more each day. I was going to have my own family which I had craved for so very long. When Emma arrived I just wanted to spend every second with her, nuzzling my nose into her fluffy hair and inhaling her powdery scent. She is the best thing that has ever happened to me. I've been so preoccupied by her that somehow, I've pushed you to the back of my mind, rather than the front where you always used to be.

Yet despite my overwhelming love for Emma I have to admit, and I know I can tell you anything Julie, is that I'm not entirely happy. I love Elliot and Emma and I know how lucky I am. But I feel sad and I don't feel normal. I think about Mum a lot and what she went through. Now that I have my own daughter it has given me a different perspective on things. I feel a whole myriad of emotions. I feel sorry for her, guilty about what happened to her but I'm also angry. I am so very angry. Not just with her but with him. That's why I needed to start talking to you again Julie. There's nobody else I can talk to about this and that's why I'm reconnecting with you. I need to tell you what's been happening. I need to tell you what I'm going to do.

I've been back in the UK now for a few weeks. I can't quite believe that it's been nearly twelve years since I left. Sydney feels like home now and we will definitely go back. We're just here for a year so Elliot can get some international experience under his belt. He always wanted to work in London and when the opening came up at the newspaper, his editor asked if he would be interested. We decided it would be a great opportunity for us as a family and also for his career. But I was excited too. I've been wanting to come to London for some time now. I've some unfinished business I need to attend to.

I hope by telling you all this, it will help me make sense of things Julie. And I hope that one day we can become close again. I know we will be together again one day. I miss you so much. I loved you as much as anyone could love their little sister. Except I would say that I loved you even more.

1

PRESENT

The last time I spoke to James MacIntyre M.P. was the day after my mother died. I called to let him know out of courtesy, given they had been married for more than a decade. His tone was curt — empathy and compassion were never among his strong points — and he said he was sorry. I wondered what for. He didn't come to her funeral or even send flowers.

Today, twelve years later, I am making my way to Portcullis House to see him again. He is expecting me, Sophie Lewis, a campaigner for a new children's charity. He thinks he's going to get some easy headlines, some good publicity. But he's in for a big surprise.

I'm still in awe of myself for having the guts to do this. I can't believe that I am here and so close to him after all this time. As I make my way through the entrance, I focus on the sound of my heels clicking on the polished floor. I'm longing to pause and really savour the moment, but a security guard points me towards the X-ray scan and I hand over my bag to have it searched. As I smile at the guard, I notice that he's really quite good looking, I think about the kitchen knife I'd considered packing. Would it have set the alarms off immediately? Would I have been carted off the premises and branded a threat to national security? I continue to smile as he deftly plucks out my make-up bag, spare tissues, chewing gum, an old banana — at which he grimaces —some crayons and a few random bits of Lego. He raises a well-groomed eyebrow as he hands back my bag. As I turn away I notice him wiping his hands on his trousers and see the shiny trail of squashed banana that is now on the crease of his slacks.

Walking towards the lifts, I stare up at the atrium ceiling above, still not quite believing I am here. There's a hum of chatter all around and people clutch sheaves of paper to their chest as they stride past me trying their best to look as though they are hurrying to an important meeting. I suspect most of them are on their way to the toilet or just upping their daily step count. The throng of folk milling around is strangely reassuring though.

'Ms Lewis,' I hear a voice behind me call.

Spinning round I see a petite woman with long brown hair emerging from the lift and walking towards me smiling. 'Yes.' I breathe a huge sigh of relief.

'I'm Joy Hughes. Mr MacIntyre's assistant.' She extends her hand to shake mine. 'Delighted that you could make it here. Let me show you to his office.'

I follow her and politely answer the questions she is asking about the children's charity that I am setting up. But as she chats away, I feel panic descend. My tongue swells inside my mouth, my armpits are dripping and oh God is that my own sweat I can smell? Have I really forgotten to put on deodorant? I'm now gripped with disgust at my careless personal hygiene. I wonder if I can go to the toilet and freshen myself up. But it's all I can do just to follow Joy's path. My eyes focus on her hair which is curled down her back in a long ponytail, and I have an urge to reach out and touch it.

'This is us right here,' says Joy as she turns to me, just as I pull my hand back, and she ushers me towards a small office off the wide corridor we're in. 'Can I get you a tea or coffee?

'Just some water please.' I am trying to work out what the familiar smell is which is creeping up my nostrils and fighting for attention with my BO. My nose crinkles in disgust as I sniff it in again just to make sure. It's that after-shave. He's still wearing the same cloying aftershave.

'Mr MacIntyre will see you now,' says Joy, opening the office door.

I clutch my handbag to my body and feel the beginning of bile starting to swish around the pit of my stomach.

Joy cocks her head to the side. 'Are you okay, Ms Lewis?'

I try to visualise myself moving forward and take a deep breath. All I can focus on is the empty arch of the door. Crossing over that threshold will change things for ever.

I manage to nod but I can feel my legs starting to shake beneath me. *Sophie Lewis* pull yourself together.

'Ms Lewis?' Joy is now clicking her teeth together, and walking towards me. 'Are you okay? You've gone very pale.'

I grab the back of a chair. 'I think I need to use your loo. I do feel a bit faint all of a sudden.'

She frowns and glances at her watch. 'Of course.' There is a tense smile on her face. 'Come right this way.'

In the cubicle, I sit on the toilet, my trousers and pants gathered around my ankles. I try to breathe deeply as I pee. I give myself a few moments, just sitting there, before creeping out towards the washbasins. Then I splash cool water over my face and wash my hands. Rummaging around in my handbag for my brush and some perfume, my hand meets the squashed banana. Yuck. I do my best to pat my messy hair down. The chalky pallor of my face doesn't really help to create the radiant, confident look I was trying to achieve. Oh well, I tell my reflection, better head out there for round two. I walk back outside and towards Joy who is now craning her neck to check I'm coming. She smiles in relief.

'All okay,' she says. More of a statement than a question.

'Yes, fine thanks.' She would be disgusted if I told her the truth.

'Come on then, Mr MacIntyre is waiting for you and he has another appointment straight after.'

Forcing myself to take a step forward and then another, I see MacIntyre come towards me confidently, smiling and ready to greet his visitor. Then there is a brief moment when panic flutters across his face. Does he look perplexed? His musky scent is back now, invading my nose, and it's getting stronger. There he is. Dressed in a navy suit, with a crisp white shirt and a red tie. He's maybe a bit greyer round the edges and is that a paunch I can see gently nudging at his belt? But there is no doubt about it. It is him. Just an older version. It is James MacIntyre. I try and relish the moment I've been anticipating for so long. I don't feel how I imagined I always would when I came face to face with him again. Strangely, the numbness is still there, but as we move towards each other I feel plain scared. I notice the worry in his face has now been replaced by a smile. A smirking, stupid grimace which intermittently appears, as if he has a beeper in his pocket reminding him to do it. Yet, let's face it, he has fooled all the voters and everyone for years so it must work for some. Never me though. As I stand just a few inches away from him, the man who invaded my sleep, dreams and nightmares for years it all feels surreal. I still can't believe I've made it.

'Mr MacIntyre.' I stare straight at his dark eyes.

'Come. Come in,' he says not breaking my gaze as a look of confusion crosses his face. 'Sophie, is it?'

My memories are now flooding back, the bile is rising and as he reaches his hairy hand out towards me I promptly vomit all over his feet.

2

PAST

I was singing along to *The Spice Girls' Two Become One* and trying to do some English revision when Mum rushed into my bedroom, her face flushed, her hands covered in flour. 'Julie's not back yet,' she said, her voice tense. 'I just saw the time. Do you know what she was doing after school? Did she say she was going somewhere?' I closed my book, *Kidnapped,* one of my favourites, and reached over to turn off the radio. 'Um, no. I don't think so.' I could hear the water trickling through my radiator.

'Where is she? Where could she be?' She was wringing her hands together and I tried not to wince at the puff of flour which floated onto my lavender carpet.

'I'm sure she's fine, Mum.' I hoped my voice was soothing. 'She's probably on her way home. Or maybe she's gone to the library?'

'But it's dark.' She stared at me, blankly. Then shook her head and stomped out the room.

That's the thing with Mum. She always flew into a panic at the slightest thing that might happen. Not the things that were actually happening around her at that moment. She worried about what *might* go wrong. I heard her go into the bathroom and turn on the taps. I knew she'd be rinsing her hands and splashing water over her flushed cheeks. The tactics she used to try and calm herself down. They wouldn't work, though, and soon she'd move onto her next strategy. A glass of wine. I heard her yank the bathroom door open, then a moment later the front door slammed. There was the thwack of a bag on the hall floor. Julie, my little sister, was back.

Mum clattered down the stairs. 'Where have you been?' she screeched.

'Sorry, Mum. I was at the library.' Julie's voice was breezy. 'I lost track of time.'

I uncurled myself from my beanbag and padded onto the landing, loitering and listening.

'Okay, dear. Sorry — I must have forgotten you said that. You gave me an awful fright.'

'Sorry, Mum,' she said again. 'I didn't mean to scare you.'

I peeked over the rails and watched Mum hugging Julie in a way she never did with me. She kissed the top of her head and then walked into the kitchen. I could hear her pouring herself a glass of wine even though the drama was over. I looked at Julie as she breathed a huge sigh of relief, slipped off her jacket, hung it on the bannister and then skipped up the stairs. I backed away so she couldn't see me until she was at the top. She was smiling, her face bright and animated, her eyes sparkling. I stood, my arms folded, and when she saw me the grin slid from her mouth because she knew that I knew she hadn't been anywhere near the library. Julie was up to something. I could always tell when my sister was lying.

3

PRESENT

Somehow, I manage to get myself away from Portcullis House to the underground and take the first tube I can squeeze on to. I slump in a corner seat, my head down and my gaze fixed on the ground. How could that have all gone so wrong? I thought I would just walk in there and confront him and . . . well, to be honest I didn't really think about what would happen next. Why, oh why did I think it would be a good idea?

When the train pulls into Richmond station I wait for everyone to walk off ahead of me. My stomach is still contracting in spasms and I decide I need to eat and try and calm myself down before I go to collect Emma from school. I'm desperate for a fag or a strong drink but opt for the nearest Starbucks where I order myself a ham panini and a latte. Sitting in a quiet corner I run through the events of the morning in my head once again. Am I going mad? Did I make all of this up? I think about Elliot, and what he will say. The thought of him usually calms me down and I can feel my breath slowing again. Until I realise how shocked he will be that I have kept this huge thing a secret from him, and I clench my hands tighter around the mug. If only I could have kept the door on my past closed. I urge myself to breathe slowly. Just breathe slowly and calm down.

To think that just a few weeks ago my life in Sydney was utterly normal and straight-forward. Part of me wishes I could rewind and be sitting outside my favourite cafe, with a warm breeze ruffling my hair. Not sitting here watching pigeons hop about the damp concourse wondering if this morning actually happened. Now, as I bite into the salty sandwich and take a sip of my lukewarm latte I am starting to wonder if confronting James was such a good idea. Perhaps I should have tried to stay anonymous. But then I've been through this so many times. I want closure from it all and most of all I want revenge. James MacIntyre was my step-father. He married my mother when I was a little girl and he always *said* he loved me as his own daughter. But I hate him. He ruined my life and my family and he was the reason my daughter won't ever know her maternal grandmother or her aunt. Emma. Shit. I look at my watch and realise that if I'm going to get to her school on time I'd better run.

It's now approaching 3pm and as I make my way to Emma's school. I can finally feel a sense of joy and elation washing over me. She's in the reception class, but in my eyes she is very much still a baby. At four she seems too young to be at school. Yet she seems to have taken it all in her stride. We've only been living in London for a few weeks after relocating from Sydney with Elliot's job. He is a journalist and when he was offered the chance to spend some time in his newspaper's London office, I encouraged him to go for it. It's been ten years since I left Glasgow, where I was brought up, for a fresh start in Australia. I never ever thought I would return. However, motherhood has unsettled me and shaken my resolve. I mean, having Emma has been amazing but being a mum and responsible for this precious girl has made me think once again about my own childhood. It's made me think long and hard about things I would rather leave buried in the past. But I can't keep them hidden any longer. I need to deal with them so I can finally move on.

I stand waiting in my usual spot, just outside the classroom door, making sure I avoid everyone's gaze. As I weigh up options on macaroni cheese or fish and chips for dinner, I glance up to see a woman marching towards me. She's wearing a white trench coat, which makes her look like a dentist, and her hair has obviously been recently styled as it remains welded in place despite the forceful breeze which has gathered pace this afternoon. I dig my hands further into my pockets, feeling the lint and crumbs bed themselves under my fingernails. I glance away and then back, and my eyes briefly meet her steely glare. As she forces a smile I flicker my eyes towards the ground watching the scuffed toes of my Converse trainers move slowly, one then the other like I'm treading through treacle. Then I feel a hand clamp my shoulder from behind and I freeze.

'Excuse me,' says a clipped voice from behind.

I turn around to face the owner of the hand. It's the woman in the dentist's coat and she is clutching a navy-blue clipboard in her other hand.

I try to smile. 'Hi.'

'Hello . . . You must be one of the mums in the Elf class?' she says brightly.

I nod.

'Name?'

'My name?'

'No,' she says with a withering shake of her head. 'Your child's name.'

'Emma. She's called Emma. Lewis.'

I notice that the clip-board has a bundle of white paper attached. They are fluttering in the breeze and she keeps jabbing at them with her long, manicured fingers.

'Mmmmm. Emma Lewis .... Where is she? Ah yes,' she says nodding and then ticks her name off with a fancy ball-point pen which seems to be an extension of those fingers. 'Super. That's great.'

'And you are?' I ask, finally managing to string some words together.

'Oh, I am sorry. Of course. Let me introduce myself. I'm Davina Rossiter. Class rep. I'm in charge of organising all the social events.'

Social events. For four-year-olds? 'Ah, I see.' I smile. 'Is that for the discos and nights outs for the kids?'

'No,' she says, her voice now becoming clipped. 'The social events for the parents. There is a very big tradition of it here at Spencer School.'

'Oh,' I manage to puff.

'Look,' she points over to a tall woman striding towards us. 'Here is Lucinda. She's my co-worker for the year and will be helping me to co-ordinate it all.'

Co-worker? I frown. What is this woman going on about? I stare as a woman dressed in slim-fitting jeans, high-heeled boots, and a teal wool coat glides over towards us.

'Hello.' She grins and shakes my hand firmly. 'I'm Lucinda. Hope Davina's not frightening you off with her clip-board. Davina, you look like you're ready to lead a tour group around a stately home.'

I stifle a giggle as Lucinda winks at me. Davina glares at both of us.

'Lucinda. Meet Sophie.'

'Hello Sophie,' said Lucinda.'

'Sophie Lewis. My daughter is Emma.'

'Ah yes. I am sure Daisy has mentioned Emma,' she says. 'We must get them together for a little play.

'That would be lovely,' I say.

'Yes. Though we haven't got your details yet,' says Davina as if she is talking to a small child.

'Details? What details do you want?' I ask.

'I am composing a list of all parents of children in Elf class, with all the parents' addresses, phone numbers and email addresses and then I will circulate it to everyone. Just makes it all *so* much easier for planning things.' She sighs.

'What sort of things?' I ask, but my question seems to float over the top of her caramel-highlighted bob.

'Parties, social events.' Again, she speaks as if addressing a small and very stupid child.

Lucinda raises an eyebrow and then .... does she wink at me? I'm beginning to like her, despite myself.

'Okay . . . I live at is 84 Muirfield Avenue. I don't remember the postcode — we haven't been here long.'

Lucinda laughs. 'I don't believe it. That's just around the corner from me.'

'Oh . . .' I start and then become distracted when I see Emma's face light up when she sees me. She's clutching a pile of drawings as well as her book bag and water bottle, and just looks so small. She runs towards me and I sink to my knees, ignoring the sharp crumbs of tarmac pressing into my kneecaps. For a moment, I think it's my little sister running towards me. That blonde curly hair and the big smile. Then as she gets closer, she looks more like my Emma. She throws her hands around my neck and I bury my nose in the soft skin of her neck.

'Hello poppet,' I say, clasping my arms around her.

'I'm hungry, Mummy — have you brought a snack?' she

says, her wide brown eyes staring up at me like little pools of chocolate. 'Snack, Mummy, I want a snack please.'

I open my bag and fumbled around for a small packet of yogurt-raisins. All I can find is that squashed banana.

'Thanks, Mummy,' she says, not even complaining slightly.

'Come on sweetie pie. Let's get you home and all organised for your swimming class.' Then I remember Davina and Lucinda and say, 'Lovely to meet you both.' I suddenly feel exhausted as events of earlier slip back into my mind. Emma grips onto my hand and I let my shoulders relax. I must focus on this little girl now, I tell myself. Until I work out what to do next. Elliot knows nothing of my past. He thinks all my relatives are dead.

4

PAST

Julie and I went into town today on our own. We took the train into Queen Street station and I laughed when I saw her crumple up her nose as we stepped onto the platform. The rush of warm air from the tunnel opposite brought a waft of stale pee, farts and rotting rubbish. We climbed the steps, panting and giggling and rushed out into the fresh air and round the row of waiting black taxis that looked like a row of shiny cockroaches. Mum gave us money for our lunch and we were going to go to McDonald's. I loved their burgers. We had also raided our money boxes. I managed to scrape together about eight pounds and Julie, who was always better than me with money, had fifteen pounds. We walked up Sauchiehall Street. Julie stared up at the street signs in awe. She wanted to go to Dorothy Perkins for a new top, so we dashed in and collected a pile of turquoise, pink and sparkly fabrics and headed to a changing room. It was one of those big communal rooms I hated. The lights were harsh, the mirrors reflected every single inch of you to everyone. Julie wasn't bothered though. Maybe it was just me, because my body was changing. I was so self-conscious of my growing hips and boobs. She asked me what I thought when she tried on a bright pink T-shirt. Her long hair cascaded down her back and her eyes sparkled even more than usual. She grinned when I told her she looked beautiful. I tried on an emerald green top which had little daisies stitched into the neckline. Julie smiled and nodded. It suits you, she said. Then she looked away. I asked her what was wrong and she turned and said she wished she looked like me.

I told my sister she was beautiful and desperately tried to keep away the wild panic I could feel rising from the pit of my stomach. I grabbed her and hugged her hard, staring at my reflection in the mirror illuminated under the strip lighting. I looked away and instead focused on the dirty patches on the white embossed wallpaper. I wondered if she had something to tell me. 'You are wonderful, Julie. Just always be yourself.' I made myself smile at her and said we should go and look at the necklaces and bangles. She giggled and I followed her out of the changing rom and to the corner of the shop where a multi-coloured tower of cheap bead necklaces and bracelets stood.

I didn't want my little sister to look up to me. I didn't want her to be like me. I hated being me. I didn't like being fifteen. I didn't like being in my life. I wished I could be the girl in *Dallas* or my *Sweet Valley High* books — the one with long blonde hair and a perfect figure — be smart and live in a place where it is sunny all the time. I wished I had parents called Chad and Molly who were good-looking and always smiled at me with their perfect, straight white teeth.

I felt like my life was different shades of grey. I felt like I was treading through a big bog which I couldn't get out of. I didn't want Julie to feel like that, ever. I wanted her to be happy. I wanted her to have sunshine and shades of yellow. I wished *I* was like *her*. I wished I wasn't me. I grabbed her hand and said we should go and get some lunch.

5

PRESENT

Depending on the time of day, the stained glass of our front-door casts a lovely glow across the hallway. I'm sitting on the top landing just outside Emma's bedroom watching the rainbow colours dance across the floorboards. Emma's safely tucked up in bed and fast asleep. My head is thumping but I somehow managed to get through the rest of the day, do a load of washing, cook spaghetti bolognese for dinner and hold a conversation with a stressed neighbour who rang my doorbell just before Emma had her bath. She'd lost her cat and wanted to check with me whether I'd seen it. I tried to nod sympathetically but my stomach was a twisting mess and the throb behind my eyes was about to explode. Fortunately, Emma appeared sleepily rubbing her eyes and so the neighbour took the hint.

Now I'm wondering what on earth I should tell Elliot. How can I ever begin to tell him who I am and what has happened? Will he ever trust me again when he realises that I'm not the woman he thinks he married? I just don't think I have the strength any more to stop it all from rising to the surface and for the truth to come out. But I don't want Elliot to leave me or to take Emma away, which he might well do when it does. I mean, I'm disgusted by it, so why wouldn't he be?

Coming to London was supposed to be a great experience for us all. I didn't want it to be like this. I sit there trying to rehearse what I will say but the explanations in my head feel woolly and weird. I just want to go to sleep. The colours in the hall are starting to fade now and I realise it must be getting late. I glance at my watch. Elliot should be home by now. Then I hear my phone beep in the kitchen. Maybe that's him. Usually I can't wait for him to get home, but this evening I feel a knot of dread at how he'll react when I tell him.

Sorry Sophie. Trains all down at Waterloo. Not sure when I'll be back. E x

I sigh in relief. Maybe his delayed arrival is a sign that tonight is not the right time to tell him. Perhaps it can wait.

OK. Thumping head. Emma fine. Going to bed. Love you x

I wander into the living room and plump up the cushions on the sofa, straighten the rug and tidy Emma's scattered Lego away. Then I go back into the kitchen, put the dishwasher on and give the worktops one last wipe. I reach up into the cupboard where I keep the Calpol and paracetamol and reach my fingers to the back to find my stash of herbal, sleeping tablets. I press two from the dimples in the foil and swallow them. Then I climb the stairs and check on Emma. I sit beside her bed watching her in amazement. Her pink lips are slightly ajar, her hands flung above her head and her hair fanned out on her pillow. I kiss her forehead and whisper in her ear. Then I leave her sleeping peacefully behind me and go to my own room, climb into bed and pull the duvet up to my chin. I find myself humming *Ally Bally Bee*. It's Emma's favourite nursery rhyme — and mine too. We had a lovely neighbour, Agnes, who sang it to me when I was little. Before MacIntyre appeared on the scene and ruined everything. When I close my eyes, I can see Agnes sitting there singing the words to me and getting me to repeat them back.

Ally bally, ally bally bee,
Sittin' on yer mammy's knee,
Greetin' for a wee bawbee,
Tae buy some Coulter's candy.

Still to this day I have never tried Coulter's candy. I don't even think it's made anymore. It must sound like something magic from a fairy tale to Emma, but she understands that "greetin'" means "crying" and that the "wee bawbee" is an old-fashioned Scottish silver coin.

As I keep humming, I try to let my mind drift to happier times and hope that I haven't put my new, perfect life with Elliot and Emma in jeopardy.

6

PAST

We walked into MacDonald's and Julie looked up at the menu, chewing her bottom lip while she decided what to have. I didn't need any time, I knew. Just as I stepped forward into the queue, I heard a squeal and then felt a hand on my shoulder.

'Sophie. Is that really you?'

I spun round and saw Agnes, our old neighbour from before. I threw my arms around her in delight. 'Julie,' I called. 'Look who's here.'

Agnes' smile widened, the lines in her forehead deep and wrinkled. But she was still the same Agnes. She even smelt the same, of vanilla mixed with Lulu perfume. I had always wondered what had happened to Agnes. She used to look after us before Mum married James. She lived in the flat below us in Hyndland, that's in the west end of Glasgow. Leafy and lovely. She cleaned the local school, worked as a cleaner at the hospital and also cleaned private flats. But she never complained and always smiled. I had so many memories of her taking me to the swing park and then to the sweetie shop for a ten-pence mix. Sometimes she would take me on an orange double-decker bus up Great Western Road, to the Botanic Gardens. When it was wet, which was often, we would walk through the glasshouses giggling at the heat. She didn't mind me pulling off my jacket, then my sweater and handing it to her while I stroked the leaves on the rubber plants.

'Girls, look how grown up you both are,' she said, standing back to take a proper look at us. 'It's been that long since I last saw you.'

She is right. It must have been three or four years since she visited. We have James to thank for that.

'How are you? How's Mum?'

Julie was smiling but glancing up at the menu. She never really had the same connection with Agnes as I did.

'Mum is fine, thanks. Busy, you know.'

'I know, hen,' said Agnes. 'She always was. Och, I've missed you girls. You need to come and see me sometime.'

I felt bad standing there looking at Agnes, her hair grey and her small stooped shoulders laden with bags, as I remembered what Mum said. She said it was time to move on and start afresh. I couldn't understand why we couldn't still see Agnes and kept badgering Mum about it, but then I overheard her talking to James one night and I heard him say that he didn't think a cleaning lady was the kind of friend that Mum should have now that she was an M.P.'s wife. I didn't understand what her job had to do with Mum being friends with her. It was only years later that I realised what the problem was: James was a snob.

'I'd better let you girls get your lunch,' she said. 'I just came in for a cuppa. I needed a wee break. I'm off to get the rest of my messages.' I hadn't heard anyone use that word for ages. It was another Scottish word for shopping or groceries and one that Agnes had always said.

'It is lovely to see you, Agnes,' and I hugged her, feeling my eyes well up.

'You too hen. You too. Remember to come and see me sometime. Anytime. It would be lovely to see you.'

'I will. Thanks Agnes.' I stood and watched her go.

7

PRESENT

Elliot kisses me on the forehead this morning and strokes my hair, and I realise all over again just how much he loves me. I force my eyelids to open, but the bright morning sun which is flowing through the open shutters is too much. I feel groggy, my head is still sore and my stomach feels as though it's done a million crunches.

'Morning, sweetheart. You were out for the count when I got in last night, so I didn't want to wake you. I can go in a bit later this morning, so I'll take Emma to school, give you a bit more time to come round.'

I try to sit up. 'What about her breakfast and . . .'

Emma runs into the room already dressed, with two plaits, and a huge smile. 'Daddy's taking me to school. Hooray! And he did my hair.'

'Just take it easy. Have a lie-in for a change,' he says. 'Are you okay? You're as tired as.' He cocks his head to one side. His blonde hair is ruffled and he is still golden brown despite the lack of sunshine.

'Just tired. Maybe a bit run down.'

'You're not . . . you know? You couldn't be . . . ?' His blue eyes start to shine.

'No. Definitely not,' I say, feeling guilty.

'Oh. Okay. Fair dinkum.' He does sound quite crestfallen.

'I'll call you later.' I reach up and pull him back for a kiss.

'Okay, sweetheart.'

'Bye, Mummy,' says Emma and she bounces onto the bed and gives me a huge cuddle.

'Bye, darling girl.' I watch as she runs after Elliot. 'Elliot,' I call.

He pauses at the door and turns. 'Yes?'

'Are you back for dinner?' *When* am I going to tell him? *When* will we get a chance to talk?

'Not sure, darling. There's talk of some late meeting. And a Sevens game is on. I'll call you this arvo and let you know.'

I feel my heart sink, and I grip the covers around me. I hear Emma plop down the stairs and Elliot calling on her to put on her shoes. Then the front door closes and the house falls silent again and I'm alone. I can smell fennel wafting across the room and I notice that Elliot has left a mug of tea for me on the bedside table. Sometimes I have to pinch myself as it somehow feels too good to be true that he is actually mine. Perhaps I should forget about all of this stuff with MacIntyre and just focus on all the good things in my life. I'll throw myself into getting us established and settled here in London. I'll make more of an effort to meet people and make friends. At least Lucinda is a start.

But I can't help myself and I reach down the side of the bed and pull open my laptop, quickly scrolling through my inbox in case there are any emails following my visit to see

James. I'm nervous in case there is an angry comeback from him or his assistant. There's nothing. I've never been a fan of social media sites like Facebook and Twitter. It scares me, which is why I don't have an online presence. I can never understand why people make so much of their life so public in such an exposed way. I have never wanted to have an online audience or online friends. The thought of posting a picture of myself in a bikini — or any picture at all come to that — onto the web makes me shudder. You just never know who could be trawling through your homepage. That said, I've found it quite a handy tool for keeping tabs on what everyone else is up to. I don't have a Linkedin account either. I just don't want people to be able to track me down out of the blue. I was aghast at the carelessness of some of my colleagues back at the hospital. They disclosed so much information about themselves without bothering about their privacy settings. A nurse I worked with in Sydney was later inadvertently outed to all her Facebook friends after deciding to RSVP a lesbian dating event on the site. She didn't realise it showed up on her profile and was visible to all her friends and family in her hometown, a small place in the Northern Territory where being gay was very much taboo. Her mother disowned her and lots of friends she'd known since she was a little girl unfriended her. That had made me even more determined never to have a social media profile. I really wasn't even all that interested in the internet if I'm honest. Until I met Elliot I didn't own a laptop. If I did need to send an email or whatever then I would use one of the online cafes near the house or go to the library.

But when Elliot and I moved in together I often borrowed his so I could check which running routes would be good to do or where the latest yoga sessions were being held in our neighbourhood. Then when Emma was born and I sat breastfeeding her for hours Elliot's laptop was handy for catching up with TV programmes I had missed or checking out parenting forums. After that I started dabbling with American and Australian gossip sites which told me all the vacuous celebrity gossip — just about all I could manage to read. I started to become addicted to Google and on more than one occasion my fingers hovered above the keyboard while I thought about typing his name in. I did it once and then forgot to clear the browsing history. 'Have you developed a sudden interest in British politics?" asked Elliot one night when he slipped into bed beside me.

My blood ran cold. 'What do you mean?'

He laughed. 'It's just that you seem to have been doing a lot of research into a particular M.P. I just wondered if there was a reason.'

'Were you spying on me?' I had to try hard not to sound defensive.

'No.' He brushed his hand over mine. 'I was looking for a site I was in yesterday and went to the history page to find it, then realised you'd been busy. Who is this James MacIntyre guy anyway? A relative?'

'Oh. No . . . just a name I recognised from the hospital I used to work in back in Glasgow. I wondered if one of the consultants had decided to go into politics.'

'And had he?'

'Nope. Different person.'

My breathing becomes ragged as I think about my confrontation with MacIntyre. Taking a deep breath, I close my laptop and then swing my legs round and hop out of bed. I decide a shower will make me feel better and wake me up. I scrub myself with a loofah and some peach shower gel and watch as the soap suds swirl away down the plughole. I finish with a quick blast of icy water to try and give myself a boost.

'Remember you are safe and you are loved,' I say to my reflection in the mirror. 'You are safe and you are loved.' I've been trying out Louise Hay's words of wisdom, talking to myself every morning. I need to tell myself how special I am and how wonderful I am and it's supposed to help with my confidence and general well-being. I've been trying it most mornings — although sometimes I do forget. 'You are wonderful, Sophie,' I say to myself — and I try to smile. The only thing is I don't believe it at all. I'm not wonderful. I'm horrid. I'm a liar.

8

PAST

There were just a few weeks to go until the general election and so James was busy campaigning. He said he felt quite confident that he would be re-elected. I agreed. In the eyes of the public, he could do no wrong. I saw the way heads turned when he walked down to the local village shops and the way the old ladies all queued up for his surgeries as if he was Cliff Richard or the Pope. I watched him talk to the neighbours and listened to his deep, throaty laugh and saw the way he ran his hand through his hair. I noticed the way the old lady next door giggled like a teenager when he made a joke. I smiled and for a moment felt proud. Excited that he was my Dad. The man who everyone looked up to and adored. The man who could fix almost anything for his constituents. Then a ripple of something else flooded through me and the pride and excitement drained away and were replaced with feelings of guilt until I just felt numb.

It was James' birthday and I had completely forgotten! I came rushing back from school with Matthew as we were planning on working on our geography project together.

(Matthew was not my boyfriend by the way, just my very good buddy.) Anyway, Mum gave me one of her tense smiles and a curious look. 'Have you forgotten something, Sophie?'

Matthew stood in the hallway wondering whether to slip off his blazer, which was kind of hanging half-way down his back anyway.

'Sorry, Matthew. I completely forgot. We are having a special dinner tonight for Dad. It's his birthday.'

Matthew just shrugged. 'No worries. We can do it another time.'

Julie appeared from the kitchen at that point, holding an apple, which she then took a loud and deliberate bite from. As she munched loudly I noticed Matthew looking at her a bit longer than usual.

'Right, I will see you tomorrow at school,' I said, ushering him out of the door.

Mum set the table with the best cutlery, laid out napkins and asked Julie and me to help polish the crystal wine glasses. It all looked fit for royalty. But then that was how Mum treated James. He was her very own VIP. I did sometimes wonder if she would have treated my real dad like that if he had still been alive. I hoped so. He died when I was two, and Julie almost one. We don't remember anything about him, and there aren't many pictures. He was killed in a terrible car crash— he was travelling back from a conference in Aberdeen and hit black ice on the motorway. I hope he died quickly and didn't lie there in the car in pain. That was something that I often wondered about. So, unfortunately, James was the only father I'd known.

Anyway, for dinner that night we were having prawn cocktail to start, then roast chicken and pavlova for pudding. Mum was in a good mood — I think she had been drinking wine — and she danced around the kitchen, her perfume wafting, her beads gently clinking together. James was, as usual, running late. But he gave us all a hug when he came through the door carrying a massive bunch of roses for Mum and a box of Dairy Milk for me and Julie. Because James was an M.P representing the Labour Party he *said* he was a man of the people. Mum said he had the gift of the gab and that's what made him so popular. It helped that he was good-looking too, with his dark, wavy hair and olive skin. He was tall, around 6ft, and had an air of confidence about him too. Because he spoke gently and firmly, rather than arrogantly and loudly, this seemed to appeal to people too. Then Julie piped up that she had a debate to prepare for and could James help her with it? James said of course, and that he thought Julie would make a good politician one day. Then I saw him wink at her and she beamed back. Mum smiled approvingly. I felt the prawns and their mayonnaise congealing in a big, fatty lump at the bottom of my stomach.

9

PRESENT

Our street is quiet when I walk back home after taking Emma to school. It's a wide, tree-lined road with a mixture of terraced, detached and semi-detached Victorian houses. Most of the shutters and curtains have been opened and the hedges and gardens are neat and well-maintained. It's very different to where I grew up in the suburbs of Glasgow and to our home in Sydney. I think briefly about the bungalow which I lived in with my sister. It was a modern, detached house with a large lawn at the front and the back. I smile as I think about the days when we would spend hours and hours perfecting our cartwheels in the garden, not caring about the grass stains on our jeans.

As I walk up the front path to our house, I feel a pang of guilt when I see the sprawling weeds. I make a mental note to do a spot of gardening later. There are so many jobs that I need to attend to. I keep telling myself that I'll get round to them once we've settled in. Since we arrived, Elliot has been so busy with work, at weekends too. I think he's desperate to prove himself. I don't mind though. I've tried to make sure that I always do something interesting with Emma at the weekend, even if Elliot's not there. We've done some fun stuff, like a boat down the river to Hampton Court Palace and a trip to the Natural History Museum, but sometimes it's just been Richmond Park, which we're lucky enough to have on our doorstep. I'm so glad that she's seemed to be quite happy at school. It's just me who has been struggling with it. I felt as though I was abandoning her as in my eyes she is still very much a baby.

Reaching for my key, I slot it into the lock. But the door isn't properly shut and it swings open. I could have sworn I locked it. I'm usually so security-conscious — I normally check I've locked the door several times. I've even arrived at the train station only to return home to check it again. So much so that Elliot even teases me about it sometimes, asking if I'm developing OCD. I walk into the hallway and shut it behind me, dumping my bag in the hallway. Then I go into the kitchen and reach for the kettle, filling it with water. As I stand at the sink looking into the garden, I look towards the shed. I really must go and sort things in there out too. I put a few of my boxes in there when we arrived. Books, papers and some old diaries.

I stand with my back against the worktop as I wait for the kettle to boil. Reaching for a mug, I'm debating whether to have peppermint or fennel tea, when I hear a clatter. I jump and gently place the mug down. I hold my breath and listen. Then I see that it's just the post that has been pushed through the letterbox. Sighing, I reach for the box of peppermint tea and throw a bag in my mug. I pour boiling water over it and turn back to the sink, to top it up with a splash of cold water from the tap. I'm about to turn it on when I hear something.

Is that footsteps? I glance around and my heartbeat

starts to quicken. Shit. I *did* lock the door when I went out this morning. I *didn't* leave it open. Someone is in the house. I pull my mobile phone from the back pocket of my jeans and start to tap a message out to Elliot.

I THINK there's someone in the house. What should I do?

I PRESS SEND, then curse as the phone pings back and tells me the text has failed to deliver. I keep forgetting about the patchy mobile reception in this house. I hear a creak. Then the bathroom door open and close. Is that what burglars do these days? Nip to the loo in between rifling? I tiptoe towards the back door, silently unlocking it, and I close it softly behind me. If I can just get to the spot in the garden where I can get reception I can call Elliot. I know I should probably call the police, but how long will they take to arrive? Or maybe I should go and alert a neighbour? Mind you, they're probably at work. The street is so quiet during the day. I look at the neighbour's fence to the right, wondering if I could climb over it. But although I'm fairly fit, even I would be struggling to scale a six-foot fence. I glance to the left and see our large overgrown hedge. The fence at the side of the house is locked and the agent hasn't managed to find the keys yet. The back gate which opens out onto the lane is my best bet. But if someone is in the house and looks out the window then they might see me. Come on Sophie. Get a grip of yourself. *So* what if they see you. What are your other options right now? I suddenly realise there were no signs of forced entry at the front . . . God, if only Elliot had checked with the letting agent that this was a brand-new lock, like I said to. I *said* that anyone could walk into this house if they'd previously lived here. I *asked* him — again and again — to check with the agent that nobody else had keys. I mean, *anyone* could have lived here and committed a crime. They could have been in prison and come back for something they'd buried in the garden or hidden in the attic. I try to get a grip on myself — my imagination is running riot as usual. Breathe, Sophie.

I run down to the bottom of the garden and try the gate. But of course it has a padlock on it and it's jammed shut. I could scream. I jab at my phone again and finally the message sends. Then a thought that's been needling away at the back of my mind, looms larger and larger. What if this has something to do with MacIntyre? What if he's in the house? Slowly, I turn round and look up at our bedroom window. There in the window, someone is watching. My phone rings and I'm rooted to the spot, unable to tear my gaze away from the outline of a man staring out at me.

'Hello,' I whisper, not even looking to see who is calling.

'Hi sweetheart. It's me.'

'Elliot. Help.' I'm desperately scanning the garden now, wondering how to get out. Is there time to run back through the house and out the front door? I don't think there is. He could easily run down the stairs and beat me to it. I'm stuck.

He laughs. 'Oh Sophie. What *are* you doing?'

'What do you mean?' There's a flicker of irritation in my voice. 'I'm stuck in the garden. There's a man in the house.'

'I can see that,' he says.

'What?'

'I can see you.'

I spin round, looking for him. Then I stare back up at the window and start to walk towards it. Elliot is standing there, watching and smiling.

'Shit, Elliot. You frightened me.'

'Sorry, love — didn't mean to,' he says.

I end the call and walk back down the garden and let myself into the kitchen. Elliot is waiting for me.

'What are you doing here?' I shake my head. 'I thought there was a burglar in the house.'

His eyes are crinkled in amusement. 'I *am* sorry, Sophie. I forgot some papers I was meant to take into work earlier. So I came back to collect them.' He glances at his watch. 'I've a meeting in Kingston in a bit.'

'You left the front door open, Elliot. I thought it was me. I thought I was going mad and had left it open.'

He walks over and kisses me on the lips. 'No harm done, eh?'

'Not really. Apart from the fact you've aged me a few years and done nothing to help my nerves.' I relax and laugh. 'Mind you, it would be a good idea to try and open up one of the gates. Either the one at the back or the fence at the side. Just in case I ever do need an escape route.'

'Okay love. I'll chase up that idiot agent for the keys and make sure we can get in and out the side gate.'

'Do you have time for a cup of tea before you go back to work? I could certainly do with one after that fright.'

After Elliot leaves, I decide I may as well start to do some of the sorting out I keep promising myself to do. I make a start with one of the boxes in the shed which is tucked away in the corner behind a lawnmower and an old watering can. I know if Elliot saw my boxes he would insist on bringing them into the house. But I'd rather they were outside and locked away.

I carry the box into the kitchen where I dump it on the table, then give it a bit of a wipe as it's covered in bits of grass. I pull out a slim diary with a yellow cover, and I start to flick through it. I dithered over whether I should keep my diaries from before. Especially when I'd got rid of everything else. However I wanted to have something to hold onto. I never expected to look at them again. But something told me they might come in useful. Flicking through it, I stop to read.

February 6th, 1996

Julie always says that my room is better than hers. My bedroom is upstairs and tucked down the end of the hall. You have to go down a small step to get to it which makes it feel a bit more removed from everyone else. The walls are lavender and I've got white curtains with a tiny purple polka dot. The floor is purple too and my bedspread matches the curtains. Sometimes I think the purple is a bit much and I feel like I'm a Ribena advert but I can't complain about it now. It was a present for my thirteenth birthday from Mum and James. They said I could choose any colour I wanted and James would decorate it for me. I was going through a purple phase then. That was back when I used to notice things, like the colour of flowers on the walk to school. Now, if I had my way, I would paint it something much less colourful. Dove grey, or icy blue or even just white. Julie says that she would swap with me in a minute and I have seen the way she looks around my room in awe wishing it was hers. She sits on my beanbag (purple) with her elbows on her knees and studies all the pictures on my wall. The posters of Madonna and Michael Jackson. I would do almost_anything for my sister but I don't ever want her to have my room. I like the thought of her being in her own pink haven where the floorboards creak every time you walk down the hall past her door. Tonight, I heard the reassuring creak as someone walks along the hall.

. . .

I CAN REMEMBER that creak so well and the rhythm of the floorboards of that house. But I would never have thought to describe it as reassuring. I keep flicking on, looking at the pages and pages of neat, handwritten notes.

FEBRUARY 25, 1997

I caught my reflection in the bathroom tonight. I stood for a moment looking at myself illuminated by the bright lights shining down on me like a spotlight. Until recently I'd been quite gangly but now I was starting to fill out. My breasts were starting to swell and the hair between my legs was starting to grow thicker. Mum said she would take me to BHS to get me a training bra soon though I'm not sure I want one. A couple of the girls in my class have started their periods and seem to love showing off the fact they wear bras by leaving their straps visible at every given opportunity. But I would rather not make a big deal about it. I'm not sure I want to grow up yet though I suppose I already have in lots of ways. I swept my hand over my nipples. They felt like hard peas.

Mum said my mood swings were all down to changes in my hormones and the fact I was becoming a woman. I couldn't understand why girls had to go through all they did when they grew up. Boys seemed to get off much more lightly.

I pulled on my nightie and dressing gown, brushed my teeth and then rubbed some of Mum's moisturiser onto my face. Mum was downstairs watching EastEnders, James was away working and Julie was in her room. I knocked on her door and she told me to come in. She was sitting cross-legged on her beanbag plaiting her hair. She looked like Rapunzel. Julie never got moody or grumpy like me, she was so happy-go-lucky. She never shouted at Mum or James and never lost her temper with me either. She's really the perfect little girl. Her friends at school love her, the teachers think she's fab and she's good at everything. Even though I should hate her, I don't. She's a perfect little sister. Most of the time. So I can understand why she is Mum's favourite. Her skin is flawless and her hair a mass of gold. She's tall and slender but has also started to fill out where it counts. Mum says she must take after her as she started puberty early. She says I take after my dad. He was a bit podgy when he was younger, she said. So really I don't have that much going for me. But at least I can be someone else's favourite. Well for the moment anyway. That may very well change.

I SHUDDER AND turn the page. The last few pages are filled with doodle drawings of flowers and dogs. A few pages have also been ripped out. Then I notice something on the inside of the cover at the very back.

AFTER MY BIRTHDAY things began to change . . .

I FEEL a chill running through my spine as I read it.

I DIDN'T FEEL SAFE. I felt different and I didn't't dare write it down in case anyone found it. But I've found a good hiding place for my diary now where nobody will ever guess.

I CLOSE the diary and slip it back into the box. I sit at the table for a very long time, staring at the wall.

10

PAST

I sat in the bath feeling so detached as I watched my submerged body underneath the water. My skin looked pale and smooth and untouched. It didn't matter how much of Mum's body scrub I used to try and slough away the dead cells. I'd even tried her loofah too, but it made no difference. I was still all there and when I pulled myself out of the water I would still feel heavy and clumsy and fat. I knew it was a mixture of my hormones and the fact that Julie was delicate and slim. I thought that was another reason why Mum loved me less than her.

Our bathroom was beige and had a mauve bathmat which I always left wet footprints on after I'd stepped out. Mum and James had their own bathroom; Mum proudly called it the en-suite but pronounced it 'en sweet'. It was pink and a bit eighties with its bidet but Mum said that some people used bidets for washing their bottoms, but as far as she was concerned it was just a handy place to soak laundry in. She said. Julie and I sniggered when she said that. We couldn't imagine how Mum would fit her bottom in it. When we were younger we used it as a mini harbour to float our paper boats in.

As I lay back, I thought about school. I did quite like it. My best subjects were PE and English. I loved my English teacher, Miss Bell. She was so pretty and smiled all the time. She kept telling us that we should read everything that we could and write stories. Or keep journals. Most of my class were more focused on their hair or how they smelt, but I couldn't think why. A while ago, I admit I *was* getting a bit obsessed about the way I looked and gave myself plus or minus points for different things. I had a bit of acne over my forehead but I told myself it wasn't as bad as loads of the girls in my class. I could grab a bit of flesh around my tummy but I hoped it would melt away eventually and leave me with a nice figure. So when the PE teacher said she was going to set up a running club I decided I would give it a go. It would be something else to focus on and it might stop me getting any fatter. Matthew said he would do it too, though he never put in as much effort as me. He was annoyingly and effortlessly good at everything. I loved the feel of the wind, or the sun or rain in my face. It made me feel alive. Today was very wet and my trainers squelched through the mud. Yesterday when I ran I cracked all the dry twigs underneath. I loved the different sounds. Best of all there was nobody else around. Nobody to talk at me or to me. Just me on my own, feeling free and light. One day I thought I might just keep running and not come back.

Just then there was a knock at the door and I splashed around as I tried sit up. Julie never knocked — she just barged in, so I knew it wasn't her. I held my breath when I saw the handle turn and the door opened.

11

PRESENT

It's been nearly a week since the confrontation with James and I still haven't told Elliot. I'm now wondering if maybe I should just forget it ever happened. But the trouble is that now I've stirred things up, I can't. The sky is a beautiful shade of blue this afternoon and I know I should feel excited as I walk towards the school to collect Emma. However, I just feel anxious about bumping into any other mums and having make polite chit-chat. I just want to scoop up Emma and get back home. I wish I could be more relaxed and confident.

When Emma was born I was so focused on feeding and nurturing my little bundle that I didn't think too much about socialising with other mums. When I was pregnant I was still working shifts at the hospital and so could never commit to a regular antenatal or yoga class. By then the staff had all changed at St Vincent's and lots of the girls I had gone out drinking with had moved on and away. But I didn't mind as I was so used to my own company and really, after work all I wanted to do was come home and nest.

Elliot's mother Joan was nice, and fortunately not at all

overbearing. She was basically a warm-hearted person, yet kept her distance. Elliot said she had built up a shield around herself ever since she and his father went through a nasty divorce when he was a teenager. Joan was in her sixties, very fit, and she kept herself busy with golf, bridge and tennis. She loved to travel, too, and so was always organising trips with her single friends. I was glad she was so independent as I couldn't have coped with a needy mother-in-law. Elliot's brother Tim was a lawyer in Perth and so we didn't see much of him either. Which was fine. I was happiest when it was just Elliot and me, and then the two of us and Emma.

The only time I missed my own mum, or the idea of her, anyway, was when I was waiting at the doctor's to have my check-ups and I watched other women sitting with their mothers oohing and aching as they flicked through pregnancy or home decor magazines, working out which shade of yellow to paint the nursery. By the time Emma got to eight months old I had started to gaze slightly wistfully as the groups of mothers who huddled together with their designer prams outside cafes sipping lattes and swapping baby-weaning tips as their babies slept peacefully.

So I decided to take the plunge and try a music class. It went okay and Emma seemed to like it. By this time, she had started to clap her hands and smile at everyone. The other mums and nannies were friendly enough but I never felt particularly drawn to any of them, so when that block of classes ended I didn't sign up for the next one.

After that we tried the baby gym and the soft play sessions at the local leisure centre. Emma loved pulling herself up on the soft blocks and trying to throw herself into the pool of balls. So because it was close to our house we would go quite often. I started to recognise a few faces and would sit and make polite conversation with other mums but there was just never really anyone I particularly wanted to be friends with. One woman I did like, Tricia, was lovely — but then she announced that she was moving to New York with her husband's job. I suppose that perhaps sowed the seed in my own mind that I needed a change.

I was spending more and more time and effort trying to control my own memories which were popping up now like a demented Whack-a-Mole game. Every time I managed to hammer one back down another would surface. I had wondered if going back to work might help because at least my mind would be busy — but I couldn't bear the thought of leaving Emma with a nanny or at a nursery. Elliot seemed to like me being at home and said there was no pressure for me to go back, and so I decided to take an extended period of leave from the hospital and concentrated on Emma.

I hear someone call my name, just as I reach the school gates, and I look round to see Lucinda on the other side of the road. Pausing, I lift my hand to shield my eyes from the sun, and smiling I stand and wait. She jogs round a man waiting by the railing opposite and then crosses the road.

'Hi there,' she says when she reaches me. 'How are you? How's your day been?'

'Good, thanks.' I smile again and we walk towards the girls' classroom. 'How about you?'

'Yes, not bad at all. Though running late as always. I was just catching up with an old friend for a coffee and lost track of time.' She exhales loudly and giggles. 'Though I'm feeling a little bit out of breath. Must do something about getting fit.'

'You should come out running with me sometime,' I say and then stop. *Why* on earth would she want to do that? And do I really want her to?

'You know, I may well just take you up on that.'

Just then the girls came running out of the classroom, clutching their bags and some pictures they had drawn that day.

'Mummy, can we go now?' Emma yawns and rubs her eyes.

'Are you tired, sweetie?"

She nods.

'Come on then, let's go.' I tap Lucinda on the shoulder. 'See you soon. We're going to head off. She's tired. Bye, Daisy.'

'No worries. See you soon.'

Emma and I walk out the gate and cross the pavement and I listen to her chatter about her day. Then I feel a shiver run down my spine. I turn and see that the man who was loitering earlier is still there, and he is watching us.

12

PAST

Something exciting happened today. Miss Bell took me aside after class and told me that my short story assignment was fantastic. I'd written about a girl lost at sea.

'Your writing is really superb, Sophie. You are so descriptive. It's very atmospheric. You have a wonderful imagination,' she said, and smiled at me.

I felt a warm glow spread across my chest and I cupped my hands together, so pleased to have done something well and to have some praise for a change.

'I wondered, with your permission of course, whether I could enter it into the short story competition that the council is running for all the local schools?'

I nodded in excitement. 'Yes please.'

'Great.' She clapped her hands and smiled. 'I think you have something special there with that talent of yours, Sophie. I really think you are in with a chance of winning . . . although of course I'm not supposed to say that.' She winked.

As we walked out the classroom she told me about a

couple of books she thought I would enjoy. 'Read as much as you can, Sophie,' she said. 'And don't be afraid to tackle even the books that look too hard — those are the ones that will help to stimulate and feed your imagination.'

'Thanks.' I felt as if I'd won the lottery. I couldn't wipe the grin from my face. 'I will.' I started to make my way down the corridor towards my locker but was distracted when I saw Julie. She was turning and walking down the stairs and I could see someone ahead of her. Someone who looked vaguely familiar. But then I felt a hand on my arm and I turned to look. It was Miss Bell, her piercing blue eyes fixed on me.

'Sophie,' she said in a gentle voice.

'Yes.'

'I . . . I just wondered if everything else is okay with you?'

I stared back at her. What did she mean? What did she know? 'Um,' I started. 'I am fine thanks. Maybe just a bit busy.' It was more of an offering rather than a statement.

She took a step back. 'Well, you do look a bit pale. Make sure you have an early night. You're not overdoing the running, are you?'

'No. Thanks Miss Bell. But I'd better go.' I wanted to get away and try and catch up with Julie.

'Well just remember I am here if you ever need someone to talk to.'

I smiled, shut my locker and pulled my coat tighter around my shoulders. 'Thanks Miss Bell. See you tomorrow.'

'I'll let you know about the competition,' she called after me.

I turned, smiled and gave a little wave. She was still there watching me and I wondered what she has noticed about me. I wondered what she knew. I wonder *if* she knew.

13

PRESENT

'How could you *do* this to me?' I'm standing in the kitchen, clutching my mug of coffee and shaking in anger. This morning Elliot is unrecognisable as the man I fell in love with. In fact, I want to kill him.

'Sophie, Sophie, Sophie,' he says, his voice soothing. 'You've got to calm down. You're going to give yourself a heart attack.' He pauses for a moment, running his hands through his hair. 'I'm sorry. I didn't think it would be a big deal.'

'That's your problem, Elliot. You *never* think.' I hate myself for being like this. I sound like a fishwife. I watch him straighten his tie. He's wearing a dark blue suit with a pale blue shirt and a red tie which I feel myself wanting to reach for to throttle him. I watch him glance over my shoulder to look at the clock on the wall behind. 'Am I holding you up?' I ask sarcastically.

He opens his mouth to answer, like a goldfish, and finally manages to stutter, 'Er no, not really. It's just that there's a meeting I need to be at in the office. Very soon. I'd better go.'

Turning my back to him, I slam my mug down on the faded wooden worktop. Digging my nails into my palms, I take a few deep breaths.

'Will you just calm down?' he says, walking towards me and resting his hand on my shoulder. His voice is reassuring and, as I catch a whiff of his familiar citrusy aftershave, I'm lulled into thinking he'll say the words that will make my rage disappear. He's sorry, he knows it's too much, he'll sort something out. 'Look, Sophie, when are you going to snap out of this? For weeks now I've been living on the edge waiting for you to lose your temper. All you have to do is look after our daughter and go to coffee shops, yet you think you've got it bad, while I . . .' He pauses.

I'm frantically scanning the kitchen for something to throw at him. My eyes settle on the iron — still sitting out after I was up until midnight pressing shirts – then my gaze switches to the toaster and for a second I think about picking it up but think of the crumbs I'll have to sweep up. I lunge for a colander and in one graceful movement swing it as hard as I can across the breakfast bar towards Elliot's newly shaved face. He bats it harmlessly out of the way.

'Whoa,' he smirks. 'Easy, Tiger.'

The sight of him laughing at my pathetic attempt at violence makes me wish I'd gone for something heavy. I know what is wrong with me. I'm on edge because of the man outside the school yesterday. And it's not just that. Last night the phone rang twice and when I answered, nobody spoke. I'm trying not to be paranoid. But I can't help thinking that MacIntyre is out there watching. But I can't tell Elliot that. He still knows nothing. 'I just want to go home,' I say, feeling the tears trickling down my cheeks. 'I want to go home. Why did you do it? Why did you bring us here?' I know I am pathetic, standing in my crumpled pyjamas with my pale face and wild eyes. But I think we've made a mistake coming here. It's damp and the house is cold and doesn't have any of my things in it. Elliot has just announced that his mother is arriving to stay with us tomorrow for an unspecified amount of time. 'I just can't believe you'd land this on me at such short notice,' I say, knowing I am being unreasonable but unable to stop myself from talking. I am very fond of Joan, actually, and if I'd had time to get used to the idea I might have quite looked forward to her coming to visit. It's just that I don't like last-minute arrangements. I like to be prepared.

'Look — I didn't know she was coming either until she called and told me . . .'

'And when was that exactly?' I say.

'Um . . . the other day,' he says, but looks unconvinced. 'Maybe last week?' he adds, at least now looking sheepish.

'Last week? And you didn't think to mention it to me?' I shake my head in disbelief. 'I know you're busy at work Elliot. But, *really*?

He shrugs apologetically. 'Look, think of it as a bonus — you'll have some support and some company during the day for a change. Isn't that what you keep going on about?'

'Your mum takes more looking after than our daughter,' I say, thinking of my mother in law who I am fond of, really I am, and I know I am being unfair. Emma loves her, and she does mean well — I think. But I'm wondering what it will be like to have her in the house all the time. In Sydney she is busy with her own life, and at least when she visits she goes home at night. Now I will be stuck with her twenty- four hours a day, no escape, and what if she expects me to wait on her hand and foot? I feel the walls closing in already and she hasn't even arrived. What is wrong with me? I mean I'm sure she will help me if I ask and at least she'll be company.

But I do feel anxious at the thought of a house guest with everything else that is going on. How long is she planning to stay, anyway?

'I thought you would be excited to see Mum,' he says. 'I thought she might cheer you up. You always get on so well.'

In short, sharp bursts, I want to scream at him. 'I'm sorry,' I sniff. 'You're right. Of course, it will be nice to see her. It's just that I'm so tired. Emma was up last night and I couldn't get back to sleep and . . . I want my life back.'

Elliot stretches his arms out wide and engulfs me. He's blissfully aware of my loaded comment and I sob into his chest for a while. Emma has been a bit unsettled the last few days. Me too. I can feel that horrid sense of dread creeping up around my shoulders again.

'Look, I know it's hard but remember what we said. We said we'd review it after six months and see how we get on. But come on, hun, it's early days and the time will fly. I think you just need a really good sleep too. Everything always seems worse when you're tired.'

That strikes a chord. It was something my mother always said to me when I was little. The thought of spending six months here, never mind 12 months, suddenly fills me with dread. But I need to try for Elliot's sake. I pushed him and encouraged him to take this job. 'You're right. Maybe I'll try and grab a snooze while Emma is at school.'

'Great,' says Elliot. 'That sounds like a plan. And remember I'm out for the footb . . .'

'The what?!' I look at him sharply.

'Erm, nothing.'

The doorbell rings.

'Who can that be?' I say, glancing at my watch. 'It's not even seven o'clock yet. Maybe the postman? Did you order something online?'

I'm on my way to the front door and catch sight of my reflection in the hallway mirror. My long brown hair looks like a ravaged bird's nest. The bags under my eyes are big enough to fit in luggage for a fortnight.

'Sophie, honey, I really need to go . . .'

I open the door to find my mother-in-law, Joan, standing on the doorstep. She's wearing her preferred travel wear of dark slacks, an anorak and plimsolls.

'Aw Sophie, it is so good to see you,' she says, throwing her arms around me. She smells of soap and roses and her breath is minty. 'Elliot, my darling,' she says, bustling past me to get to her boy.

I turn to Elliot who is loitering in the hall. 'Sorry,' he mouths over his mother's shoulder as he wraps his arms around her. 'Mum. This is a surprise. We weren't expecting you until tomorrow.'

'Oh darling.' She chuckles. 'Did you not read my email? I said it was today.'

Elliot frowns, and shrugs at me. He is clearly as mystified as I am.

'What a lovely surprise.' Despite the shock, I am actually quite genuinely happy to see her.

'You look tired, lovely,' she says to me. 'Sorry, did I get you up? Didn't you get my text that the flight had landed and I was on the way?'

I can't even bring myself to look at Elliot.

'Any chance of a nice cup of tea? Feels like I've been travelling for hours. And let me see this house of yours. It's dark, isn't it? And cold,' she says, shivering. 'And where is that gorgeous grand-daughter of mine?'

'Look lovelies, I am so sorry but I really need to run. I

need to be on the next train,' says Elliot. He pulls on his jacket, kisses the top of my head and hugs his mum again. 'It's great to see you, Mum. Sophie, I'll call later.' Then he walks briskly out the door and off down the street.

I close the door and immediately stub my toe on her large, hard suitcase which she has dumped in the narrow hallway. Shifting it out of the way, I point to the living room. 'Joan why don't you take a seat in there and I'll stick the kettle on. Emma is still asleep but I'm sure she'll be down soon.'

'Don't mind if I do,' she says, sinking into the sofa. 'I am just *exhausted*.' I mentally concede that, after a 24-hour journey, she can be allowed to be exhausted.

I manage to haul her bag upstairs to the spare room, which is filled with cardboard boxes which we are yet to unpack. The bed is covered in ironing, which I hastily gather in my arms and take through to dump on my own bed. Then I go back into the room and stack as many of the boxes as I can in the corner. It's not great but it will have to do for now. Then I hastily pull some fresh linen from the cupboard on the landing and quickly make her bed. I use a spare sheet to cover up the boxes. Tiptoeing through to Emma's room, I smile when I see her lying on her back, fast asleep, her mouth open and her arms flung above her head. I wish I had her ability to sleep through it all. I run into the bathroom and pull a brush through my hair, quickly wipe my face, then pad down the stairs to make Joan that cup of tea.

'Oh, you are a gem,' she says as I hand her a mug of Earl Grey with milk, just the way she likes it. 'I am *so* tired,' she says, flickering her gaze back to the TV which she must have switched on when I was upstairs.

'So how was your journey, Joan?' I say, waiting to hear

the full, detailed breakdown of it all including her seat number on both legs of the flight and her critique of the airline meals. But as she starts to talk about the lukewarm chicken she had for dinner, her voice fades into the background as my attention is drawn to the screen in the corner of the room. There, sitting on a sofa on the morning chat show, staring at me is MacIntyre. He's sitting on national TV, smiling and nodding without a care in the world. I hear Emma calling me, yet I am glued to the screen. The room starts to spin around me and I feel a wave of nausea rising from the pit of my stomach.

'Sophie, are you okay?' says Joan. 'You've gone awfully pale.' Her eyes follow mine to the man on the television. 'What is it?' she says. 'He sounds like you, doesn't he? Same accent. Oh listen, Emma's calling.' I can't move and she repeats, more loudly, 'Sophie, Emma is calling. Do you want me to go to her?' She stands up and puts her mug on the coffee table.

Ignoring her, I continue to stare at the television in horror. disbelief.

14

PAST

February 4, 1997

Mum has been staying in bed longer than usual. Not quite sure if she's got some sort of virus but she keeps telling us that she'll be okay. Ellie and I are used to getting ourselves up and sorted for school ourselves. I make the breakfast - normally Rice Krispies, sometimes Weetabix or toast with melted butter and honey though I prefer jam - while she does the sandwiches. I love her sandwiches. Potted salmon meat on white bread with a thick layer of margarine. Yum. And she always tries to cut them into triangles which are usually a bit raggedy. This morning when we were both in the kitchen getting sorted we heard the floorboards creak upstairs. Then we heard her retching and the toilet flushing. Julie screwed her face up and looked at me.

MUM WAS sick again this morning and so I went upstairs to check on her.

'I'm just feeling a bit delicate,' she said quietly. 'Can you bring me a cup of tea and a ginger biscuit please?'

The room smelt slightly sour and her skin was yellow,

her greasy hair matted against her head. I asked her if I should I call the doctor. But she shook her head, said it was a bug and she was sure it would pass. 'I'll be fine. I just need to sleep.'

After school, I walked home as fast as I could. Mum was still in bed, looking the same. Later when James phoned she was sleeping. I asked him if I should ring the doctor. But he laughed and said no. Mum was fine, she just needed some rest. He said he was sure she'd be better in the morning. Then he told me what a great job I was doing of looking after her. He said he was very proud of me and he'd make it up to me when he was back at the weekend. When he asked to speak to Julie, I lied and said she was out. I don't know why. He asked me about school and I told him about my day. I filled him in on the writing competition and he made ooh and ah sounds. When I hung up, I decided I should make some dinner for us all. I walked over to the fridge and opened the door. As I rummaged through the drawer of limp lettuce and squashy tomatoes I felt someone watching me. I looked over at the doorway and saw Julie scowling at me. She wanted to know why I'd told Dad that she wasn't in. 'Why didn't you let me speak to him?' she asked. I paused for a moment, as I weighed up whether to make an omelette or some pasta, and I looked blankly at my sister. 'Why did you say I was out?'

Why did I lie? Because I wanted all of his attention. Because I wanted him to forget he had another daughter and just focus on me. I buried the secret with another lie. The words were tumbling out of my mouth before I could filter what I was saying. 'Because you and I need to have a little talk.'

15

PRESENT

Heart pounding, I feel like the new girl at school as I make myself walk through the double doors of the Landmark Centre, a former church which is now used for kids' clubs and concerts. I'm clutching Emma's hand and to be honest I would much rather be at home with her watching *Angelina Ballerina* on TV, but with Joan a fixture in the house I feel a bit guilty about slouching about in my leggings and sweatshirts all day. And I need to make the effort for Emma. I can feel a bead of sweat begin its slow trickle down my back. My only task this afternoon has been to get Emma out of the door, after school, in time for this venture, but what should have been a straightforward operation has escalated into a huge war of attrition. I keep seeing someone in my peripheral vision, but whenever I turn to look there's nobody there. I know I'm probably being paranoid, but I do feel as if I'm being followed. When we arrive, I'm extremely twitchy and half expect the BBC's John Simpson to be reporting from outside the front gate.

Now I'm here, I'm not quite sure what to do. I know Emma is excited about doing this gym class, especially as

Lucinda's daughter Daisy is doing it too. But I'm tempted to retreat and go back the way we came, to the safety of the sofa. Perhaps we could buy some biscuits in M&S on the way home. It's a comforting thought. But then I remember Joan. I'm quite sure she is enjoying having the place to herself for a while. She's been quite badly affected by jet-lag and seems to be napping quite a lot. She's also being very non-committal about how long she intends to stay for. She has mentioned a few times that she'd like to visit Scotland and could I take her and show her the sights? I would like to do something nice for her, really, I would. But I have no desire to go back there, ever.

'Sophie,' I hear a woman call. Turning, I see Lucinda, her long dark hair immaculate as always. She's smiling and gesturing towards the hall ahead. 'Class is just about to begin.

I follow her lead and we are welcomed to the class by a petite woman with a glossy bob, wearing a leotard and tights. For a moment, I panic and wonder if I should have dressed Emma and myself in a leotard. Especially as some of the other women are wearing their Sweaty Betty leisure gear. Then I shake myself when I realise Lucinda is dressed normally in jeans and a sweater. Daisy, like Emma, is wearing leggings and sparkly T-shirt. Despite our daughters' tender age, the leaflet for this class promises that it would improve their 'agility and co-ordination'. I had thought it was a smooth marketing ploy which I'd bought into in a bid to settle Emma. Chloe asks us parents and carers to take a seat at the side of the room while our offspring run around.

Lucinda and I lower ourselves onto a small bench at the side and quietly chat as the girls tumble in front of us.

'So how has your week been?' she asks.

'Mmm, okay, I guess. Had a surprise visit from the mother in law at the start.'

'Oh,' says Lucinda, raising an eyebrow.

'Indeed,' I say glancing over at Emma who is now attempting a cartwheel.

'I would die if my mother-in-law turned up unannounced.' Lucinda twirls her diamond ring around her finger. 'The woman is a *nightmare.*'

'Well, mine is okay, in small doses. Which is how it usually is at home. I hope we'll be able to get on under the same roof.' I'm trying my best to be gracious.

'How long is she staying?'

'I'm not too sure,' I say, noticing the man who is sitting alone by the door. He's around my age, with dark cropped hair and a small goatee, and I don't know why but I can feel a shiver of something going down my spine.

'You okay?' Lucinda's eyes follow my gaze.

My heart is racing now. *What is wrong with me*? 'Yes, I'm fine thanks.' I pause, trying desperately to distract myself. 'Just a bit tired.'

'Oh tell me about it,' says Lucinda, stifling a yawn. 'I can't remember what it feels like not to be tired. I have fantasies about staying in bed all day and just sleeping. Can you imagine.'

I nod and force a smile but can't stop my eyes from flickering over to the man.

'Are you sure everything is okay,' says Lucinda who looks over to the man I am so fascinated with.

'Yes, yes. Honestly, everything is fine.' I glance back at the girls who are tumbling and running around and the other adults watch them with rapt attention. But I can't stop fidgeting and at last I just can't stand it anymore. I stand up to walk towards him. His eyes are fixed on the children. Why is he staring at them like that? Something is propelling me forward and I don't like this man at all. He shouldn't be here. He looks up at me and I am about to say something when I hear Chloe. 'Okay, wonderful, everyone. You all did so well. Right — I'll see you next week. It's coffee time.' Her voice is cheery.

The man looks at me in surprise. 'Are you okay?' He stands up. 'You look like you've seen a ghost.'

'I . . . I. Yes. I'm fine . . .'

'Daddy,' calls a cute little girl with blonde curls, flinging herself at his legs.

'You did so well,' he says to her, trying to edge away from me.

'Mummy,' I hear Emma call.

Turning, I mumble 'sorry' and go back to where Lucinda is sitting. Emma and Daisy are trying to pull their shoes back on. Their cheeks are flushed and Emma's eyes are dancing in excitement.

'I did a forward roll,' she says, clapping her hands together.

'Well done, darling.' I bury my nose in her hair. 'That's fantastic!'

'Okay well who wants to go and get a babyccino?' Lucinda's still looking at me questioningly but waits until we are out of the hall until she says anything. 'Are you okay?' she asks, holding the door open for me.

'I'm fine. He just reminded me of someone.' I am desperately trying to gather my thoughts. 'That's all. Just brought back a . . . bad memory.'

'I think you need a coffee.'

I nod and trot behind her gratefully, as we follow the girls out into the gardens and to the small cafe which is tucked in the corner of the grounds.

'Look, you grab that table over there and I'll get the coffees. Latte?'

'Thanks.' I'm grateful that she is taking charge. 'Come on girls, come with me. Let's go sit down.'

While we wait for Lucinda to come back with the drinks, I pass the girls my hand sanitiser which I carry everywhere with me. I take a baby wipe from my bag and automatically sweep the crumbs from the table. Then I delve around my bag for some paper and pencils. 'There you go, girls. How about you draw a nice picture?'

I'm not sure what happened back there in that class. What has happened to me these last few days? Although I know exactly what has caused my anxiety. MacIntyre and my old diaries. It isn't the first time that I feel a flash of regret for going to see him.

'Here you are, little ladies. Two special drinks for you with extra marshmallows. She places a mug, next to me.

'Thanks.' I take a long sip of the warm, milky coffee.

Her voice is gentle when she asks, 'Are you okay love?'

'Yes, sorry. Just a bit tired this morning.'

She reaches over to steal one of Daisy's marshmallows. 'Well, I'm not surprised. Sounds like you've had quite a lot to deal with.'

I gulp the scalding coffee and burn my mouth. What does she know?

'I mean, moving halfway around the world to a strange city is a huge thing. Even more so when you've got a child and you don't know anyone. Sorry, that's a very big assumption to make. Do you have any other family here?'

I shake my head. 'No. It's just me. My parents are both dead.'

'Where are you originally from? I can definitely hear a

bit of a Scottish twang there in your accent. Along with a bit of an Aussie one too.'

I smile. 'Just outside Edinburgh.' It's a lie and I'm not quite sure why I've said that. 'How about you?'

'Birmingham.' She laughs. 'Though with a name like Lucinda you wouldn't think it, would you. My parents were romantics.'

'And have you lived here long?'

'Years. Came to London after uni and never left. Though probably I should have. I keep thinking about it. But my husband loves London. He would never leave.'

'Oh,' I say. 'What does he do?'

'He runs a TV production company and he works all the time. And I mean *all* the time. I feel like a single parent and when he does come back I get quite annoyed. I mean I have all my viewing quite tightly scheduled once Daisy is in bed.' She giggles and raises an eyebrow. '*Grey's Anatomy*? I love it.'

It's hard not to warm to Lucinda, and I smile. 'I used to work in a hospital and I can assure you that the doctors never looked like that.'

'Don't tell me that. I need to dream.' She takes a sip of coffee. 'So, what does your husband do? Is he like mine and working all the time?'

'He's a journalist.'

'Oh, now that is exciting. Where does he work?'

'*The Orbital*, it's the sister paper of the one he's with back home. He had the chance of a placement here and wanted to give it a go.'

'I used to be a journalist before I had Daisy. It feels like a long time ago.'

'Do you miss it?'

She shrugs. 'Sometimes I do.'

'It's not exactly family friendly,' I say. 'He works long hours.' I glance at the girls who are furiously scribbling away. 'Do you want to go and play with the balls now?' I point at the pit behind us which is stuffed with brightly-coloured plastic balls. Daisy and Emma squeal in excitement, push their chairs back with a clatter and launch themselves at the balls. All of a sudden, I feel myself gulping back a sob. I'm *so* annoyed with myself for allowing my emotions to overwhelm me. I need to try and get a grip of what's going on inside my head. Perhaps it's Lucinda's kindness and the fact she seems to actually like *me* – it is something I'm so not used to.

'What is it? What's wrong?' Lucinda touches me gently on the arm.

Her kindness is too much and I burst into tears.

16

PAST

Julie stood next to me in the bathroom as we brushed our teeth. She was wearing her old pink and white striped nightie, even though it was far too small for her and the transfer picture of a cat had almost worn off. I watched her in the mirror, her blonde hair tumbling over her shoulders, toothpaste foaming at her mouth. She wouldn't meet my gaze. I spat into the sink and rinsed my mouth, then turned the tap on and watched it all swirl down the plughole. Then I wiped my mouth and looked back in the mirror just in time to catch her staring at me. We both burst out laughing.

'When are we going to have that little talk?'

Crap. Why did I say that? Now she was expecting me to have a deep and meaningful with her. But I didn't know what to say. Not yet. I wasn't ready to have that conversation with her. I paused to wet a cloth and wiped my mouth again, anything to buy myself some more time. She was still looking at me, waiting. 'I want to chat to you about the . . . library. And why you lied to Mum the other night.' I needed to stall her. 'Is there something going on?' There. That would do.

Julie was gazing curiously at me. She shrugged. 'I just went to the park with some friends. But I knew if I told Mum that she would be freaked.'

I nodded in agreement. 'Who were the friends?' I noticed her blush.

'Just some of the girls from my class.'

I knew about some of the girls from her class. They were thirteen going on twenty-five. Drinking in the park, giving boys blow-jobs in the bushes. Not the kinds of girls I wanted my sister hanging around with. 'Who?' I said sharply.

'You probably won't know them.'

'Julie,' I began. 'You need to be careful who you hang about with. Some of the girls in your class have a reputation . . .'

'I know,' she said defiantly, standing taller to face me. 'But I'm not like that. I'm not.'

'Okay.' I handed her the facecloth. 'I'm just saying that you need to be careful.'

Who was I to talk? I was a rubbish big sister. What did I know?

I dried my hands with the towel and muttered something about checking on Mum.

'Sophie,' she said. 'Have you ever seen a guy's thing?'

Did she just say what I thought she did? 'What did you just say?'

Her face was red now. 'Have you ever, you know, seen a guy's thing?'

'Why are you asking that?' My heart is racing.

'Just curious,' she says.

'Well yes . . . in pictures and on the telly and stuff like

that. But it's not like the boys at school wander around with it hanging out.'

She giggled, a bit too knowingly for my liking. 'Are you sure?'

'Yes,' I lied. 'I am sure.'

17

PRESENT

I didn't tell Lucinda the real reason I was crying. How could I even begin to explain? Especially when I still need to speak to Elliot. So, remembering what she'd just said about her own mother-in-law, I just exaggerated a couple of Joan's more annoying traits and soon had her nodding in sympathy. Actually, it's not all made up. In truth, I am feeling slightly suffocated with her constant presence. She keeps following me around, trying to tidy up but putting things where I can't find them. This morning I found the butter in the bread bin. Mind you, to be fair, I have been known to do things like that myself. Anyway, I'm trying to tell myself that having Joan around is actually a good thing. She accepts all offers of cups of tea and loves to chat, mainly about herself, so having to steer her away from awkward conversations hasn't been an issue until this morning. Today, we're sitting in the kitchen sipping coffee and she comes straight out with it.

'Tell me my lovely,' she says, wiping her mouth. 'Do you think you might have a little brother or sister for Emma any time soon?'

I try my best not to spit out my tea. She's never normally so direct.

'I would love that, Joan. But, you know, I think it will happen when it's meant to.'

Smiling at her I go on, 'All good things come to those who wait. That's what my mum always used to say to me.' I don't add that I never, ever believed what my mum told me — about *anything*.

'Wise words,' says Joan and she reaches for another biscuit. 'I am sure you must miss her.'

I nod, feeling the tears begin to well up. 'It's been ages since anyone asked me such a simple question. 'A bit, yes.' Although I think what I mean is that I miss the mother that I never had and the mother that I should have had.

She reaches across for my hand and gives it a squeeze. 'Well you know I think of you as the daughter I never had.'

I manage a small smile and nod. 'Thanks Joan.' I realise that I am actually quite fond of her, despite my reservations about her staying with us. I've just been worried about us all living together in such close proximity, especially as the house feels so small and dark. But, actually, just as Elliot said I would, I'm kind of enjoying her company. Elliot seems to be working all hours and having Joan here means my mind is taken up with something other than MacIntyre. I haven't had any time either to read any more from my diaries. I can't help thinking that's a good thing, although part of me is desperate to have another look. I fleetingly wonder what Joan's reaction would be if I told her everything just now. I do trust her and, yes, we are close. But then I remind myself that I am deluding myself. I need to speak to Elliot first and tell him before I say *anything* to his mother.

I don't mean that I look on her as a surrogate mum or

anything like that or that I will start to confide in her about private matters. I mean there is no need for her to know that I'm still on the Pill, is there?

'Do you want to come and see Emma swim later?' I ask, trying to steer the conversation back to safer territory.

She yawns. 'Oh, you know I would really love that. But I think I may be too tired.'

She still seems to be struggling with jet-lag and has taken to having a regular afternoon nap. In a way I'm relieved, I like it when I have Emma to myself. She adores the water and is a real water baby, just like I was at her age, but things changed after *that* holiday and I was never so confident in water after that. .

We spend almost an hour in the water, Emma giggling in delight, especially when I manage to throw her up in the air and into the water. We are in the changing cubicle and I am gently towelling her dry when I hear the girl in the cubicle next to us.

'Stop it, Daddy. I don't like it,' she says in a tearful voice.

My blood runs cold. I lift Emma onto the seat and tell her to keep drying herself. Then I unlock the door and stand outside the changing room. By now I can hear the girl crying. I knock the door firmly. The hard, grey plastic feels sweaty against my clammy knuckles. I stare at the ground, the cold, damp tiles the colour of clotted cream with dark hairs looping against them. Kids are shouting in the background, the smell of fried food wafts through the air and I am starting to feel a bit foolish standing there with my towel wrapped around me. But the girl is still crying. I knock again. The door slowly opens and a man who looks a bit like a grown-up Harry Potter bewilderedly peers out.

'Is everything okay?' I ask.

The man doesn't even blink. 'Yes,' he says. 'What do you want?'

'I could hear the little girl crying and I wanted to check she was okay.'

He shrugs his shoulders. 'She's fine. She just doesn't like having her hair brushed.'

I crane my neck over his shoulder and see the girl sitting on the bench with a detangler brush in her hand. Her hair resembles a bird's nest.

I try to put my foolish blunder right. 'Um, try some conditioner. That sometimes helps,' I suggest. 'Sorry to bother you.'

The man sighs and shuts the cubicle door. Back in our space, a flimsy couple of inches separating us, I finish dressing Emma as fast as I can and get out of there. My cheeks are burning in embarrassment.

I'll be honest. It wasn't the first time I'd got it wrong. One day at the park, just after we arrived here, I became anxious when I spotted a man with a pale face, a few days of stubble and sunken eyes sitting staring vacantly at the opposite side of the park. Next to him sat a large black bag which I decided he was using to camouflage his video recorder or camera. I watched his every move intently. He didn't seem to be interacting with any of the children. Quite frankly, I didn't think he had any right to be there and I was just gearing myself up to tell him that when a little boy, around Emma's age, came hurting towards him.

'Daddy, Daddy. Can we play football now?'

The man scratched his head and looked at his watch. 'Sorry, Josh but I'll need to get you back to your mum. She said we only had an hour.'

Josh's lip wobbled and I thought his tears were going to spill over. His father reached out and ruffled his hair.

'Come on. Josh. How about an ice-cream on the way home?'

A glimmer of excitement passed over his face. 'But Mummy doesn't like me having ice-cream before lunch.'

His dad, who now I realised just looked tired and weary perhaps from the effects of divorce, smiled. 'Well we just won't tell her. It will be our little secret.'

I felt the park lurch around me and some memories came rushing at me from around the trees. I stumbled and sat down.

'Mummy, Mummy,' said Emma. 'Mummy okay?"

Josh and his father were passing me at this point. They stopped.

'Are you okay?'

'Yes, yes thanks,' I said. My cheeks had flashed crimson as I thought about the wicked things I'd been accusing that man of in my head just five minutes ago.

'You look a bit white,' he said.

I nodded and remembered what to do. I held Emma's hand and breathed in and out as calmly as I could.

'Water? Here, take this.' He produced a bottle from his bag.

I didn't want it, I didn't want the kindness of strangers. But Emma reached out and took it.

'Thank you,' she said.

I drank it to please Emma and smiled weakly at the man and his son. Once they were sure I was okay they left the park. Emma and I sat there on the chipped bench, which was splattered with bird droppings, for some time after. I enjoyed feeling the warmth of the sun on my face and the breeze ruffle my hair.

'Come on Emma, I said eventually. 'Let's go home and have some lunch.'

Today's episode at the pool is just a further reminder to me that I need to face up to my demons. As Emma and I walk home, I am decidedly jumpy, especially when a car slows down as we are walking along. I hear a window being buzzed open and a voice calls, 'Excuse me, excuse me.' I ignore her until Emma says, 'Mummy that lady is calling to you.'

I stop and nervously turn to see a woman sitting in the passenger seat, leaning out. 'I'm so sorry to bother you, but can you direct me to the high street please?'

I breathe out in relief and give her the directions. Then she and her husband drive away. However, I know I can't go on much longer like this. I need to tell Elliot exactly what happened before we met. I just need to pick my moment. It could change things forever.

18

PAST

March 3, 1997

When Miss Bell asked me to stay after school today, I thought it must be for a good reason. I sat as patiently as I could in maths, which was the last period, although I couldn't stop tapping my foot. The teacher was talking us through donkeys and apples and carts - the joys of standard grade maths - and I normally hated maths. But I made a real effort, put my hand up and tried to enjoy it as much as I could because surely if I was good then only nice things would happen to me.

When the bell rang, I shoved my books and pencils into my bag, jogged out the door and down the corridor towards Miss Bell's classroom. She was seated at her desk, marking papers, and wearing her green which I always thought made her look extra pretty. The sunlight was streaming through the window and caught her strawberry-blonde hair. I knocked gently and she looked up and smiled. Then I noticed a flicker of something flash across her face. That's when I knew that it wasn't good news.

. . .

'Come in, Sophie,' she said, beckoning me with her long, slim fingers. 'Please take a seat.' She pulled out the chair opposite and I sat down. 'So, how have you been?'

'Okay, I guess.'

Twirling the funky silver pendant necklace round her neck, she sighed. 'Look there's no easy way of telling you this so let me just tell you how it is,' she began. 'I'm afraid we're having to withdraw your story from the competition.'

My eyes widened. 'Isn't it good enough?'

Miss Bell shook her head and clicked her teeth together. 'No Sophie, not at all. In fact quite the opposite.' Leaning towards me she went on, 'You are not the problem. The problem is . . . with your father.'

'What do you mean?' I was aware my voice sounded high-pitched and odd. Then I started to feel the room spin around me. What did she know?

'Sophie, the crazy thing is that you are on the shortlist. You made it to the shortlist! But he has been asked to be on the judging panel to select the winning entry.' She sat back, suddenly exhausted, and gave a weak smile. 'I'm sorry Sophie.'

I felt the blood pounding in my ears.

'I'm just so very sorry. I think you are so talented and I really did think you had a good shot at winning. But apparently,' she said in a slow and deliberate voice, 'it's against the rules.'

'Oh.'

'Sophie, are you sure you are okay?"

Miss Bell wasn't going to let this rest. 'Yes.' I forced a smile.

'Are you sure?'

I wanted to tell her. I *really* wanted to tell her. I needed to talk to someone. The concern in her eyes, the kindness in her voice, it was all so overwhelming. But I *couldn't* tell anyone. I *mustn't* tell anyone. I promptly burst into tears.

19

PRESENT

Joan and Emma have gone to the shops and so I have a rare half hour to myself at home. I decide to use my time wisely. I nip into the garden and into the shed, sticking my hand into the box and pulling out a few of the notebooks. I take them upstairs and curl up on my bed. Taking a deep breath, I start to flick.

April 22, 1997

I hate my life. I feel so alone. Nobody understands me. Sometimes I just want to go to sleep and never wake up. What is the point?

THAT WAS all I wrote that day and, despite its tone, I can't even remember writing it. Was it general teenage angst? Or had something else happened that day? I close my eyes tightly and try so hard to remember and grasp at anything which might fill in the blanks. But of course, I could have been writing about anything and everything. So I read on.

. . .

May 1, 1997

I'm just back from school and I had to tell you my good news! It was the cross-country competition today and I came third! Yay!! Third out of fifty kids in the region. I was so, so chuffed. I'm so glad I've been practicing so hard. It has really paid off. I managed to pace myself really well and then sped up just at the right time and overtook another couple of girls who trailed in behind me. It was amazing to cross that finishing line knowing I was third! I ran through the door and into the kitchen to tell Mum. She was in the kitchen, sitting at the table and she looked up when I came flying in. But she told me off for running in the house. She must have realized that she'd been a bit sharp with me because then she offered me an Empire biscuit from the tin.

I REACH for a tissue from the box next to the bed and wipe away a tear. How well I remember that day. I was so desperate for my mum's approval and was sure she'd be happy that I'd done so well. After the biscuit, she went onto change the subject completely.

MUM PUT AWAY the tin and said that James had been asked to sit on the board of a women's refuge. She said it was a bit like a charity that looked after women and their children who aren't safe at home. Suddenly I didn't want the biscuit any more. I asked her what she meant. Her back was to me now and she stood at the sink, her hands in the soapy water. She said it was for women whose husbands shouted at them or hit them. I kept willing her to turn round but she seemed very fascinated by the pot in the sink and stood there scrubbing and scrubbing. She said it was a very prestigious position and it would be very good for his career.

I walked over to the sink and stood beside her. Barney followed. Her eyes wouldn't meet mine though and that's when it dawned on me that she really didn't have a clue.

I HEAR the front door open and quickly slip the notebooks underneath the mattress.

'Hi Sophie. We're back,' calls Joan. 'Do you want to go for a run?'

She's been at the shops with Emma and shrugs off her coat. Emma brandishes a lollipop at me, which I pretend not to see, and quickly vanishes into the kitchen before I take it from her.

'Well, only if you're sure. I was going to make a start on dinner.'

'Nonsense,' says Joan. 'Leave that to me. I'm just going to have a nice cup of tea and then I'll get started. Off you go. Fresh air will do you good.'

'Okay, but please don't worry about dinner, Joan. I'll sort it when I get back.' It takes me just a few minutes to dash back upstairs and quickly change into my running gear. 'Bye then, see you soon,' I call out as I shut the door behind me. I feel relief when I get out of the house and roll my shoulders as I briskly walk down the street towards the park. If I do my usual loop it shouldn't take more than half an hour or so. I am *so* glad that it's finally Friday. It has been such a long week. Mainly because I've been trying to convince myself that I'm over-tired which is making me paranoid that someone is watching our house. Watching our lives.

I take a deep breath. I know that running will clear my head and make me feel better. Elliot has also promised to be around all weekend and so we're going to take Joan and Emma to Kew Gardens. I just need to try and focus on the good things in my life. I start jogging and begin to sort out the jumble of thoughts that are floating around in my head. I think about Joan and, actually, how much I do appreciate her being here. Then I feel a flash of guilt when I think of Elliot and the argument we had the morning she arrived. Especially after she said that she looks on me as her own daughter. The one that she never had. Yet I have to admit that although I'm fond of her, I never saw her as a replacement for my own mother. I'm not quite sure why but I never wanted someone else to fill her place, although I am fond of her. My breath is settling now and so I pick up my pace and think about my own mum again. What would she think of all of this? What would she think of the way my life has turned out? Would she like Elliot? And what about Joan? Would she approve of her? And Emma? Would she like Emma? Would she love her grand-daughter more than she had loved her own daughter? I think she did love me once upon a time, and I don't know what made her stop. For a while I'm lost in my own thoughts as I run through the park, admiring the orange and yellow leaves and listening to the gravel gently crunching under my trainers.

I glance down at my watch and see that I'm making good time. Usually I can run five kilometres in about twenty-eight minutes and today is a good running day. My pace is strong, my breathe is even and so I decide to push myself and go on a bit further. I may as well make the most of having Joan here to baby-sit. My thoughts turn back to Emma again and I smile. She is my world and she is what drives me to get up every day. I really can't imagine what my life would be like if I didn't have her. It was when she turned two, that she really started to remind me of Julie. She made me think of my mum too. When I look at Emma I know what it feels like to truly love someone. Her peachy skin and fuzzy hair make me want to inhale her. I mean I fell in love with Elliot or I wouldn't have married him. But if he died life would go on. If anything happened to Emma that would be it. There would be no reason to go on. I would do anything to keep her safe. Every little girl deserves to be loved and looked after by their mum. The feelings remind me of the way I felt about Julie. I would have done anything to protect her because I loved her so much.

My breathing is now becoming laboured, my limbs are starting to ache and I slow my pace down to a quick walk. So much for pushing myself, yet although I am exhausted I do feel quite exhilarated. Running really does clear my head and make me feel calm. Glancing at my Fitbit again, I see that I am almost at seven kilometres and have been running for forty minutes. When I reach the park gates I slow down and walk the rest of the way home to cool down. I'm idly thinking about what to make dinner and whether to open a bottle of red or white wine. Should I make a chicken and mango salad? Or would the spinach and ricotta filled pasta with tomato sauce be better. Or maybe the salmon? I can feel sweat trickling down my back and I'm looking forward to a long shower. When I open the front-door, I slip off my trainers and decide that perhaps fish would be better for dinner. Joan loves salmon and it would be nice to make her favourite to make her feel more welcome. Throwing my keys in the jar by the door, I mull over how to cook the fish when I realise the house is very still. I frown when I see Emma's shoes aren't in their usual spot by the door. I shrug. She and Joan have perhaps gone to the shops again or to the park. Although it is now getting a bit dark. I wouldn't put it past Joan to have taken her up to the High Street to get

Emma the triple chocolate ice-cream she loves for after dinner.

When I come out of the shower, I run lightly down the stairs noticing Emma's shoes are still not there. I walk into the kitchen and, glancing at the clock, I turn on the oven and reach to check my phone. There is a message from Elliot saying he'll be home by 6.30pm which is perfect timing. That gives me half an hour or so to get organized. As I reach into the fridge for the salmon, I hear a noise in the front room. I stop, my hand suspended in the air. I hear it again and I feel a trickle of fear at the pit of my stomach. Shit. Burglars. Breathe, I tell myself. Just *breathe*. Slowly, I close the fridge door and tip-toe towards the back-door. I'm not quite sure what I'm going to do. The door is bolted and I'm not quite sure how quickly I can open it. How I wish I'd oiled it the other day when I meant to. Then I hear a creak in the hallway. I stop breathing.

'Oh, hello,' says a voice.

I turn to look and see Joan, standing in the kitchen doorway.

She's stretching her arms up, linking her hands together and she yawns. Then she looks around in confusion. 'I must have fallen asleep. That was such a lovely nap.'

'Joan,' I say, 'Joan, wake up.'

But she just looks at me for a minute, as if she doesn't know who I am.

'Joan.' My voice is sharp this time and I run over to her and shake her arm gently. 'Joan. Where is Emma?'

She smiles at me, her eyes bright. 'I was asleep,' she says, almost casually.

'Where is Emma?' I repeat, looking at the empty space by the door where her shoes should be. 'Where is Emma?' I grab both her shoulders, willing her to answer me. But she won't and so I push her aside and check the front room and then run upstairs to look in her bedroom. I thump down the stairs trying to push away the bile that is rising into my mouth. 'Where is she?' I scream at Joan. 'What has happened? Where is Emma?'

'Oh . . . Emma,' says Joan. 'She's gone to the park.'

'What do you mean? Did Elliot come back early?' My heart rate starts to slow slightly. Maybe this is all a misunderstanding and Elliot has come back earlier than planned. Then I remember his text. 'Joan. Please. Think carefully. Emma is only four. Who did she go to the park with?' I look at her in horror. 'You didn't let her go on her own, did you?'

'No,' she says, aghast. 'I wouldn't do that. That man . . . the one . . .what's his name again? You know him,' says Joan, though she now looks worried.

'A man?' I whisper. Then the room lurches around me and I double-over, gasping for air.

20

PAST

When I got home after school, I told him that, thanks to his role as a judge, my competition entry was disqualified. He tried to laugh it off, said there would be other competitions. Mum told me to stop taking myself so seriously.

Later as I lay in bed I thought about what Miss Bell said to me. She told me I should always use my imagination. I should read to feed my imagination and it would help with my writing. But the disappointment over the competition was massive. I didn't know if I wanted to write anything ever again. Then I heard the creak of the floorboards along the hall and I started counting slowly in my head one, two, three. Sometimes I counted backwards ten, nine, eight, seven. Or if I was feeling really worried and needed to try and focus I would do a bit of both. One, two, ten, nine, three, four, eight, seven, five, six. I could always manage to hold my breath until I reached ten and then I had to gulp in the air. By then my heart was thudding. It was always the same routine.

'Sssh, Sophie,' he said. 'It's okay. I'm here now.' He

wrapped his strong arms around me and pulled me close to his chest. The soft cotton of his T-shirt tickled my nose and I knew I shouldn't want comfort from him — but I did. The scent of laundry detergent and his aftershave made me feel for a few seconds that everything was okay. But it wasn't okay. And it was all my fault. This was all my fault.

21

PRESENT

Joan is biting the corner of her lip and averts her gaze from mine. I have to stop myself from reaching out and shaking her or slapping her hard.

'Joan. I need you to start talking. Tell me what has happened. Where is Emma?' My voice is desperate and Joan tilts her head to the side. 'Please, Joan. *Please.* Think.'

'The man that took her,' she says slowly. 'He said . . . he said he was her grandfather. He said it would be fine.' Joan smiles at me. 'They've just gone to the park.'

I clasp my hands to my chest, a mixture of fear and terror rippling through me. Calm. I *must* stay calm. 'What do you mean he said he was her grandfather?'

Joan sits down at the kitchen table and drops her head into her hands. Then she looks up, her face ashen. 'I'm sorry Sophie. I'm sorry. It's the jet-lag I think. I'm a bit all over the place.'

Oh God, I know I must stay calm and not lose it but I need to find Emma. My whole body is shaking and I want to grab Joan by the throat and shake her. What *was* she thinking? Should I call Elliot? Or the police? What I *want* to do is scour the streets looking for my daughter even though I know it will be impossible on my own. My four-year-old baby. What if something awful has happened to her? Frantically I wipe away the tears that are sliding down my face. 'Joan,' I shout. 'Please, *please* tell me what happened.'

She shrugs. 'The nice man said he was Sophie's grandfather.'

'But she doesn't have a grandfather. Why would you think that? You know my parents are dead. I've told you loads of times.' My voice is pleading now as I pace the floor.

'Because he said he was. He knew all about you and told me his name and your name and showed me his pass. He's a Member of Parliament, you know.' She closes her eyes and smiles. 'We had a nice cup of tea together.'

I glance at the two mugs sitting on the table. I want to smash them off the fucking wall. How *dare* he do this. And why is Joan suddenly being so stupid?

'Why didn't you tell me about him, Sophie?' She frowns. 'Or did you, and I'm just getting mixed up?'

'No I didn't tell you about him. My father is dead and that man definitely isn't Emma's grandfather.'

'He said he would love to take Emma to the park. He said I could have a lovely nap. I told him about my terrible jet-lag and he was very sympathetic.'

'But Emma wouldn't go with a stranger,' I shriek, fixing my watering eyes on her.

'He isn't a stranger though,' says Joan brightly. 'He's her grandfather. Haven't I met him before? His face looked familiar.' Of course it does. He was on TV the day she arrived.

At that moment, I have a horrid mental image of MacIntyre pushing my daughter in a swing in the park. He's reaching out to push her back, holding her hand, hugging her . . . Running to the door, I pull on my trainers and I scream when Joan suddenly appears from behind and grabs my arm.

'He said to Emma that she reminded him of his daughter. That he loved taking her to the park and that he had chocolate buttons in his pocket.'

'Oh God . . . just wait here, Joan. Stay here in case they come back. I'm going to the park.' Using chocolate as a bribe? Seriously? He may as well have offered to take her to see some puppies.

'I'm sorry Emma . . . I didn't realise I was doing something wrong . . . I thought it was okay . . . he's her grandfather.' Joan's stumbling over her words now and I shrug her off. Now is not the time to point out that he's not her bloody grandfather and that she has just also got my name wrong. Pulling the door open, I rush down the path and out onto the street. I scan my eyes to the right and left. But I can't see a soul. I start to run as fast as I can in the direction of the park. Then I stop and turn and run back the other way. Then I stop. Which park? There are so many parks around here. That was the reason we wanted to come and live in this area. I try and steady my ragged breathing, taking a moment to try and frantically clear my head. Then I hear the roar of a car engine, there's a shout, a horn honking and the screech of brakes. Then a child's cry. I gasp and look behind me. It's her. It's my baby. And she's standing in the middle of the road. And he is clutching her hand. The driver in the car looks shaken and I can see MacIntyre mouthing 'sorry' to her.

'Mummy, Mummy. You didn't hear me. I had to run to try and catch you.' Fortunately, she is oblivious to what almost happened there on the road. 'Look what I got.' She runs over and flings her arms around me. My precious, darling daughter. She's smiling, that gap-toothed grin, and proudly holding up a purple bag of chocolate buttons. Sinking to the ground, I pull her to me and bury my nose in her hair.

'Oh Emma. Are you okay? You gave me such a fright.'

'Well, well, well,' says the voice which makes me shudder.

I stand up and tell Emma that we need to get back home. Grabbing her hand, I start walking back up the street towards our house.

'Lovely to see you too, dear,' says MacIntyre, falling into step with us. 'Though if you don't mind me saying, you're not looking your best today Sophie.' He touches my arm lightly and I recoil, shaking him off. 'Have you been crying?'

'Come on Emma,' I say firmly. 'Gran will be wondering where we are.'

'Lovely lady,' he says.

I don't like the menacing tone he's using and I grip Emma's hand tighter. 'Ouch, Mummy, you're hurting me.'

'Oh now we can't have that,' says MacIntyre. 'Bad Mummy. Tsk.'

'*Come* on Emma.' It doesn't matter that our front door is only now a matter of metres away, it feels like miles.

'Well bye Emma,' he says, kneeling down to stroke her hair. 'I had a lot of fun today.'

'Get your hands off my daughter,' I say slowly.

He stands up and glares at me, his eyes dark and his jaw rigid.

Moving to block her from his gaze, I tell Emma to go inside and check on gran.

'Okay Mummy. Um . . . thanks for the chocolates, Grandpa,' she calls. 'Bye.'

'It's been so very lovely getting to know my grand-daughter. Such good fun at that age, don't you think?'

I am shaking. 'How dare you. How *dare* you come to my home and kidnap my daughter. I'm going to be reporting you to the police.'

He sneers at me. 'And say what? That I took my grand-daughter to the park with the permission of your mother-in-law. What are they going to do?'

I can't answer. I clench my fists, wishing I could just scoop them up and smack him. He was right, of course. What would the police do?

As if to prove his point, he twirls the parliamentary lanyard that hangs around his neck.

'How did you know where we live?'

He gives a dry chuckle. 'It's not that difficult in this day and age Sophie.'

I think of the man at the school who was watching me. 'You had me *followed*?'

He frowns and looks at me in concern. 'Followed? Why would I do that Sophie?' His voice is soothing and he pauses for a minute. 'Sounds like you're becoming a bit paranoid. Oh dearie me. Some things just never change, do they?'

'You had me followed, you fucker.'

'Now, now, Sophie. Calm down. Watch your language. You don't want to end up like you did before. So much rage.' He strokes his moustache. 'Or maybe you've never changed. Are you still just an angry wee girl?'

Stop it, I want to scream at him. Stop. 'You had me followed.'

He looks around the front garden and beyond to the house, taking everything in. 'There are other ways you know,' he says, his voice a whisper.

'Stay away from me and my family.' I turn and walk

away, digging my nails into the sides of my legs. He is right behind me, I can feel his breath on me and smell *that* aftershave.

'It was lovely to meet Joan and hear all about your family. Just lovely to hear all the news.'

Quickly, I push my way through the front door and then slam it behind me but he is there, holding it ajar with his foot. Staring at me with those menacing eyes. Through the crack in the door he whispers, 'Remember, Sophie. Remember that I know where you and your daughter live. Isn't she beautiful?' His voice is so quiet now that I can barely hear him. But I think he says, 'She reminds me of you at that age.' He clears his throat. 'I'll stay away from you, Sophie, if you stay away from me.'

I push the door shut and lock it. Then I move the coat-stand in front of the door. I run into the lounge and yank the curtains shut. Then do the same upstairs. But there is no sign of MacIntyre. He has vanished.

22

PAST

May 25, 1997

Julie and I had a proper argument tonight. She borrowed my favourite top without asking and left it in a crumpled heap on the floor with a huge tomato ketchup stain on it. She knew how special that top was to me. I'm shaking with rage as I write this and the tears are falling onto the page.

'I CAN'T BELIEVE you would do that,' I shouted. She just shrugged and said she was sorry. Honestly, what had happened to her? She never used to be so careless. It was the top I'd bought when went on our shopping trip together, so she knew how special it was to me. 'It's hardly the end of the world, Sophie. Don't be so dramatic,' said Mum. 'Julie, in future don't take your sister's things without asking her. But Sophie, you really need to control that temper of yours. We have all had about enough of you in this house.'

Her words stung me and I sat there feeling shaken and alone. I really was the outsider in this family.

'Sorry,' said Julie again and tried to smile at me across

the dinner table. I avoided her gaze though and concentrated on eating Mum's deep-fried onion rings. It was like chewing on an old sock. I didn't speak for the rest of the meal. I just listened to the chit-chat around me, and tickled Barney's head which was resting on my lap. Sometimes I felt as though he was the only one who understood me. I washed the dishes in silence, went upstairs and got ready for bed without making a fuss. I muttered goodnight —though not to Julie — and I lay in bed thinking about what a mean sister I was. I should try and be nicer to everyone. I had to stop losing my temper and being horrible. I needed to do better. I needed to try harder.

But it was no good. I couldn't sleep. My mind was whirring, going around in an endless circle of wretchedness. I wished I was smarter, prettier, happier. I wished I wasn't me. I lay there staring up at the white swirls on my ceiling. I knew every single detail of the lattice print on my curtains. Then, just as I started to drift off to sleep, I heard the creak. Everyone else was asleep and that was why he was creeping into my room. I lay still, pretending to be asleep. I felt his weight on my mattress, could smell the wine on his breath. His hand snaked under my duvet and rubbed my leg for a few moments. Then he leant over and kissed me on the lips before reaching deep into his pocket and pulling out a crisp £10 note. 'Here's some money for a new top,' he said, leaving it on my pine bedside table, which was cluttered with books. He left the room shortly afterwards.

23

PRESENT

When Elliot arrives home, Joan is sitting in the front-room watching a movie with Emma. Both seem completely oblivious to the drama and panic of the last couple of hours. I beckon him through to the kitchen.

'Hey love,' he says, planting a kiss on my lips. 'Boy, am I glad it's the weekend.'

I nod tersely. Shit, where do I even *begin?* Reaching for the open bottle of red wine, I pour him a glass and hand it to him.

'Thanks, hun,' he says and takes a glug. 'What a day.'

I look at him, his shirt-sleeves rolled up, and momentarily wonder what I did to deserve a husband like him. A voice inside my head tells me that I don't deserve him, that he'll leave me after I've told him what has happened. My empty glass slips from my hand and crashes to the floor. Gasping, I curse myself as I feel the tears start to fall.

Elliot looks at me in confusion and starts to sweep up the glass, telling me not to worry about it. 'Honestly, Sophie. It's only an Ikea glass. Don't stress.'

'Sorry. I can be such a klutz sometime.' I watch my lovely husband, on his hands and knees sweeping up my mess and think how much I love him. But I wonder if he will still love me? 'Um, we need to talk.' God, now he looks worried, scared even I think.

'Sure.' He stands up and empties the shovelful of shattered glass into the bin. He tucks the dustpan and brush back under the sink, then stands and leans against the worktop, his arms folded.

I fold mine too. 'I don't know where to start.'

'Um ... why not at the beginning?' He is smiling, though I can tell from the way his eyes are flickering about my face, that he is worried.

'You're not leaving me, are you?' He is still joking. 'Or having an affair?'

When I don't immediately reply, his eyes widen in shock. 'Um, Sophie? You may want to answer?'

I gasp. 'Elliot no! How could you think that?'

Dropping his shoulders, he unfolds his arms. 'It's just you've been so quiet these past few weeks and I don't know what to do. What's the matter, love? What do you need to tell me?'

My lips are trembling and I clasp my hands together. 'I need to tell you about what happened to me before you met me and why I think everything that is happening to us now is all linked.'

He sucks in a breath and waits for me to speak.

'My stepfather was the M.P. James MacIntyre, and he was a bastard to my mum.'

The words tumble out of my mouth and hover in the air. Tell him you went to confront him, screams the voice in my head. 'I went to see him.'

Elliot's piercing blue eyes are inscrutable. I feel as

though I'm talking to him through a screen; everything feels veiled and fuzzy. He nods, encouraging me to go on. 'I went to see him at Westminster a few weeks ago. I didn't want to worry you. It was something I needed to do myself.'

Eventually he speaks. 'When was this? And why didn't you tell me anything about it, love?'

'I didn't want to worry you.'

He comes towards me. 'But I'm your husband and it's my job to look after you.' He pulls me to his chest.

But I can't cry. I don't know what I expected. I thought I would feel better. Suddenly I feel claustrophobic again. I push myself away from his hug. 'It doesn't end there though. It gets worse.'

He's really looking at me properly, I can see confusion in his eyes. I know that he's hurt that I've kept this from him. But I don't know what to do to make him feel better. I feel guilty for lying to him all this time. I gingerly step around him, dodging his arms. This is stupid. I've kissed every inch of this man, devoted myself to him. Bloody hell — we have a child together, yet I feel like I am a stranger.

'Today he came to the house. He tricked his way in and charmed your mother. Then . . . then he took Emma to the park.'

His face is etched with horror. 'He *what*?'

'He took her to the park when I was out. He convinced your mum that he was Emma's grandfather. God knows why she believed him — she knows both my parents are dead. That's a worry. She's not herself.'

I am shivering and Elliot walks towards me. 'And Emma?'

'She's fine. She came back with a huge bag of chocolates and was smiling.'

'But he can't do that. He can't just turn up on our doorstep and take our child.'

I shrug. 'Who is going to care? And who would believe my word over his? He's a member of Parliament, Elliot. And a very charming one too.' I want to yell that I blame his mother, that it's her stupid fault for letting this man talk his way into our home and take our daughter. But I leave all these words unspoken. Because there's only one person to blame here and that is me.

All of a sudden, I need to get out of the room. I need to get away. I run upstairs and Elliot follows. I stand in our bedroom and find myself digging my toes into the scratchy seagrass carpet, welcoming the pain. I'm not sure what to do. I'm a bad mother and a bad wife. Elliot deserves better than me and so does Emma. I should have told him everything, I should have been more honest. This is all my fault.

'Sophie, love, It's okay. You did the right thing telling me. Come on, let's go downstairs and talk.'

My eyes dart over his face and his gaze never leaves mine. He gently pulls me in towards him. I run my hand through his hair.

'I'm sorry, Elliot. I shouldn't have gone to see him. I'm so sorry. Really, I am. I caused this mess and I need to fix it.'

'Don't be silly, Sophie. You've not done anything wrong.'

I'm weeping now. 'I *have*, Elliot. It's my fault. *Everything* is my fault. I need to go.'

A jolt of shock runs through him. 'Go where?'

'I need some time alone.'

'But what about us? What about Emma?'

I turn to look at him. 'I'm not leaving Emma,' I say. 'Or you. I'd never do that. I just need to sort myself out. I need to get my head together. I've made such a mistake. I've caused all of this mess. Look after Emma while I'm gone.'

His eyes plead with me to stay. 'Please Sophie,' he says. 'Please don't go.'

But I can't stay. 'I just need to get out and get some air,' I say. 'Please. Just let me have some space.' He follows me downstairs and I pull on my shoes. I watch him as he bends towards me and lightly kisses my head. I inhale his scent as much as I can. He's warm and it's just the reassuring scent of Elliot. The tears start to slide down my face. I may as well be going to the moon and never returning. This is what I was afraid of. I should have kept quiet. I glance into the front room and see Emma curled up beside Joan. She's fast asleep and I don't want to disturb her, so I blow her a kiss. As the front door clunks behind me, I stand alone on the doorstep. That's when it all hits me. But I force myself not to crumple. I have no idea where I'm going. I just start to walk.

24

PAST

They wouldn't let me go running with my Walkman on. I just wanted to have a quick jog before tea to clear my head. It was raining again but I didn't mind; if I let the weather dictate what I do then I would never do anything. It was always raining. Glasgow was the wettest place in the world. I was definitely going to move somewhere hot and dry as soon as I could. Far away from here. Anyway, I was standing in the hallway stretching and I shouted I wouldn't be long. Mum came out of the kitchen and said I wasn't to wear my headphones. She said she and James agreed it wasn't safe for me to be out in the dark with no idea if there was a car behind me or someone following me on foot. I sighed and untangled the cord of earphones from within my top and slammed the Walkman down on the hallway table.

'Sophie, we just don't want anything to happen to you, we want you to be safe,' she said.

A bitter gurgle of a laugh came flying out of my mouth. Mum just stared at me and took a sip from her glass. I tried my best to hold her gaze but she turned away and headed back into the kitchen, calling out that I shouldn't be too long as tea was almost ready. She said she was expecting Julie back from the library any time soon. As I jogged down our street past the houses surrounding us, I smelt the damp scents of autumn and a light drizzle begins to fall. I concentrated on my breathing and the pounding of my feet as I turned the corner and headed towards the small thicket ahead which was just through the park gates.

There was a trail around it and through it and, despite the darkness, I headed straight for the middle of it. As I ran into the darkness, I felt protected by the solidity of the trees and began to calm down and my chilled body began to warm. The twigs and branches crunched under my feet and I could barely see a few centimetres in front of me. Then I heard a cough and was seized by terror. Someone was in there with me. But I couldn't see a thing. I kept running as fast as I could, hearing noises behind me and imagining people grabbing at me. I needed to keep going. I needed to get out of there and get home. I reached the end of the trees and sprinted out back towards the trail, through the gate and towards the streetlights on the main road. I slowed down to catch my breath; my heart was racing and I was panting. I focused on the cracks in the slabs of pavement, watched my feet and kept moving forward. At least there were people about. I couldn't believe I'd been so stupid as to go into the park and through the bushes in the dark. Mum would freak if she knew. I couldn't stop shaking. I needed to get home, have a hot shower and sit down. The wind whipped my hair across my face and for a moment I couldn't see. I reached to sweep it away. That's when I felt a hand on my shoulder.

25

PRESENT

I walk for miles, following the main road which leads into Twickenham, then I pass St Margaret's and then I'm walking over the bridge into Richmond. The night is still and the full moon dominates the sky. My head is swirling with so many thoughts and I just don't know how to fix this. I still can't believe what has happened and that MacIntyre had the nerve to do what he did. But then why should I be surprised? The memories I have of him may have dimmed slightly over the years but they are always there, packed away at the back of my mind. He is a very bad man. I allow myself to think about what happened that day I visited him in his office.

Once my watery sick was wiped off his shoes, we stood opposite each other. I looked at him, an old man in front of me who had withered over time. I realised that his eyes weren't as fierce as I remembered. He wasn't the same man I'd carried an image of around in my head all these years. In fact, I'd never ever planned to see this man again. What good would it do? Although I had tried to prepare for that moment as much as possible, being in the same space as him again unsettled me. I felt the room lurch around me. Then the memories of tangled limbs and heavy breaths came through the window behind him, allowed me clarity to focus on why I was there.

'Ms Lewis? How can I help you?'

'Hello James,' I said, my voice cool.

His smile was less certain and I saw a flicker of recognition dance across his eyes, and then the shutters fell. 'Please sit down.' He gestured to the chair in front of his desk. 'You are here to talk about a children's charity you're setting up?'

I paused for a moment. The atmosphere in the room suddenly became thick and I watched him sit back down in his chair making a steeple with his fingers. 'You don't know who I am, do you?' I let my question linger for a minute. 'Or are you just pretending?'

He licked his lips in that way he always did. His tongue darting out between his tongue. A strange mixture of shock, fear and surprise crossed his face. 'I do. You are Sophie Lewis.'

'No, James. I'm Sophie. Sophie MacIntyre. Your daughter.' The words hung in the air for a moment or two. Of course he knew who I was.

'Sophie.' He leaned forward. 'It's been a long time. How are you?'

Suddenly, I felt flustered.

'You look different. Have you done something with your hair?'

I instinctively reached up to touch my hair. 'Well yes . . .' I bit my tongue. I needed to pull myself together. 'I think you know why I am here, James.'

'You haven't told me how you are, Sophie?' His voice was soft as he said, 'It's been a long time.'

'I'm fine, James.' Then I paused. 'Though it's a wonder

that I am.' Leaning back, I crossed my arms across my chest. 'I never forgot you, James. Or what you did.'

He sighed lightly and loosened the top button of his shirt. 'Oh dear. It seems like things haven't really changed much for you, dear. I was hoping that you'd have moved on and away. Made a fresh start for yourself. Clearly that is not the case.'

I unfurled my hands and dug my fingers into my lap, willing myself to rise up and away from becoming a helpless teenager again in his presence. 'Oh yes — I have moved and made a new life for myself, James,' I said, slowly. 'The only problem is that I can't forget what you did.'

He leaned forward and looked me straight in the eyes. 'You've always been so highly-strung, Sophie. So very like your mother, with that vivid imagination.'

He relaxed back into his seat. I glanced over at his desk noticing the framed photograph of a woman with a young girl. 'Have you seen a doctor recently? Are you still on medication?'

I could feel his gaze slowly wandering over me. My skin felt as though it was crawling with ants. I swallowed, urging myself to remember why I was here. 'You made my mother's life a misery.'

'That's enough, Sophie,' he said smoothly. 'I think this is all getting quite of hand and you're being your usual melodramatic self.' He stood up and moved to look out the window. 'Are you married now? Do you have family? Someone to look after you?'

The room started to spin before me and I grabbed onto the edge of the seat. Had I imagined everything? Was he right? *Was* I making this up? I shook myself. It didn't matter that I was now a thirty-two-year-old woman. I felt like a vulnerable child again.

'But . . .'

He interjected effortlessly, smiling kindly. 'Come on now, dear. Tell me what's going on with you. I can see from your wedding ring that you are married.'

That soothing voice. 'Yes,' I said automatically. 'I'm married. Married to Elliot.'

'Elliot.' He nodded his head. 'And what about children? Do you have any?' His voice was reassuring, almost hypnotic.

'I . . .' Then I wanted to slap myself. *What am I doing?* I stared at James as he ran his thumb up and down his pen, his head cocked to one side waiting for my reply. 'It's really none of your business.'

His brows knotted together. 'There's no need to be like that, Sophie, I was just showing an interest. We used to be family, after all . . . but then you always were so contrary.'

I looked at him in disbelief as I'm sure I heard him whisper, 'There's nothing to tell, Sophie. Who would believe you?'

Maybe I had imagined it all. Had I? My palms were sweaty. I wanted, I *needed* to get out of the room.

An image of my sister, wearing a new bathing suit, on that last holiday together in the Lake District, floated into my head at that moment.

'You were such an odd child. Always twisting things and lying.'

A heat was now spreading up from my belly and reddening my cheeks.

'Why are you dredging things up now, Sophie and raking over the past? Has something happened?' He paused.

I couldn't find any words. I couldn't retaliate.

'Your mother would be horrified that you are bringing this up again. You should be ashamed of yourself.'

The tears began to well up but anger stopped them from spilling over. Finally, I found my voice. 'How *dare* you say that to me. You drove my mother to an early grave. You wicked old man.'

'What an odd thing to say, Sophie. Now you're worrying me. You are sounding like you used to. Paranoid. Maybe it's time you considered going back on the medication.'

No, no, no. That wasn't how it was. Was it? Visions flick through my mind like snapshots. I remember the sweet tea he'd deliver to me first thing in the morning. I can still hear the creak of the door swinging open and him padding over, the floor always groaning lightly just as he reached my bedside table. The taste of tea makes me vomit even to this day.

Was that confrontation really only just a few weeks ago? I catch a glimpse of myself in a shop window and see a stranger staring back. I don't recognise myself, that woman with the dark circles under her eyes and the hollow cheeks, and I don't like what's happening in my world. Why on earth did I think raking over the past would be a good idea? I should have left all of this buried in the past. This was my choice. This is my fault.

I cough and am suddenly so very thirsty and realise I can't remember when I last ate or drank. It has been such a long day. But I left the house without anything. No money, phone or keys and I feel vulnerable and alone. I walk past women, in make-up and heels, and think that used to be me. In Sydney that was me. Anonymous and just part of the crowd. Now I feel like an outsider and I don't like it. This is all a harsh reminder of why I wanted to leave everything behind before and start afresh in Sydney. Why did I think coming back to the UK would be a good idea?

I find myself approaching the station and have a burning

desire to go home. I need to be with my family. Glancing up at the board, I see a train is due any minute. Fortunately, the barriers are open and so I make my way to the platform and just hope that there is no guard on duty to check tickets. I get on an empty carriage and stare out the window into the darkness as the train trundles along.

When I get off at the station closest to our house, the street is in complete darkness. There must be a problem with the street-lamps. Thank goodness the moon is at least offering some light otherwise the road would be pitch black. I shiver as I walk along this familiar road which suddenly seems eerie at night. My eyes adjust to the dark and I stifle a small scream when a fox brushes past my leg. A shadow looms out from the parked cars ahead. Another fox. I'm cold, my teeth are chattering, and I pull my cardigan tightly around me. Focusing on walking briskly, I'm sure I can hear someone or something behind. I bite my lip, telling myself to focus on breathing. It's probably just another fox. They come out in their droves at night and take over the streets around here. Yet, I think to myself, foxes have four feet and they pad along whereas I can definitely hear just two feet behind me. And they're pounding quite firmly, slapping against the pavement. Oh why did I think this was a good idea? I keep walking, my heart is racing, and I wonder if I should start to run. Or will that make it worse? Maybe the feet belong to someone who was on that train. It's probably just someone walking home, exactly the same as I am. I clench my hands together. But what if they've followed me? What if it's MacIntyre? Or someone else he has sent to scare me.

I was so absorbed in my own thoughts I didn't even bother to check to see who else got off the train. Idiot. Maybe they haven't noticed me. It *is* dark and I *am* dressed in black, I tell myself trying to rationalise that it will be okay. I just want to get home to Elliot and Emma. Please just let me get home to my family. But the steps are quickening behind and I don't have a good feeling about this. If only I had brought my phone with me. I don't even have keys to use as a weapon. I have nothing and I am completely alone. I need to do something. Think, Sophie, think. I need to move faster. So I start to jog, blinking to keep the tears of fear away that are threatening to fall. Shit. The feet behind me have started getting faster too. I start to run. If I can just keep going a wee bit longer, if I can just get home. I don't have far to go, I'm almost there. I can make it. If I just keep going. But stupidly I decide to look back and I trip and fall on the pavement, landing with a bump. I try to haul myself up, but my arm is bruised, and now I'm panicking and I can't get up. I see two feet stop beside me and I gasp. Because I recognise the shoes. I know who it is.

26

PAST

I screamed and tried to keep running, but someone or something had hold of the hood of my top. I was jolted backwards and stumbled.

'Sophie,' I heard a voice say. 'Are you Sophie?'

I turned around and saw a middle-aged man, in jeans and a jacket, standing there.

'I'm sorry,' he said. 'I didn't mean to frighten you. Are you okay?'

No. I wasn't. I was scared, shaking and stuck to the spot.

'Look you don't know me, at least, you do, but you won't remember me. I'm sorry to accost you in the street. But I have been trying to contact you for a while now.'

I stared blankly at him. What was he going on about?

'Did you get my letters?'

'Your letters?' I said, confused as to what this man was going on about.

'Yes. Every year I've been writing you letters.'

Okay, I thought. This is weird. What on earth was he going on about? 'I'm sorry,' I muttered. 'I don't know what you're talking about.'

He shrugged and shook his head, his eyes downcast. 'Of course you didn't. What an idiot I am.'

'Why did you write me letters? And why did I not get them?'

Puffing through his mouth, he said, 'Maggie. Your mother. That's why.'

I scanned the street, desperate for someone to walk past. Typically, it was empty. The chemist's illuminated by lights, the baker's locked up, a couple of cars passing by. I turned to move away from him; if I could just run I would be home before he could catch up with me. He looked respectable enough, but how did he know my name? Who was he?

'Sophie — do you know who I am?'

'No,' I said, my teeth chattering against my tongue.

'Look,' he said. 'Please, Sophie. Really, I don't mean to frighten you. But this is the only way I could get you on your own.'

'You followed me,' I whispered in disbelief.

He looked sheepish. 'Not really, not in a stalker kind of way.'

'Well what then?'

'How about we go and have a cup of tea somewhere?' he said, looking over his shoulder at the cafe on the corner.

I shook my head. 'No. No,' I said, trying to shout it but the words came out like a squeak. 'Get away from me. I don't know who you are.'

He sighed heavily. 'I know you don't. I want to find out what Maggie told you about me.'

'My mother?' I said again. 'How do you know her? What's she got to do with it?'

He stuffed his hand inside his jacket pocket and stared at me. 'Sophie, there are things you don't know. Things you need to know. That's why we need to talk.'

I started to edge away then turned and ran. But I could hear the thud of his footsteps behind me, smacking off the pavement. Feeling thankful for going to running club at school, I upped my pace and kept going. Focusing on my breathing, I fixed my gaze on the red letterbox ahead. If I could just get there then I would be okay. I would almost be home.

'Sophie,' he called after me. 'Please stop, Sophie.'

I told myself to keep going. I was almost there. The letterbox was about fifty metres away, if I just kept running. But I heard the feet slamming up fast and hard behind me, then a hand gripped my shoulder and yanked me back.

'Sophie,' shouted the man. 'Stop. Please stop.'

I tried to scream, tried to punch the man but my hands were too weak.

'Sophie,' he said again. 'I'm your dad.'

27

PRESENT

It's him. It's Elliot. He reaches his hand out and helps me up and I burst into tears as I collapse into his arms.

'You scared me Elliot,' I say. 'I thought I was being followed.'

'Aw, Sophie. Are you okay? You scared me.' He clasps his arms tightly around me. 'I've been out of my mind with worry. You didn't take your phone and I had no idea where you had gone . . . or if you were coming back.'

'I'm sorry,' I whisper. 'I just needed to be alone. I was just walking and the time disappeared and I kept walking . . . then I was desperate to get home and I didn't have any money . . .'

'Ssh,' he says, his voice soothing. 'It's okay. You're here now.'

'I went to Richmond.' I pull away from him, rubbing my arm.

'To Richmond?' he says in surprise. 'Wow. No wonder I couldn't find you.'

'I got the train home. But oh my God, you frightened me. I thought I was being followed.'

'Oh sweetheart, I didn't mean to frighten you. I didn't see you until you started running and that's why I ran after you.'

My breathing has steadied now and I clutch Elliot's hand.

'Come on. Let's get you home.'

When I walk through the front door, the first thing I want to do is check on Emma. I creep upstairs. She's fast asleep, her arms flung above her head. My angel. I shudder as I think of MacIntyre being anywhere near her. I kiss her gently on the forehead and tuck her blanket around her shoulders. Then I pad gently across the hall and glance in on Joan. Her gentle snores confirm she is not losing sleep over what happened, and I know it's wrong but I can't help feeling annoyed. I'm not sure how quickly I can forgive her. I go back to Elliot, who is waiting for me at the bottom of the stairs.

'Sophie. God, you had me worried.' He reaches to hug me.

'I'm fine. Honesty love. I just needed some space.'

'I know. I get it. Jeez.' He scratches his chin. 'What a right day.'

'Was Emma okay after I went?'

'Yip. Right as rain.'

'And your mum?'

'Mmm, seems to be. Didn't say a lot.'

'Really?' I can't quite get my head round the fact that she doesn't realise how serious this is. But I decide not to press the issue just now. I'm exhausted. 'Come on, let's get to bed.'

But as I lie there, I'm unable to sleep. My mind is buzzing with thoughts and images. When I do manage to drift off I feel myself suffocating and I wake sweating.

The rest of the weekend passes in a blur. We go to Kew

Gardens but it's busy and Emma and I are irritated by the crowds. Joan doesn't seem to be enjoying the visit and keeps sighing. Even Elliot is getting exasperated and suggests we leave early after Joan decides the café is too busy for lunch. He goes out for a run when we get back and Joan keeps following me around, trying to tidy up after me. I think it's her way of saying sorry about what happened. I am tearful, thinking of my own mother, though never in a good way, and I just want my own space back. I need my own safe little world again. I don't feel I am in control of things with her here in my territory and in my home. I'm longing for her to head away for a few days, like she always planned to. I feel guilty for even thinking it, but I don't trust myself — I have to make her go before I do something I'll regret.

Tonight, we're all gathered around the kitchen table eating cheese and biscuits. Joan's had a couple of glasses of wine and as I go to refill her glass she covers it with her beautifully manicured hand. Her long fingers stretch across the mouth of the goblet.

'Oh no, Sophie. Really, I mustn't have any more. I'll be up all night.'

'Are you sure?' I hover the bottle in mid-air. 'It does go awfully well with that cheese.' I start moving it away and see her relax her grip on the glass.

'Oh well maybe just a little,' she says and I smile as I listen to the thick red wine swoosh into her glass. Her cheeks are flushed and she is giggling as Elliot tells her about something Emma did earlier. She's gazing at him across the table as though he is a rock star.

'This is just so lovely. I am so enjoying my time here.' She looks at us and smiles.

I nudge Elliot under the table but he just frowns at me,

clearly missing the cue to ask his mum if she has any plans at all to leave. I smile back at him then slip off my shoe and stretch my foot up into his crotch. He raises an eyebrow and smirks. He is lovable but he can be an idiot sometimes.

Elliot's annoyed with me because I have refused to have sex with him while his mother is staying. The thought of us banging the headboard against the wall where her bed is positioned is hardly an aphrodisiac.

'Come on Sophie,' he says every night. 'I'll be quiet. I promise.'

Elliot doesn't know the meaning of quiet sex. He likes to punch the air, moan, groan and pant. I am wondering now, though, if a spot of loud nocturnal amorousness could perhaps be the key to cutting Joan's visit short. Elliot's getting increasingly grumpy with his lack of action and keeps trying to persuade me to have a quickie whenever he thinks the coast is clear. I've not exactly been in the mood lately anyway and the thought of being caught in the act by my mother-in-law is hardly fuelling my desire. But tonight, needs must.

It's getting late and I stifle a (not entirely fake) yawn which prompts Joan to start yawning too.

'Yes, I'm tired too. I think I'll head to bed. Though do let me give you a hand clearing up,' she says.

'Oh no, please don't worry about that. Off you go — you get ready for bed and Elliot and I will tidy up here. It won't take long.'

She turns and walks in a quite sprightly way from the room and as soon as I hear her padding up the stairs I turn to Elliot. Holding his head in my hands I kiss him deeply, wrapping my tongue around his. He holds me back for a moment and then kisses me back, his hands slip under my shirt and he brushes his fingers against my nipples. For a moment, I allow myself to forget everything and just enjoy the sensation of my husband's touch. Then I push him away.

'Come on. Let's get tidied up first.'

'Sophie,' he says, his voice thick.

'Good things come to those who wait.' I turn away and start to clear the table using every opportunity I can to brush up against him or touch him. I can tell from the bulge in his jeans that he is desperate for me. I feel a warm rush of satisfaction that this is all going to work out rather well.

When we creep upstairs we try not to giggle when we hear Joan's gentle snores. While Elliot uses the bathroom, I poke my head around Emma's door and see her tucked up and fast asleep with her Anna and Elsa dolls on either side. Joan's door is ajar and I push it open further with my foot. Slipping into my bedroom I quickly rummage in my drawer and pull out my laciest underwear, undress and put it on so that when Elliot comes into the bedroom I am ready for him. His pent-up frustration seems to be making him even noisier than usual and the headboard slams against the wall as he shrieks and moans. Lying beneath him, I try my best to stifle my giggles but just as he's about to climax I hear movement next door and the bed creak. I hear her calling out and asking is everything okay, but her voice is drowned out as Elliot groans loudly, then collapses on top of me in a panting heap.

'That was your mother,' I say.

'What?' He looks bemused.

'She just called out as you came.'

He snorts just as the toilet flushes. 'Oh God. There's no way she missed anything, then?"

'No.' I try not to laugh.

'Love you, Soph,' he says, resting a hand on my breast, then quickly falling asleep. He's soon snoring but I am wide awake and I can hear Joan pad back to her room. I lie there, twirling my hair and staring at the ceiling, wondering whether she might take the hint.

28

PAST

I managed to listen to him for two minutes. A tumble of words came out of his mouth and it was all too much to take in. 'I'm your dad. Left when you were two. Always loved you. But couldn't be a good dad or husband. I am sorry. That is why I have come to find you. To say I am sorry. But your mum won't let me. You're almost fifteen now and I can't wait any longer to talk to you.' His voice was frenzied as he spoke, and some spittle flew from his mouth.

All I could think was that he must have done something bad for Mum to shut him out completely. 'What did you do to Mum?' I asked.

He held up his hands. 'Look — I wasn't perfect but I loved your mother. I loved you. But I was young and mixed up and I couldn't be the type of man she wanted me to be. I didn't earn enough. Nothing I ever did was good enough for her. So she told me to go. And, stupidly, I did.'

'But where you have been all this time, then?'

His eyes flitted across my face. 'Here and there,' he said. 'I went abroad for a bit.'

I was scared. I didn't know if this man was telling the

truth. I looked at him and for a minute thought I could see some familiar traits. He had dark hair and the same shape of eyebrows as mine. When he smiled, I saw the tiny dimple in his right cheek. I had one of them too. 'Look, please I need to go now. I need to go home.'

'Sophie,' he said, pulling a piece of paper from his pocket. 'Look — take this. It has my number on it. Have a think about what I said. Call me if you want to talk more.'

I took it from him, turned, and fled.

When I got home, I shut the door quietly behind me and pulled off my trainers. Then I scampered up the stairs and into the bathroom. Turning on the shower, I pulled off my clothes and stepped in, letting the water cascade over my head. I closed my eyes and stood there until my mother hammered at the door.

'Get out of there, Sophie. You're using up all the hot water,' she said.

The shower was electric, so I knew that couldn't be true. She just wanted an excuse to nag at me. Is that why he left? Because of her? I flicked it off, grabbed a towel and roughly dried myself. Should I confront her directly? Should I ask Mum more about him? Or should I do my own digging?

It was only as I was towel-drying my hair that I wondered why he hadn't asked after Julie. Did he even know she existed?

29

PRESENT

'How are you feeling this morning, Joan?' I say brightly, as she creeps into the kitchen. She's wearing a summer dress, and her eyes have shrunk into the back of her head.

'Oh ...okay I suppose, dear. Just a bit tired.' She rakes her hands through her hair.

'Granny.' Emma runs through from the living room and is tugging at Joan's hand. 'Come and play *Elefun* with me.'

She shudders. I think Granny has a hangover.

'Oh darling, I will, I will, but first let me have a cup of tea.'

'Okay.' Emma skips back through the door. 'I'll go and set it all up.'

Joan gingerly lowers herself onto a seat and rests her forehead in her hands.

'I'll get you that cuppa. And how about a piece of toast?'

'Mmm, please,' she says.

I move around the kitchen fixing her a mug of Earl Grey tea, then spreading the toast with butter. 'Jam? Honey? Marmite?'

'Marmite this morning please, Sophie.' She pauses. 'Where is Elliot?'

'Ah — left already. Had to be in work for a meeting first thing that he'd forgotten about until he woke up.' I pause for a moment. 'He was tired this morning.'

I see her shoulders drop and she seems to sigh in relief.

'Here you go, Joan.' I place the toast in front of her next to her tea. She takes a sip and I return to the kettle and reach into the cupboard for a bag of camomile tea. As I sit down beside her she screws up her nose and points at my flowery Cath Kidston bucket of a mug.

'Urgh. I don't know how you can drink that stuff.'

I shrug. 'I don't mind it. I'm trying to cut down on caffeine and be a bit healthier, as it's not mean to be that good for you if . . .' I pause for effect. 'You catch my drift?' She looks back at me blankly. Like mother, like son. Cocking my head to the side I frown. 'Joan, you do look tired this morning. Didn't you sleep well? Too much red wine?'

Her cheeks flush again and she pulls her dressing gown tighter around her chest, which I am thinking looks a bit like a deflated balloon. She won't meet my gaze.

'Oh no,' I say, clasping my hand over my mouth in a simulation of shock.

Neither of us speaks.

'Oh, Joan. I am so very, very embarrassed.'

Still she refuses to make eye contact.

'Were you cold? I *knew* I should have given you some extra blankets or a hot water bottle. That room can get a bit chilly.'

She briskly shakes her head and then sinks her teeth into the toast. I watch as the Marmite coats her two front teeth.

'I should have been more polite,' I say. 'I just wasn't

thinking. I'll make sure that I'm a better hostess tonight.' I take a sip of the herbal tea and frown. I really don't like the taste of it at all. But I need to show Joan that I'm taking all of this baby stuff seriously. Joan continues to chew her toast and traces a shape with her finger around the swirly pattern on the tablecloth.

'I guess I can let you in on a secret.' I lean towards her conspiratorially. 'We're trying for another baby.' I beam my brightest smile at her. 'I'm ovulating right now so it's the key time to try and get pregnant.'

Her eyes widen and her lips draw together in a tight pout.

'Granny, are you ready?' asks Emma as she wanders back into the kitchen twirling a small, red feathery twist from her game. She reaches for a piece of Joan's toast. 'It's all set up and ready to go.'

Joan shoots her chair back and stands up. 'Of course, come on dear. Let's go and play.' It's the quickest I've seen her move since she arrived here. She picks up her mug and mutters to me that that is 'nice news' but she just can't meet my gaze. I've obviously crossed the line.

'Aren't you cold, Granny?' Emma is pointing at her dress.

'I am a bit, actually. I'll go and put a sweater on. Thanks for the toast, dear,' she says, following Emma out of the kitchen. I lean back into my chair and feel satisfied that the job is almost done.

In fact it doesn't take much longer to convince Joan it's time for her to go on her travels. She can barely look at Elliot when he gets back from work and when he asks me if she's okay as she seems a bit upset, I assure him that she is fine but perhaps just a little bit hungover from the excess of Rioja.

Elliot can hardly believe his luck when he comes to bed

later and I reach for him. He immediately stiffens next to me and I straddle him straight away pouring every ounce of effort I can muster into giving him the night of his life. It works a treat. The next morning Joan tells us that she is planning to head to Cardiff to visit friends.

'You two need your space.'

'Oh Joan you don't have to go,' I say. 'It's been so lovely to have you. You will come back before you head back home?'

'Yes,' she says. 'I'll go and see Elspeth and Frank and then maybe go up north. I'm keen to try and visit some of my historical roots. Then I can think about arranging my flight home.'

I'm so relieved she doesn't mention visiting Scotland. She's made a couple of suggestions that we go to Glasgow and Edinburgh for a long weekend together. Hopefully she will just go alone. There is no way I'm going back there. Never, ever. Elliot still hasn't noticed that his mum is still acting quite coolly towards him and is fully accepting of her hastily arranged departure. 'I'll take you to the station,' he says.

'Thank you. That would be nice, then I won't have to get a cab.'

The next morning, she hugs me and Emma goodbye. She does shed a tear when Emma grabs her leg and holds onto her tightly. Bending towards her, she wraps her arm around her and holds her close, and I feel slightly ashamed that I have conspired to get rid of her. She stands up and wipes away a tear, then offers her bag to Elliot. As I watch them walk off down the street I feel a sudden rush of elation that she is gone and we are back to being just us.

30

PAST

June 2, 1997

It was parents' night tonight and both Mum and James, went leaving me and Julie home alone. They said they wouldn't be long, which I doubted; most of the teachers were so impressed that my stepfather was an M.P. that they always ended up talking to him for the longest, and most of the other parents didn't mind waiting their turn. Though those with opposing political views must have cursed him. When they got back, they smiled at me and said I was doing 'just fine'. I sat on the bottom step, scuffing my feet against the beige carpet, wondering what that meant.

'HOW HAS YOUR WEEK BEEN?' James asked me politely when Mum called me through for a mug of cocoa.

'Good, thanks,' I mumbled. What I wanted to scream at him was that I had been accosted by a man in the street who had told me he was my real dad. 'We are going to Stirling Castle next week for our history project.'

He took a sip from his large glass of wine and nodded.

'Well, do let me know if I can help you with that too. I'm sure I have a book about the place somewhere in my study.'

'Did you meet Miss Bell?' But his eyes moved to the door as Julie appeared. I put my mug down. My appetite had gone. Why did I always have to compare myself to Julie? He'd offered to help me, hadn't he? I tipped the rest of the cocoa down the sink while Mum switched on the dishwasher and Julie and James discussed the finer points of the Prime Minister's debating technique.

Mum patted me on the shoulder as I stood at the sink washing my mug. She never said anything, just touched me awkwardly as if I was supposed to know what the touch meant. Was she saying, 'There, there, Sophie. I know how hard it is being you and I get it. But I do love you despite everything.' Or was she saying, 'Come on love, try a bit harder. Try and make more effort. Smile more, sparkle more. Be like your sister.' I just didn't know. Her loaded gestures just made me feel more confused than ever.

'Mum,' I said. 'Can you tell me more about my real dad?'

Her lips formed a tight, pinched line. 'Why?'

'I just want to know more about him.'

Breathing in hard, she said, 'Please don't mention his name around here again. It is too upsetting for all of us.'

Later James stuck his head around my door and watched me for a moment before speaking.

'We did meet Miss Bell. She said you have a real talent for writing. Said you were really disappointed at the debacle over the writing competition. Why didn't you say anything?'

I just shrugged. The truth was that I did say something to him at the time. He obviously didn't listen.

'Not sure what I could have done about it. But you should have told us.' He smiled.

He had now slipped himself around the door and into

the room. He crouched down beside me and spoke very quietly.

'Watch that Miss Bell,' he said, his voice trailing away. 'There's something funny about her. She asked me too many questions. A bit too nosey for her own good.' His expression was blank, his voice flat as he said, 'Just watch your step, Sophie. Keep your head down and work hard.' He put his finger to his lips and made a 'shh' sound. 'It's always better to be a good girl and do as you're told. Don't tell tales.'

I didn't move for a long time after he left the room.

31

PRESENT

With Joan now out of the way I thought I would feel better, but I don't. I know it's weird, but I actually do miss having her around. Even though she drives me mad and, despite what happened with Emma, it was nice having another adult in the house. She's not the problem anyway. The problem is me and MacIntyre.

I really do need to tell Elliot what happened that day in his office. I need to tell him the truth and why I went to see him. I have been replaying that day over and over in my head.

I stood there, at his desk, and I said, 'I think everyone needs to know just what you did, James. A man in your position . . .'

He laughed at me. His lips were twisted in a sneer. 'What — are you one of the hashtag-me-too movement now? Trying to jump on the bandwagon?' Pointing to the door, he said, 'I think you had better leave now, Sophie. Otherwise I'll be forced to call security. You have no proof and these allegations are not only malicious but completely frivolous. You sound like a very disturbed young woman. I hoped that you had made a fresh start somewhere for yourself. God knows I tried to help you when your mother died, but you threw it all in my face.'

'Tried to help me? You didn't even come to her funeral.'

'You didn't let me,' he said, his voice quiet. 'You said I wouldn't be welcome and you sent back all the letters I wrote and never returned my calls.'

'Why would I want anything to do with you? It was your fault she died.'

I kept prodding at him for a reaction. 'What about your family? Your new family? Do they know of your background? Your family from the past?' I gestured at the picture on his desk. It's the flashpoint I had been probing for and I saw his mask slip for a second, his hands gripped the back of his chair.

'This . . . you . . . have nothing to do with my family.' His knuckles were white, he relaxed his grip from the chair and leaned towards the phone. 'Yes, it's James MacIntyre here. I have an unwanted visitor who is refusing to leave my office. Could you send security up please.' He slammed down the phone. 'You know Sophie, perhaps you are right. Perhaps things would have turned out differently if Julie was still here. Your mother might even still be alive.'

'You bastard,' I whispered. 'This is not the last you will hear of this.'

'Yes, it is, Sophie. It has to be, if you know what's good for you.'

I made no move to stand up.

'For your own sake, *dear*, leave me alone. Or there may well be repercussions.' He stood up and lunged towards me.

I jumped up and turned away, then spun back round, catching him off guard. 'Don't threaten me James. I'm not a child anymore. I'm an adult. And you need to pay for what you did.' I could see his fists clenching as he moved towards me and I strode to the door, exiting quietly.

'Just remember,' he called after me, 'Just remember, Sophie. I know things about you.'

I kept walking and smiled as I passed Joy, whose cheeks flushed when she realised she'd been caught doing her Sainsbury's online shop.

'Did you get everything you need?' she asked as she quickly shut down the site.

'Not quite. But don't worry,' I managed to say. 'I'll be back for more.'

Tonight, when Emma is safely tucked up in bed and fast asleep, I walk into the kitchen and tell Elliot we need to talk.

'Sure,' he says, without looking up from his phone.

'Elliot. I need to speak to you.'

'Mmm.'

'I need to tell you the truth.'

He looks up and frowns. 'What do you mean?'

'I threatened to tell everyone what he did.'

'To your mum?'

'No.'

'I don't understand.'

I sigh. 'I didn't tell you the whole story. I need to tell you what he did to me.'

An hour later, Elliot sits holding his head in his hands. I start to speak but he holds up his hand to stop me. My husband looks older than he did a couple of hours ago. I think I've aged him. 'Ssh,' he says. 'I just need a minute.'

I have told him everything about James MacIntyre. My step-father, the only Dad I knew. To the public, the gifted and charismatic politician. To me, a monster.

Elliot takes a few deep breaths, reaches over the table to me and grips my hand. 'I want to help you work through this, Sophie. It's too much for you to deal with by yourself and I want to help.'

I nod tentatively, unsure where he is going with this. I'm not sure what I was expecting. Shock, horror, revulsion? Not this calm, measured approach.

'I will be here for you and support you. I love you Sophie.'

I'm still not quite sure where he is going with this but I force myself to give a small smile.

'We'll get you help. I'll get you a counsellor. Someone who you can talk to.' His face is earnest and pleading and once again I'm reminded of just how much and why I love my husband.

'I'm sorry I didn't say anything to you before now.' My voice is a whisper. 'I wanted to, but I just didn't know where to start.' He's now beside me and I sink into his arms.

'I know,' he says soothingly and strokes my hair. 'I know.'

The sense of relief I'm feeling is massive and I feel some of the tension in my shoulders start to slip away.

'Before I knew you . . . when I was starting out as a court reporter, I covered so many court cases of victims of sexual abuse, Sophie.' He sighs. 'I spent hours sitting there in the courtrooms and listening to all these graphic accounts of what perverted old men did to young girls. It wasn't just old guys either. It was disgusting, Sophie, and it sickens me to think that's something you went through.' He squeezes my hand. 'I would kill anyone who ever hurt Emma. I really think I would. And part of me wants to kill James MacIntyre.'

I say nothing and we both sit there for a while in silence, just listening to the faint sound of a siren outside. I am starting to wonder if that is a possibility.

'I'm sorry, Elliot,' I say. I'm now digging my nails into the palms of my hands and when I look down I see the pattern they have left. 'I've been thinking about this, Elliot, and — well, especially with all the coverage of the Savile case and those celebrities who were arrested ....' I fix him with my best serious glare. 'And I can't help thinking that I don't want to let him get away with it.'

Elliot rubs his chin.

'What do you think?'

'I'll support you whatever you decide, Sophie.' His voice is now husky with tiredness. 'But,' — he frowns — 'you can't enter into any of this lightly. If you're going to make a complaint against him then you have to be prepared for it to blow up all over the press. You've got to be prepared to give a statement to the police and . . . evidence in a trial if it goes to court.'

'I know.' I nod vigorously. 'I've thought about the repercussions. But I keep thinking about Emma and how I need to do it for her so she knows her mum stood up to bullies. And I know he's got grandchildren — or step-grandchildren, anyway — around about her age.'

Elliot's mouth is set in a firm line. 'It's your decision. But I'll stand by you, whatever you decide.'

'I'd never forgive myself if he hurt another child. I know I'm years too late but I need to do this. For myself and for Mum and . . .' I let my voice trail off.

'Okay,' says Elliot. 'Well we'll go to the police and make a complaint.'

I love him for that, how promptly and simply he says it, and I manage a small smile at the thought of what is to come.

'Let's go to bed. Its late and it's been an emotionally draining couple of days. We both need to sleep.'

I feel elated at the thought of Elliot being on my side.

Crawling into bed I snuggle into his chest ad grip him as tight as I can. Elliot?'

'Mmm,' he says on the verge of sleep.

'I love you.'

He mumbles, 'Love you too,' hugs me to him, and within a few moments is asleep. I free myself from his grip and roll onto my side and exhale in relief. I think of my diaries that are now under the mattress. Still there, like a ticking time-bomb. Elliot is now snoring and so I hop out of bed and reach for them, and tip-toe downstairs.

I pull the blinds, just in case anyone may be watching from outside, flick on the light and sit at the kitchen table. And I start to read.

June 4, 1997

It used to just happen in the dark. At least I had the cover of thick blackness to hide in. Now things have changed. I now know every single detail of the lattice print on my curtains. It's not just visits in the night though.

I was in the kitchen helping to tidy up after dinner tonight and stood by the bin scraping sweetcorn from the plates and watching them drop onto the pile of brown coffee grains. That's when he pushed past me and then paused to push into me grasping my hips with his hands. I stood there concentrating on pushing the blobs of ketchup off and into the bin until he moved away. When I turned round he had his back to me and was reaching up into a cupboard. I longed to shove my knife into his back and smash the plate over his head. I wanted the blunt knife to tear through his skin, through his muscles and for his blood to spill. I hate him. He turned towards me just as Mum appeared in the doorway. She wanted to know why I was taking so long. You're always dawdling, she said and then she left the room. He stared at me, shook his head in disappointment and then went after Mum. And I stood there stuck to the spot, useless idiot that I am. My mouth full of treacle and my lips somehow glued shut.

June **6, 1997**

When I walked into my bedroom tonight I could tell someone had been in it. I'm so tidy, I know exactly where everything is otherwise I can't relax. Nothing was obviously messy. But straightaway I just knew that someone had been snooping. I looked in all of my drawers and saw papers and pencils which had been nudged aside. A stack of papers on my desk, slightly out of kilter. I could tell someone had been in my underwear drawer, which I was obsessively neat about, and it wasn't Mum as she knows to leave things on my bed so that I can put them away in my own special way. I stood on my rug for a moment, digging my toes into the soft pile. I stared at my dressing table. My hair-brush and accessories were all there. What was missing?

I stomped through to Julie's room. She was lying on her tummy flicking through a book. I shouted at her to stay out of my room. She said she hadn't been in my room and I called her a liar. Mum shouted up at us to keep the noise down. It's never worth the hassle of telling her anything as she always blames me. I walked back to my room and slammed the door. That's when I realized it wasn't Julie. It was him. I'm sure he was looking for something. I'm sure he was looking for this diary. Why else would he be going through my things? I ran over to my hiding place. It's in the corner of my room under my bed. I wriggled underneath my bed and moved boxes and papers aside. Then I carefully peeled back the carpet. It was okay. You, my diary, were still there. When I smoothed everything over and wriggled back out I noticed someone had been on my bed. There was a dent on the duvet and I wanted to vomit at the thought of his hands touching my pillow and my pyjamas. They were poking out. I never leave them like that. They're always tucked away and out of sight. Oh how I want to punch him. And kill him. I hate him. He's obviously worried that I might be writing things about him. Making a written record of his sordid little secret. I'll need to be really careful from now on. I'm not even sure I'll be able to take you on holiday, diary. There might not be anywhere to hide you. Nowhere will be safe.

IT DOESN'T MATTER that this happened such a long time ago. It makes no difference that I'm an adult, with my own family and sitting in my own house. Reading this takes me right back to that moment. I'm in my bedroom and I can remember feeling fear and panic that he'd been rifling through my stuff. Most of all, I feel overwhelming guilt at calling my sister a liar. I flick through some more pages, reading more entries.

JUNE 15, 1997

Tonight, for the first time, I tried to push him away. I tried to say NO! This is not okay. I DON'T WANT THIS!! It didn't work. He just gripped me harder and told me to be quiet. Told me it was all okay. That what he was doing was all okay. He's leaving in the morning to go to Brussels for parliamentary business.

I CAN'T READ any more. I know that once I've made a formal complaint to the police there will be no going back. And I don't want to. This is about dealing with the past and moving on.

32

PAST

I lay in bed trying to focus on the sounds of the birds outside singing and scratching around and the sound of their gentle thumps as they hopped around the roof. I focused on the throb of the car engines as they passed and the gentle rumble of the milk van as it started the day. Usually depending on the time of night, late or early morning, there was something I could fixate on to take me to another place. Then I thought of the shower I could have, the warm water washing away the grubbiness. But only if I scrubbed . . . and scrubbed . . . and scrubbed.

When I was at school I wondered if anyone noticed anything strange about me. Did they think I was weird? I felt different. I didn't want to be a freak. There was nobody I could tell, either. What could I possibly say? Then I started to question myself and wondered if maybe I'd imagined it. Could this really be happening? I was curled up in a ball and I didn't want to get up. I didn't want to speak to anyone. Mum came into the room, her face expressionless as she stood there on the threshold.

'Get up — you're going to be late.' Her voice was flat.

How I longed for her to cross the room to my bed, to sit next to me and stroke my hair and ask me what was wrong. Why couldn't she just ask me if I was okay? Why couldn't she say to me, 'Sophie, dear, aren't you feeling well? Is there anything on your mind?' I knew she would if it was Julie.

I would have loved her just to ask me any of these questions. Just *one*. Just to show that she cared. She was my mum and I loved her — of course I did. Though I hate her too. Which made me wicked, didn't it? I don't know why she didn't like me. I don't know what I'd done to make her hate me so much. I had a vague memory of happier times with her. When I was four or five, she would sometimes take me shopping to the supermarket. I remember that big *Safeway* sign which clashed with the backdrop of the green hills behind. Julie was at home having an afternoon nap while he worked in the study. Mum would hand me the shopping list which she'd written out carefully on a piece of lined paper. Her handwriting was curly and she looped all her letters together. I would carry her list around solemnly telling her what was on the list. Then after we'd finished with the list and packed all our shopping into bags we'd stop off at the little in-store cafe for a treat. Mum would always have Earl Grey tea and I'd have a sugar donut. I spent most of my time licking off the grains of sugar until all that was left was a sticky, anaemic looking O.

People knew she was the M.P' s wife and most let her get on with doing her weekly shop. Others would corner her in the cereal aisle or back her up against the cheese counter and vent their spleen at whatever their particular gripe of the day was.

'Everyone loves your stepfather Sophie. He's a very good man,' she would say to me regularly.

I would smile and agree. I imagined it must be like living

with a popstar. Everyone thought he was amazing and could say or do no wrong. We'd get home and unload the car and put away all the shopping so that everything was just so. Mum was very particular about where things went. She said it all went back to her days in nursing when she was fastidious about cleanliness and tidiness and it was a trait that had carried over into family life. We had a huge kitchen, which was always spotless and I did try to imagine what it would be like to have a mum who stood at the worktop stirring a bowl of cake mixture and letting us dip our fingers into the bowl. I imagined having loads of cousins running around with lots of laughter and noise. Maybe a brother or two as well as Ellie. Maybe some grandparents or aunts and uncles too. Somehow I thought it would make life seem more fun.

Now she just looked at me, told me to remember to take my pills and shut the door. I heard her in the hallway chatting to Julie. Her voice was always bright and light when she spoke to Julie. I lay there for a moment longer staring at the pills on my bedside table. I didn't like the way they made me feel. They made me feel horrid. Tired. Lethargic. Despondent. But I knew I had to take them. Surely eventually they would make me feel better. Feel normal. Whatever that was.

There was a knock at my door and Julie stuck her head round it. 'You getting up, Sophie? Matthew said he'd call in for us this morning.'

I shook my head. 'It's okay. I'll catch up.'

'Okay,' she said. 'See you later.'

Off she went. Skipping down the stairs to walk my best friend to school. I swung my legs off the bed and stood up. Glancing at the clock I realised that, if I was quick, I could have a shower. I stood under the water and let the jets pummel my neck and I scrubbed and scrubbed and scrubbed.

33

PRESENT

We haven't spoken about going to the police for a couple of days, but I know if I don't do it soon I will lose my nerve. I keep thinking that tomorrow will be the day I go. But when I wake up, thinking that I have slept, it's not even two o'clock. Elliot is propped up next to me with his reading glasses on, looking at his laptop. Glancing over at me, he gives me a tight smile.

'Are you okay?' I rub my eyes, memories of last night seeping back into my mind. I watch him clasp his hands together and stretch them above his head.

'Just been doing a bit of research.'

'On what?'

'On MacIntyre. Just want to know more about this scumbag.'

Now, I'm sitting up, trying to look at the screen. That reminds me, I must hand in my own lap-top to that repair shop Elliot spotted in the high street. It's playing up — keeps crashing.

'I've had a brief look at Google already, but it doesn't go back as far as I want it to. I logged onto work's cuttings service and started to search for some news coverage.' He took a sharp breath. 'Seems he was quite the man back then and 1999 was quite the year.'

He passes the computer over to me and I grip the sides as I read.

SHAMED M.P. James MacIntyre 'Dumped by Wife'

THE MARRIAGE of shamed Labour leadership contender James MacIntyre is over, it was claimed yesterday. The 42-year-old, exposed for his affair with a parliamentary researcher, tried to reconcile with his wife Samantha. However, she has said she cannot go on with their marriage. The couple have been married for 12 years and have one daughter, Sophie.

MacIntyre has refused to comment further on the split referring to the public statement which he issued last week in which he said: "I am sorry for the hurt and humiliation I have caused. I will continue to work for all my constituents both locally and at Westminster. However I will step down at the next election and concentrate on other issues.'

I KEEP SCROLLING through the articles which, depending on the publication, vary in their range of salaciousness.

SHAMED M.P. Quits Labour Party's Leadership Race After Exposed as Sex Cheat

. . .

Shamed Labour M.P. James MacIntyre has quit his party's leadership race after it was revealed that he had sex with a researcher in his Westminster office. MacIntyre, touted as a rising star, dramatically resigned from frontline politics over the revelations. The married father of one said the incident had been an 'error of judgement' and apologised for the distress and embarrassment he had caused his family, friends, constituents and party. Friends said they were stunned by the revelations including claims of asking the researcher to dress as a schoolgirl.

My stomach twists as I read on. This was the same article I had read only a few weeks ago, when I decided to start out on this mission.

Shamed M.P. Makes Political Comeback

Disgraced former Labour M.P. James MacIntyre, has made a political comeback after being re-elected to Westminster. Shamed MacIntyre was forced to quit his party's leadership race, 15 years ago, when it was revealed that he used his public office as a sex den. The then married M.P. was a rising star of the Labour Party, and when news of the sex scandal broke at the height of the party's leadership contest it plunged the party into disarray.

At the time Macintyre, now 57, blamed his 'error of judgement' on the grief he felt after a family tragedy. He withdrew from the leadership contest and agreed to stand down as M.P. for Glasgow West at the next election. Since then he has been working quietly behind the scenes for a children's charity. He has since remarried and has two stepsons and a step-grand-daughter.

MacIntyre made his political comeback when the Labour

Party asked him to stand for a safe seat in Lancashire. In an interview shortly after his incredible re-election he spoke of his regret over the episode which led to his downfall.

'Politics and daily life left me stressed and feeling depressed. My wife and I had just lost our daughter and we were in pieces. Our life was shattered by her loss. I knew it was wrong but I just wanted an escape from my life. I kept telling myself each time would be the last but it was hard being in London and on my own during the week. I felt like a failure and so alone. I felt like I had let everyone down.'

His wife divorced him shortly afterwards. He later remarried and says he has learned from the mistakes of the past. 'I want to move on now with my life and leave all of that behind. This is time for a fresh start for me and my wonderful family. I'm very much looking forward to re-entering political life and serving my constituents.'

I SCROLL down the page and find another article.

SHAMED M.P. Stands Again

JAMES MACINTYRE M.P. has spoken widely about how he tried to rebuild his life after a sex scandal ruined his career and led to his downfall. A newspaper exposed him for regularly using his office for sex with a researcher which led to the breakdown of his marriage. His former wife then died a few years later.

MacIntyre said he found life at Westminster tough to juggle with family commitments and that he'd been left devastated by the loss of his 14-year-old daughter. He said the grief had overwhelmed him and the relationship between him and his wife crumbled. 'We could never really get over the loss of Julie,' he said.

Now, fifteen years later, he is very much looking forward to this new chapter in his life. 'I hope my new constituents will benefit from my hard work and commitment to serve them both locally and at Westminster.'

I CLOSE the laptop and stare ahead at the wall. 'I wonder what happened to the researcher. The girl he had the affair with.'

'She's working as a marketing manager in Spain,' says Elliot.

'Really? How on earth do you know that?'

He shrugs. 'Facebook.' He clasps my hand. 'No more secrets. Please Sophie. No more secrets. Tell me about Julie. Tell me about your sister.'

34

PAST

June 25, 1997

It feels like everyone hates me. Mum's been moping about the house and every time James walks into the room it's as though a huge raincloud follows him. He seems to be lavishing all of his attention on Julie, which she adores. I don't. It makes my skin crawl when he's nice to her. I've been trying to go out and run as much as possible whenever she's at any of her dance classes or at a friend's. I just want to keep running away from everything.

But when Julie is at home I want to be around her. I want to look after her. I just wish I could control my temper. Today she was showing off her new trainers to James. They were pink and orange with pink laces. They are lovely, and when I looked down at my grubby white ones, yes, I did feel jealous, and a swirl of rage swooshed from nowhere.

'Maybe they'll help you run faster,' he said, laughing. 'Maybe I should take up running too,' he added, raising an eyebrow in that annoying way he did.

And I know it was really stupid of me. I know I needed to control my temper, but I lunged at him and he caught me just before my ragged fingernails tore at his stupid moustache.

'Sophie. Good God. What are you doing?' he said, pushing me back. His eyes were cold, his lips forming a thin smirk as he stared at me.

'Sophie,' screeched Mum. 'You get to your room right this minute.'

'But you don't understand.' I stared at her, sobbing in frustration.

'You're crazy,' she said.

It was the first time in ages that she'd actually raised her voice, and I knew there was no point in arguing. I turned to go and then I was left reeling by what she said next. She grabbed me on the shoulder, spun me round and said, 'You are — just like your father. Crazy. Now go. Go away.'

Later on, when I was lying on my bed reading, Julie gently tapped the door and came in. 'Sophie,' she said. 'Are you okay?'

I shrugged and she came into my room, gingerly lowered herself onto the edge of my bed. Her eyes were unsure. She gripped my duvet cover with her long, slender fingers. 'It's just you always seem so cross.'

That really hurt me. 'Oh,' is all I could manage to say. 'I don't mean to be, Julie.'

'Anyway, I brought you some dinner.' She pulled a cheese sandwich and a Kit-Kat from her pocket. 'Mum doesn't know. When she was serving dinner, I asked if I should call you down, but she said no.'

I felt rage surging through me again and then defeat. My shoulders slumped. 'Oh. What did you have?'

'Spaghetti Bolognese,' she said, sheepishly.

It was her favourite.

'Did he agree?'

She nodded. 'They said they think there is something wrong with you. You're always angry.' Her face was serious. 'I don't like it when you're cross, Sophie. It scares me.'

I tried not to let her see how hurt I was again by her words. I sighed. 'I'm just fed up, Julie. I feel as though Mum hates me. She barely looks at me or talks to me. And James . . . I hate him.'

'That's a bit harsh,' said Julie.

'I can't help how I feel. I hate him.' I was tired now and just wanted to eat the snacks she'd brought and go to sleep. Maybe I could go and live with my real dad. Maybe he could save me from all of this.

'Hate is not a nice word, Sophie,' she said, standing and putting her hands on her hips. 'You know, I thought they were exaggerating when they were talking at dinner. But I think they were right. I think you are jealous.'

'Of what, Julie?'

'Of me. This is why you're in a mood. It's all about the trainers, isn't it?'

I stared at her and my eyes start to fill with tears. At least I had some left. 'Julie,' I began to say, 'You're my sister. I love you.' I saw confusion cloud her eyes.

'Mum says jealousy is a horrid emotion.'

I didn't speak. How could I? Of course I was jealous of her. She was perfect. She got the trainers, received all the praise and attention. She was beautiful and kind. She had even bewitched my best friend, Matthew, who was now currently obsessed by her. But that wasn't where my rage was coming from. If I told her, she wouldn't believe me.

She squeezed my hand. 'Cheer up,' she said. 'It might never happen.'

I rolled onto my side and stared at the wall. But it had. It already had.

35

PRESENT

I sink back into the pillows, close my eyes and think of Julie. My adored little sister, with her flowing blonde hair and her bright smile. She was perfect and I really did love her to pieces.

Opening my eyes, I stare at the intricate cornicing on the ceiling and I'm suddenly reminded of the large tenement flat Mum and I lived in before she died. Mum. She is another story altogether. Then I feel Elliot brush the hair off my face.

'Just take your time,' he says.

'Julie was my little sister,' I begin. My throat is dry and I reach for the glass of water by the bed. 'She was eighteen months younger than me and was pretty much perfect. She was kind, funny, had hair like Rapunzel and was smart.' I am wracked with sadness and guilt as I tell my husband, in dribs and drabs, snippets of information about Julie. I thought it would be easier than this. But trying to articulate the way I felt about her is tough, especially when I denied for so long that she ever existed. 'It was just me and Mum and Julie. Mum said Dad, our real dad, had died in a road accident. Then she met MacIntyre . . .' my voice trails off, as it's not quite as simple as that. But right now, I need to focus on Julie, the story of Julie. Taking a shuddering sigh, I continue. 'I did want to tell you, Elliot. You have to believe me. So many times I thought about telling you but I just wanted a fresh start. I didn't want to be reminded about before. Or be asked about her. I left it all behind when I moved to Sydney.'

His gaze remains locked on my face as I talk. 'I mean — how would I even have begun? You would have thought I was crazy.' I pause for a moment, questioning whether I am. 'I just couldn't say anything. I would have told you about MacIntyre and you would have run a mile. Do you understand?'

He nods and wipes away a tear from my cheek. Glancing over at the alarm clock, I see the red digits shimmering. It's just after three o'clock. The house is still and quiet.

'What happened to Julie? Tell me,' he says, gently.

I look across at him. 'She died.'

Elliot doesn't gasp in horror or look shocked. It's like he already knows that's what I was going to say. I continue, feeling his hand tightly clasping mine. 'The day my sister died, the weather was beautiful. The water in the lake sparkled as though it had shards of diamonds scattered across the top.' Closing my eyes, I see the dusky orange gravelly path which led towards the dark, cold water of the lake. Reeds were protruding around the shoreline and there was a gentle twitter from the birds. 'We were on a boat. Then the boat turned over. Julie screamed and I heard a plop, a huge splash and then I was in the water too.' I begin to shake as I remember how cold the water was. 'It was freezing and the shock of falling in seemed to have winded me. I could see Julie's arms flailing around in the water. Her T-shirt clinging to her, her long blonde hair blooming around her like seaweed. I reached out for her and that's when she grabbed my hair. I was trying to tread water. But all of a sudden my scalp felt like it was being hauled off.'

Panic is now rising up my throat. 'I tried to say it'll be okay, hold on. Take my hand. She was terrified. The water was splashing and slopping over us. I kept reaching for her hand. Take my hand, I called. But my voice was croaky, I was getting tired. I kept trying to hold onto her. But then she started sinking. I went under the water and looked. But she was sinking like a stone and I couldn't save her.'

My eyes are closed now and I am back in the water, feeling myself choke on the mouthfuls I swallowed in. I'm desperately reaching for Julie, for something solid to grab. My breathing becomes ragged.

'It's okay, sweetie,' says Elliot. 'It's okay. You're doing well.'

'I watched them pull her out of the lake. Mum was inconsolable. Literally. It felt so unreal.'

'What about MacIntyre?' he asks. 'What did he do?'

'Nothing. He did nothing.'

Finally, I feel a tsunami of grief hit me and the tears fall and fall until I am sore from crying and my head is thumping.

Elliot holds me for what feels like hours before he finally nods off. But I can't sleep. I lie awake thinking and listening to his gentle snores.

36

PAST

I did call him. The man who said he was my *real* dad. Ross. I had been trying to forget all about him, but I couldn't. I had to wait until I was alone in the house, and I quickly dialled his number. He answered it after two rings.

'Sophie,' he said.

'Yes. How did you know it was me?

'You are the only person who has this number,' he said.

'Oh.'

'How are you?'

'Um, okay. I . . .' my voice trailed off.

'I was hoping you would call. I was worried I'd scared you off. I am so sorry, Sophie. I just wanted to talk you. That is all.'

'Okay,' I said. 'Let's talk. But not now, over the phone. Someone might come back.'

'Right. How about after school one day? Can you manage that?''

'Yes,' I whispered into the phone.

'Okay. How about we meet near the train station. On the platform?'

'Okay,' I said slowly, thinking it was a strange place to meet.

He obviously guessed what I was thinking. 'If we go to the local cafe that will look strange. And if you're seen wandering through the village with a man people will be suspicious. We can chat at the station. And get on a train if we need to.'

'Fine,' I said. 'What time? Four o'clock? Tomorrow?'

'Great,' he said, and I knew he was smiling. 'Thank you, Sophie. Thank you for giving me a chance.'

The door slammed shut behind me, just as I put the receiver down. It was Julie standing there. 'Who were you talking to? Have you got yourself a new boyfriend? Going on a date?'

I glared at her.

'I've just come in to dump my bag and change,' she said. 'Matthew and I are going for a walk.' She stood there twirling her hair, looking way older than her fourteen years.

'Right,' I said. 'Is Matthew your boyfriend now, then?'

She blushed. 'I won't tell if you won't,' she said, gesturing her head towards the phone.

37

PRESENT

I feel Elliot's arms around me as I listen to the birds start to wake and I smile as my husband kisses the back of my neck. Everything feels brighter this morning, sharing a piece of my past feels liberating. Elliot still loves me, he isn't horrified by my past. We manage to untangle our limbs from each other just as we hear Emma start to move around next door. The floors creak and I can hear her drawers sliding open and the cupboards being banged shut.

'Mummy,' she calls.

'I'll go to her.' Elliot hops out of bed hastily pulling on a T-shirt and jeans that are lying in a heap on the floor.

'Daddy,' I hear her squeal as he goes to her room. I picture her throwing herself at him and then the giggling starts and I know he was is walking around her bedroom with her standing on his feet. Stretching, I feel strangely content for the first time in ages. For a change, I am actually looking forward to the day ahead, and it feels rather amazing. We agreed last night, or early this morning, that today we will go to the police.

But later on, the sensation of worry and the accompanying nausea have returned. I'm sitting in the police station near our home. Who would have thought such ugly words and accusations could be spoken in such a nice district of London? This is an affluent area where bankers and their immaculately dressed wives live. I wonder if the officers in front of me listening to my story have ever heard such tales. D.I. Ana Kaszuba has short brown hair and dark eyes. Her colleague, D.I. Rosalind Wells, has long, reddish hair and a kind smile. As I'm talking I notice the officers looking at each other in a certain way as I tell them what happened. I begin with the very first time and continue talking, pausing only to take a sip of water every so often as my voice becomes dry and cracked. I didn't want Elliot to be in here with me hearing it all in such detail. I want to be able to look at him in the eye again. He is sitting on a hard, plastic chair in the waiting room outside holding a polystyrene cup of lukewarm coffee.

'He was such a powerful man,' I say. 'Nobody would have believed me when I was small if I'd told them what had happened.' I wipe away a tear which has finally appeared. 'I told my mum. Or at least, I *tried* to tell my mum but she said I was wicked and I was making it all up.'

'Why did you wait so long?' asks D.I. Kaszuba. She has a round face and her eyes seem to penetrate through me. I shift uncomfortably, wondering if this is a challenge rather than a question.

'Because I'm a mother myself now and I need to do this for myself and my daughter. And because of all these other historic cases that are in the news right now. They made me think that if these victims can do it then so can I.'

Chewing on my bottom lip, I continue, 'It's not right for him to be a member of parliament and to be serving the public when he's done all of this. What if he's still doing it? I mean . . . I think he may even have a grand-daughter, or a step-grand-daughter anyway, now around my daughter's age.'

The tears are now streaming down my face as I let go of all the hurt and loss I've harboured, yet pushed away, for so long. 'I tried to go and see him at his work,' I begin and then wipe my nose with the back of one hand, while digging around in my pocket with the other hand.

D.I. Wells, like a magician, suddenly produces a box of tissues.

'When was this?' asks the redhead, making a note in her pad.

'It was about a month ago. I can check my diary for the exact date.'

'Did he know you were coming?'

I shake my head. 'No. Well, he knew he had an appointment to see a Sophie Lewis, but he didn't know I had married and changed my name.'

'Okay, and so what happened?'

'I know it was silly.' My voice is apologetic. 'I just wanted to see him face to face and for him to apologise.'

'And did he?'

'No. He said I was a liar and a fantasist and if I didn't stay away I would regret it.'

Nobody speaks and I stare at the table in front of me covered with little crisscross marks and biro stains and cup rings.

'It's only now I've been able to pluck up the courage to come and talk to you about it.' It feels like I've been in this room for hours now and when I glance up at the white clock on the wall I realise that in fact I have. I jump up from the chair, startling the officers. 'My husband? Is he still here? It's my daughter. She needs to be collected from school.'

'It's okay,' says D.I. Wells. 'He said earlier to let you know that he would collect your daughter and that you should take a taxi home afterwards.'

I didn't even notice her leaving the room. How did that happen? I must have been so engrossed in telling my story.

Okay,' I say and smile in relief that the ordeal is — hopefully — almost over.

'Mrs Lewis, thank you for being so open and honest with us. I know it can't be easy,' says D.I. Wells. 'You must be exhausted.'

I realise that I am, and hungry too. But all I want to do now is go home to my family. 'What happens now?'

'Well, obviously these are very serious allegations. If you leave them with us we will look into them and go and interview Mr MacIntyre.'

'Thank you.' I breathe a sigh of relief.

'Mrs Lewis,' says D.I. Kaszuba.

'Yes.'

'One last thing before you go. Do you have anything else in your possession which may be useful to our inquiry?'

I shrug. 'Such as?'

'Letters, diaries — anything you may have kept from that time.'

'Actually, yes I do.' I am feeling another surge of adrenaline run through me. 'I've always been a hoarder and I held onto my diaries.'

'We'll be in touch to collect them,' says D.I. Kaszuba.

There's nothing else I can do just now. But when I close my eyes all I can see is my mum. And I can hear her shouting at me. Telling me that I'm crazy. Just like my dad.

38

PAST

I went to the train station as arranged the next day after school. I waited and I waited. But he didn't show up. I was devastated, wondering if I had got the time and place wrong. But I *knew* I hadn't. When I got home, I ran up to my room and looked for the scrap of paper with his number on it. It wasn't where I'd hidden it. There was nothing I could do. I just had to wait.

I just tried my very best to be good. To be nice. I took Barney out for walks every day. I ran, in a bid to improve my mood, and I tried to be nicer to my sister. I thought if I was nice then maybe, somehow, he would find me again.

When Mum asked me if I wanted to go out for lunch I thought that maybe I had turned a corner. Perhaps things were starting to be okay and I was a bit more normal. We went to the local deli at the Cross and she asked for a table at the back of the cafe, in the conservatory where it was nice and quiet. She asked me politely about school and running and then she started. She began by telling me she was worried about me. She said I was skulking around the house in a permanent mood and the family had had enough. I stared at the table, listening as she talked, but all I could hear was the clatter of cutlery in the background. The sun was beaming through the conservatory roof and I watched as the pensioners who had come in while we were talking removed their coats and scarves, their cheeks flushed. I studied the blackboard above her head wondering why the foods were so elaborately described. You couldn't just order a sausage roll. It was a *scrummy* sausage roll with *local pork* and a *touch of apple* wrapped in *buttery puff pastry*. The cheese on Mum's sandwich was *Scottish* and *rich* and *creamy*. It just looked orange and greasy to me, hanging out of the toasted bread. I couldn't eat much of the jacket potato she ordered for me. The tuna had too much mayonnaise on it, leaving an oily film in my mouth.

'I found this,' she said, reaching into her handbag. It was the piece of paper. The one with my father's number on it.

'Oh,' I managed to say. Why was she snooping in my room? I wanted to scream that I hadn't done anything wrong.

'Do you want to tell me anything about it?'

'A man who said he was my dad approached me in the street. He said he was my dad and he'd left us when I was small. Said he'd tried to keep in touch over the years. Said he sent letters.'

Mum just stared ahead, two dark spots appearing on her cheeks. 'That man is a liar. Do you understand me?' She paused. 'Unless this is one of your little schemes to get more attention?'

I gasped and dropped my fork. How could she think that? It seemed a wild accusation, even from her.

Then Mum dropped her bombshell. 'We think it would be a good idea if you go away for a while, Sophie.'

I frowned. 'What do you mean, go away? Where to?'

'James has a good contact who works in a centre which deals with ... helps teenagers like you.'

'Why? Where?'

'In the country. In Stirlingshire.'

'But I don't want to go,' I said, the tears starting to slide down my face. 'Why do you want to send me away?'

'Now Sophie, I'll thank you to remember you are in a public place. Please behave. Remember you have your father's reputation to think of.' She dabbed her lips with her napkin. 'It's only for a couple of weeks. Hopefully they will help you manage your mood swings. Perhaps even give you some medication.'

It took every ounce of will-power for me not to turn the table upside down. That's when I knew she had planned this perfectly. She'd brought me to this public place to tell me her news, knowing that if I made a scene then everyone would just point at me and I'd be known as the M.P.'s mad step-daughter. I decided not to play into her hands.

'Okay. If that's what you think is best.'

'Oh,' she said in surprise. 'Well, I'm glad to hear that you're being sensible about this. Your father has worked very hard at pulling some strings to get you in at such short notice.'

'He's not my father,' I said, my voice flat.

'No need to be awkward, Sophie,' she said, smiling and then waving at a lady in the corner of the conservatory.

'When do I go?'

'Now. Your bag is in the car.'

39

PRESENT

It's been over a week since I made my complaint against MacIntyre to the police. Despite believing I was doing the right thing, I think my confession has driven a massive wedge between me and Elliot. Perhaps I should have kept quiet and pretended that everything was okay. But then I had to tell him. Keeping it all secret was gnawing away at me like a cancerous growth. Yet now he seems to be avoiding me. Coming to bed later when I am already asleep and getting up earlier than he normally does. I can't remember when he last touched me. It's been days. I don't feel elated or relieved about my complaint anymore. I now feel worse with each day. Too tired to get out of bed, I feel gluey and my head is constantly thumping. I certainly don't feel like telling myself how much I'm loved or how wonderful I am. In fact, I'm reminding myself of what my own mum was like and I don't like it at all. I don't want Emma to have memories of me being in bed permanently or moping around, but I really can't even drag myself out of bed. I am just exhausted. I am so petrified that all my efforts have been wasted. Joan is due back today but I'm glad, it will be good to have her company. She, of course, knows nothing of what has gone on, so we will need to tell her later. Part of me is worried about her reaction; will she reject me or be annoyed with me? Will she still want to be my mother-in-law?

This morning I'm just contemplating whether or not to try and force myself to go for a run, when the doorbell rings. Surely Joan can't be arriving back early? She's not due back for a couple of days, I think with a sigh. But standing on the doorstep are Detective Inspectors Wells and Kaszuba. 'Can we come in?'

I show them into the living room and call Elliot from upstairs where he's working in the spare room. He's based himself at home this week, to keep an eye on me maybe, in case I do anything silly.

'Hi there,' he says as he walks into the room looming large in the doorframe. He gestures at the women to sit down as he walks towards me and sits next to me on the sofa.

'We thought we would just come and give you a bit of an update as to what has happened since we last spoke,' says D.I. Wells.

'I'm sorry about the delay,' says D.I. Kaszuba. 'There was a bit of red tape to deal with,' she adds, raising an eyebrow. Her eyes don't seem so cold today and I catch her smiling at Elliot.

'We've had a look through your diaries, Mrs Lewis, and we now want to bring Mr MacIntyre in for questioning.'

The room lurches around me and I drop my head in between my knees to stop myself fainting.

'It's okay. Take deep breaths.' Elliot is rubbing my back, small circles which get bigger.

I do as I'm told and stare at the cream rug on the floor

and start to feel more in focus again, especially when I begin to make out the lettering on the green M & M which is squashed into the corner.

'Are you okay, Mrs Lewis?' asks D.I. Wells.

I sit upright. 'Yes. I'm fine.'

'What does this mean?' asks Elliot.

'It means we'll be bringing him in for questioning tomorrow.'

'Then what?'

'One step at a time,' says D.I. Wells. 'We'll see what he has to say about these allegations and then take it from there.'

Elliot asks a few more questions and I can hear them all murmuring but I start to zone out and the noise drifts away. It's as though they're having a one-way conversation while I get to grips with the fact that this is really happening. Finally. I'm making it all happen and I can feel a tiny glimmer of hope. Out of the corner of my eye I see Elliot stand up and I force my mind back to the room.

'Thanks so much for coming to tell us in person.' Elliot stretches his hand out to shake the officers' hands. They nod at me and smile, and I notice that D.I. Kaszuba maintains eye contact with my husband for just a fraction longer than I think she should, and she catches me looking at her.

'Your personal belongings will be returned to you as soon as possible, Mrs Lewis,' says D.I. Wells.

I try to smile. 'Thank you.'

'Now, as I said to your husband you will, of course, not be named when this story breaks. We will not name Mr MacIntyre either. Unfortunately, there's not much we can do to keep things out of the press these days,' says D.I. Wells. 'They'll find out who it is. All it takes is someone to leak it. I'd just advise you to get on with your daily business as best as you can and not to discuss this with anyone while our investigations are pending.'

D.I. Kaszuba keeps trying to catch my eye but I avoid her gaze — I'm not sure why. Then she puts her hand on my arm and I know it would be too rude of me to shake it off, so I force myself to raise my head and look at her. 'Mrs Lewis,' she says.

'Yes.'

'I just want to let you know that we never doubted your story. Rosalind and I have heard the same story so many times over the years. We are on your side.'

She is smiling at me and I try to return her smile, but my lips are stuck to my teeth, my mouth is dry and it must look like a grimace.

'Thank you,' I manage.

'We'll keep you posted,' says D.I. Wells.

Elliot shows them to the door and waves goodbye. He shuts the door and turns to me, but the expression on his face is unreadable.

'Are you sure you want to do this?' he asks.

'Do what?'

'Go ahead and press charges.'

Neither of us speaks.

'Why would I not be sure?'

'Because it's a huge step, Sophie. Once they arrest MacIntyre there is no going back.'

I feel a bead of worry starting to gnaw away like a worm boring its way into my gut. Elliot's face is pale and he has dark jags of stubble on his chin.

'Don't you believe me?' I take a step towards him. He remains where he is.

'Sophie,' he says. 'It's not about that.'

He doubts me, I can see the hesitation in his eyes.

'It's about what lies ahead for you, for us as a family.'

'That is why I'm doing it.' The tears are now freely falling down my face. 'I'm doing it for us, for Emma. I can't go on any more burying all these secrets.'

He takes a step towards me and pulls me to him but I no longer feel safe pressed against his chest. His body feels tense. I feel like an intruder.

'Well if you're sure this is what you want, then okay, Sophie. I just know how much stress and heartache lies ahead for you. Especially if this goes to court. To trial. Your life will be ripped apart. Our lives will be ripped apart. Nothing will ever be the same.'

Feelings of guilt and shame which are flooding through me. 'I'm sorry,' I whisper. 'But I can't be the victim anymore. I need to speak out.'

40

PAST

When I first arrived at the residential centre for problem kids, I met Patricia, who was to be my key worker. She had chubby cheeks, a wide smile and blonde hair streaked with grey. She wore wooden bangles on her wrists which clacked together when she talked. Patricia showed me to my room, gave me a tour of the rest of the centre and pointed to the recreation room where the residents could play table tennis or snooker. I glanced briefly at the girls and boys who were in there. Two girls and a tall, spotty guy with dyed black hair sat in the corner in a huddle. I quickly decided I would be avoiding them.

Patricia asked me if I'd like a drink before beckoning me to follow her through to the conservatory so we could have a chat.

I told her that I wasn't quite sure why I was there — well, other than the odd mood swing. But that was a normal teenage thing, right? All teens were prone to mood swings and tantrums. It was all to do with the hormones. Well, probably not in my case but I wasn't going to talk to her about any of that. She just nodded encouragingly at me and then scanned her eyes over my notes and sat back in her armchair. I stared at the inches of exposed skin between her sock and her trouser hem. Staring at the dark hairs sprouting from her legs, I wanted to suggest she should shave.

'Your mother seems to have some worries about you though, Sophie. Do you know why that might be?'

I shook my head. There were a million things I could suggest, but I wouldn't. I didn't want this to become about my relationship, or lack of, with my mother.

Patricia's hands were clasped on her lap. She was so peaceful and serene. I looked around the room, at the trailing plants on the window ledge, the flecks of fluff on the carpet and the spider which scuttled across the ceiling.

Her voice was soothing and gentle as she said, 'You are safe here, Sophie. Nothing you tell me will go any further than these four walls. I am here to help you.'

We sat in a comfortable silence as I thought about what she had said. It was warm and I started to feel sleepy, and wondered if I could really tell her the truth. I closed my eyes. *Could* I tell her about James? Then a harsh slap of reality jolted me from my slumber. Of course I couldn't. He was the reason I was here. His special status meant he had fast-tracked me into the place. No doubt the staff were all fooled by him too, along with the rest of the world except me.

When I opened my eyes, Patricia was gone. She'd left a dent in the blue cushions and her clipboard was sitting on the table. I wondered if I should look at it. Leaning forward, I quickly grabbed it with both hands, quickly fumbling through the pages before she returned. What did it say about me? What did it reveal? Then I saw a white page with typed notes and saw the name Ross. I gasped. My dad? I greedily read on, trying to grasp as much information as I could, feeling the blood rushing to my head. Patricia wandered back into the room and sat back down in her chair. The folder was back in place and I sat in my chair, my eyes still shut — for I knew that if I opened them, she would be able see my shock. Now I understood — kind of —why my mother had told me he was dead.

41

PRESENT

'M.P. James MacIntyre was arrested today over claims of historical sex abuse. The 57-year-old was arrested at Portcullis House and was held at a central London police station where he was questioned for more than six hours.

The claims relate to several alleged sexual assaults on a woman during the 1990s. A Scotland Yard spokesman did not name the M.P. but said his offices and an address in West London had been searched.

The probe is the latest in a long line of high-profile inquiries into the conduct of ageing celebrities and personalities as long as 40 years ago. This arrest is said not to be part of the high-profile sex crime investigation Operation Yewtree, set up in the wake of revelations about BBC presenter Jimmy Savile.

It is not the first scandal to hit the married M.P. He famously resigned from his Scottish seat in 1997 after a newspaper exposed his affair with a researcher. He later went on to relaunch his political career in 2012 and is now M.P. for Romness, Lancashire. It is unclear whether the allegations relate to the time he was an M.P. in Scotland during the 1990s.'

Elliot flicked off the radio as I sat down at the kitchen table. He handed me a cup of coffee and I clasped my hands around the scalding pottery.

'Emma was fine when she went into her class. Just wondered if you could pick her up. Oh, and your friend Lucinda came over and asked if you were okay. Said she'd not seen you for a while. Toast?'

I shake my head. 'Aren't you going to go to the office?' I'm suddenly feeling self-conscious of being in my pyjamas, which I seem to have lived in these past few days.

'No. They're fine with me working from home,' he says. 'I just said that you'd been under the weather. Taking time to adjust to life in London and had a nasty virus which you couldn't shake.'

Great. So, his colleagues must now think I'm a complete fruit-loop. Mind you they might be right. I take a sip of coffee and flinch as he noisily slurps his.

'Do they know about this?' I say gesturing at the radio.

He shakes his head. 'No. I didn't want to say anything. Thought I would see how it pans out.'

I chew my bottom lip.

'I'm doing some research anyway for an environmental feature so I am tied up with that. I expect the story will be all over Sky, and the papers too Sophie. Just to warn you.' He turns and pours the rest of his mug down the sink.

'Okay,' I say, taking a huge breath in. 'I think I'll go for a run.' I don't add that I want to run and run and keep going. I want to run away.

'Oh, by the way, before I forget. Mum says she met someone who knows you in Cardiff.'

I frown. 'I don't know anyone in Cardiff.'

'I'm sure she'll tell you all the details when she's back. Just said she was chatting to someone in a cafe, turned out they are also from Glasgow, she mentioned you and the chap said he knew you from school.'

I grip my coffee cup.

'Small world, isn't it?'

'Did she say what his name was?'

'Mmm, can't remember.' He is now staring down at his phone, scrolling through the inbox on his screen. 'Ah. Here it is. Matthew.'

My mug slips from my fingers and falls to the floor.

42

PAST

I sat on a bench beside the tall oak tree in the large, landscaped gardens. The paint was peeling away and it was splattered in bird poo, but at least it was quiet there and I was alone. The cold air bit at my cheeks, even though it was supposed to be summer, and the clouds were heavy with rain. When I felt the spits of water land on my head, I pulled up my hood. I didn't move. I wanted to stay sitting there forever. Even when the rain became torrential, I stayed there, watching it bounce off the concrete slabs of the path. The water ran down my forehead and my nose, and I wiped my face with the back of my hand. I heard a voice calling me, but I didn't turn to see who it was. I knew it was Patricia. I could hear her bangles clacking. She sat down on the bench next to me and I sighed. She didn't speak, just sat alongside me and waited. And she waited. I was getting a bit cold now, and soggy. I stood up with a shiver and she put her hand on my arm. I flinched, brushing it away. I gestured with my head towards the door. I walked away from the tree, my shelter for the past hour or so, and went towards the large Victorian house which had been my home for the past two weeks. Patricia followed me and, when we got inside, she pulled off her coat and helped me off with mine.

'Shall we go and get dried off?' she suggested, her voice firm. 'Then we can have a nice hot drink.'

She wasn't asking, she was telling. I could already hear the questions she was going to ask me. 'You can tell me how you felt about sitting outside in the rain beside the tree. How did it make you feel, Sophie? How are you feeling now, Sophie? Is there anything that makes you feel sad, Sophie?' And I knew I would shake my head again and again and reply no. For … what would she say if I told her the truth? She would shake her head in disbelief. She would surely call me a liar. For that's what I must be. It was my fault. I was imagining everything. I was a liar and I was mad. Just like my dad. It even said so in the notes. I trudged upstairs to my room, changed into a dry pair of jeans and sweater, and towel-dried my hair. I caught my reflection in the mirror and saw someone else staring back. It wasn't me. The girl looking back had hollow eyes, pale skin and limp hair. That was not the me I remembered. I remembered the old Sophie. The Sophie from before. From before it all began.

43

PRESENT

By the next morning every newspaper has splashed MacIntyre's arrest and it is all over the internet and TV too. When Emma and I walk to school, the paranoid feeling I've had on other days, that everyone was whispering and pointing their finger at me, has vanished. Emma is telling me about the art project she is doing today and that she loved *The Gruffalo* book that the teacher read to the class. She skips through her door happy and smiling and I feel strangely liberated about the way things are going now.

Davina even smiles and says good morning, which is quite unexpected. 'We missed you at the coffee morning the other week,' she says.

Really? Me? 'I'm so sorry, I've had a horrid virus,' I lie.

'A few of us are going to the Gilded Balloon now if you fancy it?' I hesitate, then smile when I see Lucinda approaching.

'Hello, stranger. Are you feeling better?'

'I am, thanks,' I say and I do genuinely feel better. 'I'm sorry I didn't get back to your messages.'

'That's okay. Your husband said you'd been under the weather. Got time for a quick cuppa and catch up then?'

'Sure.' I see Davina nodding approvingly.

Ten minutes later a group of eight mums sit nursing cappuccinos and lattes around two small coffee tables in the Gilded Balloon cafe. We are all making polite chit-chat when my ears prick up. The women at the table behind us are discussing MacIntyre's arrest.

'I mean, what is it with these old pervs,' says one woman. 'It's like Savile and all these old wrinklies off the telly. They think they're gods and they can get away with anything.'

I know,' says her friend. 'Though I do sometimes wonder if some of these women coming forward are just after a bit of compensation.'

'Mmm. I don't know if you would put yourself through that, would you, just for a bit of cash?'

'I don't know . . . I mean it just depends where you are from and what your circumstances are doesn't it? I mean look at Savile. There are hundreds of claims for compensation against him. I mean I'm not saying that they're not all genuine. But come on. Don't you think that some of those people are just jumping on the bandwagon?'

'I'm not sure. I don't think *I* could do that, make false claims against someone just for the money,' says her friend. 'I mean — it's all a bit tawdry, isn't it?'

'Some women would stoop to anything for money. Look, I'm not saying this woman is making it up about MacIntyre. I mean, he does look a bit creepy. But I'm just saying we should be ready to question everything in this compensation culture we live in where everyone is cash-obsessed.'

I have to muster all the self-control I can to stop myself from turning round and confronting them.

'Earth to Sophie,' says Lucinda, poking me in the ribs. I notice her glancing at the women too.

'Sorry — I was miles away,' I say.

'Davina was asking you something.'

'Sorry Davina, what did you say? I didn't sleep so well last night so I'm a bit absent-minded today.'

'That's okay,' she says, her voice clipped. 'I was just interested to find out where you are from in Scotland. I have relatives there.'

'Glasgow,' I say, stifling a yawn. Then I realise that Lucinda is looking at me in surprise.

'Isn't it dangerous there?' asks Davina.

'In what way?'

She shivers. 'Oh, you know — knives, murders, all that.'

'No more dangerous than London, Davina. It's quite a safe place, you know.' *Unless your stepfather is a paedophile.*

I notice Lucinda still looking at me oddly. What have I done? I'm quite grateful to her when, not long after, she is the first to suggest making a move.

'I need to go, girls. Loads to do before lunch including a leg wax and a quick trip to the supermarket.'

I stand up too. 'I'll walk you along to the shops. I have some errands to run as well.'

Once we're out on the street, I thank her for her exit strategy.

'That's okay.' But she isn't smiling and I don't know whether I've done something or said something to offend her. 'Is everything alright, Lucinda?'

'I am so, so tired,' she says and rubs her eyes. 'Daisy hasn't been sleeping at all well these past few nights. She's been tucking into my bed at night.'

I nod in sympathy. 'That lack of sleep is like a form of torture. What's keeping her up?'

'Bad dreams . . . though I think she's missing her dad. I'm sure that's at the bottom of it all. He's just never around.'

I reach over and pat her arm. 'If there's anything that I can do don't hesitate to ask. I could have Daisy back for tea after school and give you a break?'

She smiles at me. 'Thanks, Sophie. You're a pal. Really appreciate it.' She sighs and looks at her watch. 'I'd better get on. I'll see you at pick-up?'

'Sure.' I turn to walk away.

'Sophie? Do you ever wish you could just go back to your life before you had a kid?'

I stand there for a moment and say nothing. 'No,' I say. 'Never.'

'You're right,' she says. 'I couldn't imagine not having them. It's just hard. Maybe we need to do something fun,' she goes on, her eyes brightening. 'Maybe we need a night out?'

'THAT SOUNDS GOOD,' I say, hesitantly.

'Leave it with me and I'll arrange something.'

'Okay. Now off you go and get those legs waxed.'

She smiles gratefully and turns. 'Oh, Sophie,' she says again.

My heart rate quickens and I wonder what she is going to say.

'Why did you lie?' she says, her expression unreadable.

'What do you mean?' I say, feeling panic grab at my insides.

Lucinda laughs heartily and I do feel a bit more at ease. 'No need to worry. White lies are only little lies. I just wondered why you told Davina you were from Glasgow, when you told me that you are from Edinburgh?'

'Ah, well,' I say, thinking quickly, 'they're both true, in a way. I was born in Edinburgh, but brought up in the west. I was kind of interested to hear what she would say about Glasgow. She thinks it's Danger City. Did you see her edging away from me?'

Lucinda laughs. 'See you later.'

'Bye.' I'm getting careless and that was a very stupid slip of the tongue.

44

PAST

Since arriving at the centre I'd been so, so tired, which Patricia told me was quite normal. At night, I lay in the hard, narrow bed and I stared at the cornicing on the ceiling which reminded me of a wedding cake. As I studied the swirls and the intricate designs, I thought about my own room and then I thought about Julie and I started to panic. I could hear the creaks of the floorboards and I wondered if she was okay. My heart raced, I started to sweat and more than once I hammered at my door saying I needed to call home. I needed to check my sister was okay.

Soothing hands rubbed my back and told me that it was fine, everything would be okay and I just needed to calm down. Cool hands on my forehead, tissues to mop my sobs and a sip of water and some more tablets and then eventually I drifted off into a fitful sleep. I could see my dad in my dreams. I could see him standing there on the pavement that night. I could hear him on the phone saying he was looking forward to telling me more. I started to reach out for him, then recoiled and woke shaking.

I sat up in bed, pulled the beige duvet cover up around

my chin. It had been just over two weeks since I'd been away from home and I wondered when I could go back. I thought about Mum. I'd not missed her at all — but then, why would I when she seemed to dislike me so much? When I thought about James I felt nothing but indifference, not even hate. It was when I thought of Julie that I felt a yearning. I needed to get back to my sister. So when Patricia told me that I could go back to my family, I started to smile. We were in the conservatory again where it all began.

'Julie is important to you,' she said.

I nodded. 'Yes.' She smiled at me, encouraging me to go on. 'I think since our dad died I always felt I had to take care of her.'

Patricia leaned forward in her chair. 'What about your mum?'

'She's always had James,' I said.

'How does that make you feel?'

I shrugged. 'It doesn't really make me feel anything. I just miss my dad. And right now I miss my sister. I can't wait to see her.'

Patricia sat back and narrowed her eyes. 'You speak about your dad quite a lot. Do you mean James, your stepfather?'

'No. He's not my real dad.'

I shrugged.

'But he's always been like a dad to you?'

I quickly shook my head. 'No. I've never been able to call him that. He's not my real dad. He's just James.'

'Sophie,' she said and then paused. 'How much do you remember of your dad?'

'Not much,' I said. 'Why?'

'I just wondered how much you can remember of when you were small.'

I squeezed my eyes shut and I tried to remember. I saw shapes and snapshots of the past. I smelt soap, Cussons soap. I could feel his wiry hair in my hands. Then there was nothing. I snapped my eyes open. 'He died when I was two. I don't remember much about him at all. It's like he never even existed.' I meant every single word of it. He had let me down. He had appeared out of the blue, when I believed he was dead, and he failed to meet me as promised. He'd let me down again. I let the tears fall and Patricia handed me a tissue.

'How are you feeling about going home?' she said, eventually.

'Fine,' I said. 'Looking forward to seeing my family.' I forced a smile. 'Looking forward to getting back to normal.'

'And do you think the techniques we practised will help if you feel you're going to lose your temper?'

I smiled and nodded. I realised near the start of my stay that the best thing to do was tell her what she wanted to hear. I knew James and Mum would get to read my notes anyway. He would pull some strings again and read my innermost thoughts in therapy. But there will be no shocks as I have told everyone what they want to hear, rather than the truth.

45

PRESENT

The paranoia is back today and I'm sure the neighbours are talking about me behind their designer shutters and Farrow and Ball-painted doors. I can hear their voices screaming in my head as I walk up the road studying the cracks on the pavement.

Elliot's gone back to work now as I think he's fed up of being around me. The story has tailed off in the papers now that a reality TV show star is getting married. It seems that sex offenders are no longer front-page news. D.I. Wells did call to check how I was holding up, and said to stay positive. (She didn't tell me how to do that, though.) The police were still continuing their enquiries, she said, and she would be in touch again as soon as there was some more news as to whether or not they could go ahead and charge MacIntyre. Apparently, these things take time and I should just be patient.

In the meantime, life goes on even though my world has come crashing down around me. There's an impenetrable greyness about the days when the sky seems too close and heavy. Life is the same for Emma and her routine goes on as normal with her swimming lessons and now dancing too. Julie would have been proud of her. Emma seems oblivious to what is happening around her. Thank God. After I drop her at school I've taken to catching the train to somewhere, anywhere. Some days I catch up with Lucinda, other days when I want to be alone — which are increasingly common — I go to Richmond and sit in a coffee shop, watching the world pass by outside and inside. I watch the groups of groomed women gathering around the tables with their skinny cappuccinos and Americanos gossiping about their lives, their children, their sex lives (or lack of), their annoying in-laws, paint charts and whether or not they are on a fasting day, and I feel so pleased that I'm not in their clique. I am happy that I can get up and walk out whenever I want.

Other days I take the circular loop to Waterloo and back, and just sit and listen to the squeaking of the carriages as they sway and rock me. The windows are always grimy, the faces blank, but I fix my gaze on the flooring studying every single speck. Occasionally a tear will escape from my eye and I let it fall rather than brush it away. I'm amazed that I'm able to shed anything, after everything that has happened.

Elliot keeps telling me to eat more and that my clothes are hanging off me and am I okay? I'm fucking tip-top, I want to shout at him. Pass me the chocolate cake and the strawberry milkshakes. Let's open the champagne and celebrate.

I'm in the middle of going through the motions of making dinner when I hear the front door open. Elliot's back.

'Hello,' he calls.

I hear Emma slide off the sofa in the TV room and run through to see him.

'G'day princess.'

I hear her giggle as she always does when he lifts her high up in the air.

'Something smells good,' he says, when he walks into the kitchen, carrying Emma.

'Oh.' I shrug. 'It's just a casserole. It'll be ready soon.' I watch Elliot as he rolls up his shirt-sleeves.

'How about you go and tidy up next door, Emma?' he says.

'Then wash your hands,' I call after her as she disappears out the kitchen.

Elliot walks over and hugs me. 'Hi love. How was your day?'

'Fine thanks.'

He looks at me quizzically for a moment. ''You sure?'

I nod.

'I'll just go wash up too.'

I stand there for a moment thinking about what Lucinda asked me the other day. When she asked me if I would ever prefer to go back to my old life. I love being a wife and mother but, yes, some days I do wish I hadn't started all of this stuff with MacIntyre. Now I know the meaning of the phrase, let sleeping dogs lie.

The timer on the oven starts to beep dragging back into the here and now. 'Dinner's ready. Elliot. Emma. Wash your hands and come on through,' I shout, then realise that actually I'm missing Joan. She's due back in a few days and I will be pleased to see her. I've missed her, despite what happened with Emma.

'Okay, hun,' says Elliot as he walks through, his head down looking at his phone.

I catch my reflection in the window and I try a positive affirmation. I try to tell myself that I am safe and I am secure and that I will be okay. But it's not use, it doesn't work. All the reminders of the past are with me in my head and I don't know that I'll ever let them go. When I glance up, Elliot is frowning at me. 'What's wrong?'

'I think you'd better have a look at this,' he says, passing me his phone.

It's an email from Shirley, my old colleague from the hospital in Glasgow.

FAO Sophie MacIntyre

Dear Mr Lewis,

I am sorry to contact you this way and out of the blue. However, I am trying to get in touch with your wife, Sophie MacIntyre. I used to work with her in Glasgow at the Royal Hospital and I know she worked at St Vincent's Hospital in Sydney, but don't have an email address for her. Her former colleagues at St Vincent's said I could perhaps get in touch via you – they told me which paper you work for and I found your email address on the newspaper's website. I wonder if you could ask Sophie to email me please? It's a matter of urgency that I talk to her.

With best wishes,

Shirley Patel

. . .

My heart is racing and my palms sweaty. I want to throw the phone away. What does she want? What does she know? And why after so many years is she getting in touch?

46

PAST

I stopped trying to wriggle free. This was obviously my life and how it was meant to be. I had been so tired since coming home from the centre. Some nights I wanted to crawl into bed after dinner. I had lost interest in my books, I felt too heavy to run. Sometimes I just wished I could close my eyes and never wake up. I thought the time away in that place would make me feel better. That's what they said. But I felt worse. They gave me more tablets which just made me sleepy. It all felt like a foggy blur.

'Oh for God's sake Sophie,' snapped Mum at dinner. 'I wish you would blooming well cheer up a bit.'

I sat there digging my nails into my palms, desperately trying not to cry. Julie squeezed my hand under the table, then when Mum's back was turned she stuck out her tongue. That just about made me smile.

Mum had made trifle for pudding.

'Sophie, clear the plates away. Julie, dear, can you fetch some spoons please?'

The sight of the cream, the custard and the hundreds and thousands was tempting and I licked my lips like a dog.

Mum left me until last, serving herself before me, and handed me a portion. It was smaller than Julie's. She let the bowl hover in mid-air for a moment before allowing me to take it. Of course I said nothing, just felt immediately guilty for eating it —although when the sugary pudding hit my lips I did feel happy for a second. And I ate it fast, greedily eyeing up the rest that was left in the crystal bowl. I felt Mum's eyes on me, disapproving and disgusted.

'I'm full,' said Julie, pushing her bowl away. 'Thanks though Mum, that was delicious.'

The sound of the clock ticking was the only sound I could focus on. Mum didn't speak for a few moments, then she clasped her hands together and leaned forward.

'Well girls. I was hoping your father would be here to tell you this. But he's been held up again and I really think you should know.'

Julie and I exchanged glances and I held my breath. Mum ran her fingers through her hair and smiled. For a tiny moment, her face softened and she actually looked kind. Like a proper mum.

'Your father, girls, has been given a special award.' She paused for a moment, obviously trying to heighten the drama. 'He's going to be made Scotland's Politician of the Year at the Press Awards.' Her eyes sparkled. 'Isn't that marvellous?'

I watched Julie nodding in agreement and smiling. Did she look as happy as she was before I went into the centre? Had anything happened? It was hard to tell.

'There's going to be a special awards ceremony at the Hilton in Glasgow and lots of important people will be there. I know he hoped to tell you himself, but I'm just so thrilled and excited for him I couldn't wait.' She twirled her wedding band round her finger. 'He's such a good man,' she said, staring at me. 'I'm just delighted that all his hard work is finally being recognised.'

I couldn't smile back at her. Politician of the Year? Everyone loved him and in the public's eyes he could do no bloody wrong. They thought he was a saint. They probably think I'm crazy. I've just been in the mad-house, after all. I sat there and stared at my lap, listening to the ticking again. Tick tock, the minutes ticked past. Julie asked to be excused from the table. I looked over at her. I hoped she was okay. She wouldn't look at me. I hoped I wasn't too late.

47

PRESENT

After dinner, Elliot takes Emma upstairs to get her ready for bed. I follow them up and glance into the bathroom where she is submerged in bubbles. Elliot sits on the floor next to her scrolling through his phone, again. A horrid thought invades my mind and I bite down on the urge to gasp out loud.

What makes a man abusive? What makes a man do the things that MacIntyre did to me? I shake away the image of his hands, reaching and grabbing, and I make myself count slowly to ten. My skin is clammy and my heart races at the thought of anyone hurting Emma. I look at Elliot again, *really* look at him. He glances up and momentarily smiles, then reaches over to brush a bubble from Emma's nose. Then he looks back and mouths, 'Are you okay?'

His head is tipped to one side and guilt washes over me for even having such a fleeting thought. He's a good man. He's nothing like MacIntyre. *Nothing* like him at all. I pad through to our bedroom wondering if I should just wait until tomorrow before getting in touch with Shirley. But I know I'll just lie awake all night tossing and turning and wondering. In our bedroom, I reach for my laptop which is down the side of the bed. I sit up, pillows plumped behind me, and log onto my email account. Again, and again, I read over the email Elliot has forwarded me from Shirley. My hands tremble as I think about that time. Those dark days, when it was just me and Mum. Then just me, alone and desperate to escape. I feel goose-bumps forming and a wave of revulsion sweep through me. I don't want to go back to those days ever again. I shake my head. I need to face this now and get it over with. So I start to type.

Hi Shirley,

Elliot passed me on your email. How are you? It's been ages. Is everything okay?

Best wishes,

Sophie

I read it over again, wonder about redrafting it and saying something else. Is it too brief? Too bright and breezy? Too impersonal? But before I can change my mind I make myself send. There's no going back now. I realise my hands are still trembling, then I jump when I hear a ping. An email has dropped.

Sophie - thanks for getting in touch so quickly. Can you call me please asap? My number's attached.

Shirley

. . .

I SIT FOR A MINUTE, trying to stay calm. But I'm dizzy and am gulping in air. Forcing myself to breathe, I think. What is the urgency? Why, after all these years, does she want to speak to me so urgently? And why can't she just email me whatever she wants to say? Thoughts start to race through my mind, I see images of Mum, smell the hospital and feel the walls closing in.

I thought I had left all of this behind. I don't want any reminders of the past now, seeping into my mind and soiling it. Emma and Elliot are chattering quietly and I can hear the splash of water. What should I do?

Snatching up my phone which is lying on the bed beside me, I decide I take to take control of the situation. I need to have the upper hand here. I stand up, key in the number and wait. Moving towards the curtain, I peek outside at the shadows below. Rain has started to fall, and the drops are bouncing off the pavement. I stare at them, momentarily transfixed.

'Hello,' says a voice.

'Hi. I'm looking for Shirley.'

'Aye that's me . . . Sophie, darlin' is that you?'

'Yes. Yes, it is.' My voice trails off. I'm sure I can see someone out there staring up at me. Yanking the curtain firmly shut, I slump to the floor.

'How you enjoying Sydney?' She coughs.

'Fine thanks. Great. The weather's good.'

'Well, listen, I know this will be costing you a fortune. I just wanted to tell you over the phone though, not on the email.'

I hold my breath. I'm not sure why I don't correct her. Why don't I tell her where I am just now? Why do I let her believe I'm still in Sydney? Instead, I say, 'Sounds ominous.'

'Ach, well, hopefully there's nothing to worry about. But I've had an anonymous letter.'

My heart sinks. It's almost like I know what she's going to say.

''Aye, a letter claiming that we should be looking into your past. That you're not to be trusted and that the hospital should be looking into deaths at the hospital at the time you were there. It claims you were sloppy with a few things.'

I can almost picture Shirley as she tells me this. Her face will be etched with concern and she'll be worrying about whether or not she's doing the right thing. 'Oh God,' I whisper. 'Who would say such a thing?'

'Exactly. These anonymous letters are awful. Don't worry, love — you're not the first. I just wanted to warn you. It sounds like someone is out to make trouble for you.'

'And it names me personally?'

She sighs. ''I'm afraid so. Otherwise I wouldn't have bothered you with it. But I just wanted to let you know.'

My voice is hushed as I say, 'So what does this mean, Shirley?'

She gives a dry chuckle. 'Don't you worry, duckie. It doesn't mean anything because it's anonymous and there's nothing specific in the letter. No allegations are being made about particular patients. It's just a general complaint which makes me think someone is just trying their luck.'

'But will the hospital not want to investigate? Or ask questions?'

She tuts. 'As if we've got the resources to do any of that. You should see what the nurses in here are expected to do these days. The work-load has trebled since you left. So no, they won't be worrying about nuisance mail like this.'

I wanted to ask her if she was sure. How could she be

sure that this wouldn't go further? But she must have sense I wanted to say more.

'Anyway, it's just me that's seen the letter. It was addressed to the head of the ward and I opened it. Happened to be on the early shift that day. I've been sitting on it and wanted to have a good, long think about what to do with it.'

'Oh,' I manage to stutter.

'I thought it was best not to mention it to anyone else here. Especially when there's nothing to say. And anyway, Sophie, I know you wouldn't do anything wrong. You wouldn't hurt a fly. You were one of my best nurses.'

Her kind words are going over my head as I try to remember what she said a minute ago. 'Did you say you've been sitting on it for a while?' If she was talking weeks, then perhaps it was all a random coincidence that everything was going wrong just now. I glance up at the door and see Elliot frown.

'Aye,' she says. 'I never like to react too quickly to things. I've been mulling it over.'

'When did you get it?' My shoulders are almost dropping with relief as I anticipate what she's going to say next.

'A few days ago,' she says.

'Oh,' I say in a quiet voice.

'Indeed. But don't worry about it. I just wanted to flag it up to you so you know about it. Just in case . . . you never know what's round the corner.'

I close my eyes and nod. I know exactly who is behind this. I jump up and yank the curtains open. But — of course — when I look outside, the street is empty. He's got into my head now, so why would he bother coming to stalk me in person?

48

PAST

We were being dragged to the awards ceremony at the Hilton. Mum made us wear our best clothes even though my dress was clearly too tight for me. She wouldn't buy me a new one. She treated herself a new black cocktail dress, and had her hair done and her nails painted. Julie had a new red dress and she looked beautiful in it. I just felt like the fat, ugly sister. James wore his kilt and kept admiring himself in the mirror. I heard him practicing his acceptance speech and he reminded me of Tony Blair. Smarmy and insincere. I almost choked on the cloud of sickly aftershave which followed him about.

At the hotel, we sat at a table with some of his parliamentary staff and colleagues. All were clearly thrilled to be there and so close to him. The woman next to me told me what a charmer he was and how all his constituents adored him. She'd drunk quite a lot of the wine on the table and her breath was sour. She kept giggling and slurring her words.

We were having dinner before the awards ceremony

began. My place-card told me I was supposed to be having chicken in a cream sauce with roast potatoes, followed by chocolate mousse. Someone must have ordered for me when I was away. Julie was having salmon, *my* favourite. I picked at the food on my plate and pushed it away. I was worried everyone was staring at me, wondering how James had managed to have such a fat, ugly daughter. Even if she wasn't related to him by blood.

I watched him at work. He did a good job, as always. He had that way about him and tonight was no different. His eyes focused on just the person he was talking to. There was never any doubt that you had his full attention. He was charming, and his gaze didn't flicker across your shoulder assessing who else he should or could talk to.

I glanced across the table and saw Mum's face flushed from the red wine she was drinking. She looked pretty as she sat there smiling and talking animatedly to the man next to her. Julie was next to me and she was a bit subdued. I had tried asking her if everything was okay but she said everything was fine. Maybe when we went on holiday next week we'd have more of a chance to talk about things. Matthew has stopped calling in for her too. But I thought that was probably my fault too. Maybe he was too embarrassed to come round anymore because I'd been away.

When the awards ceremony started it just seemed to go on and on. I wasn't quite sure who everybody was — although I did recognise some faces — or quite why they were so deserving of their awards. When his name was announced he beamed at everyone around the table and leaned over to kiss Mum. Then he practically sprinted up to the stage, where he landed a huge kiss on the lips of the surprised TV newsreader —who immediately blushed and momentarily found herself lost for words. That was the James effect.

He stood there for a moment smiling at the audience and milking the applause. Then he raised the trophy, a large curve of engraved glass, in a bid to silence everyone, like he was Tom Cruise receiving an Oscar.

'Thank you, thank you so much. I couldn't of course do this without the hard work of my team who keep everything running smoothly behind the scenes,' he said, putting down his trophy and clapping his hands together. Everyone duly copied. They were entranced, like he was some sort of evangelistic preacher. 'And, of course, I absolutely couldn't have done this without my beautiful wife and daughters.'

Mum blushed, Julie grinned and I grimaced. I knew people were staring at us and I wanted to disappear. I knew they were thinking that I must be the sullen, chubby one. The one who was going through that awkward, hormonal time that teens just needed to get through. Mum gazed adoringly at him standing there on the stage. It made me want to puke. He gestured towards us, pausing for extra effect. I wondered what his audience would think if they knew what he did. If they knew the way he talked to Mum behind closed doors without the cameras and the adoring fans. I often caught Mum staring out of the window, and I wondered what she was thinking about. Her love for her husband? Her regrets in life? Did she want to be somewhere else? I wondered if she had her own secrets to hide?

Later that night, in the taxi home he said, 'I thought that all went rather well, don't you?' He clicked his teeth together and sat back, closing his eyes and clasping my mother's hand. And I sat there wondering, wondering if my mother really loved him. Did she even suspect what he was really like?

49

PRESENT

After I hang up, I Elliot stares at me waiting for me to speak.

I half-fill him in as much as I can. I'm unable to meet his eye because all I can think about is what a mess I have created. 'We can talk about it tomorrow,' I say. 'I just want to go to bed.'

He hugs me. 'Okay, love. That's fine. Just go and say goodnight to Emma.'

'Well, of course I will.' I am irritated that he's now telling me what to do and I check myself again for the way I'm behaving. I'm annoyed with myself for becoming so distracted that he needs to remind me what to do. I kiss Emma and tuck her into her bed and tell her I love her. Then I climb into my own bed and lie restlessly, my mind whirring.

But it's not my nerves that wake me the next morning. It's the hammering on the front door. I squint at the red digits on the clock. It's only six o'clock. Then I sit up, panicking that the noise will wake Emma. I run over to the window, pull aside the curtain and see several police cars parked haphazardly. I shake Elliot, who is in a deep sleep, after some late-night supposed baby-making, but he won't move. Grabbing my dressing gown, I shake him again.

'Elliot,' I shout. 'It's the police. The police are at the door. Oh my God — what has happened?'

Elliot finally opens his eyes and leaps out of bed naked and confused. Throwing his clothes at him, I yank our bedroom door open. By this time my heart is thumping loudly. I run down the stairs and open the door. A squad of policemen is standing on the doorstep. Surely they have the wrong address? Maybe a drug dealer or a murderer used to live in this house before us? Or a terrorist? Surely the letting agency could have warned us? Unless —oh God — I slap my hand across my mouth. This is what happens when someone dies in an accident. Please, no. Elliot would be devastated and so would Emma.

'Is it your mum?' I say, turning to Elliot beside me, 'Is it Joan?' Could MacIntyre have done something to her, to get at us?'

A man in a dark grey suit looks blankly at me.

'Is it Joan? Has something happened to Joan?'

I feel Elliot's hand heavy on my shoulder. 'No Sophie love,' he says, gently. 'I don't think this is about Mum.'

In my dazed state, I listen as the man flicks his ID and warrant card at us, then casually announces that they need to do a forensic search of the premises.

'For what?' Elliot looks aghast.

'I'm sorry,' I say, feeling a surge of panic engulf me. My teeth start to chatter and I try and tell myself to hold it together. 'I'm so sorry, Elliot. They must know. The police must know what happened.'

'Mummy. Mummy. What is happening?' I can hear a small voice from the top of the stairs.

I look up and see my daughter, her thumb in her mouth, her teddy tucked under her arm.

'It's okay, sweetie.' I push past the officers and run up the stairs towards her, snatching her into my arms.

The policemen are now swarming into the house like insects.

'Sorry, love, but we'll have to search her room,' says a gruff voice as another officer bangs up my oatmeal-carpeted stairs — which are now covered in muddy footprints.

'Mummy,' she says. 'I do *not* like these people.' Her voice is cross and normally it would make me laugh. Not this morning.

'Me neither.' I look to Elliot, standing in the hallway in his pyjamas with his hair sticking up. He's frowning and shaking his head. What on earth is going on?

'Can you at least let us get our clothes on?' he says to the man in the suit.

'Sure, but we need to watch you.'

Elliot throws him a look of disdain. 'Whatever floats your boat. Come on girls, let's get our clothes on.' He gently places his hand on my arm. 'You're okay, Soph, you're okay.'

'I'm sorry,' I say again, knowing it is all I can manage.

'This isn't your fault, Soph.'

It is, I want to scream. It *is* my fault. I did a bad thing. We traipse upstairs and I manage to grab myself and Emma some clothes. I take her into the bathroom to dress her. Although I'm made to leave the door open while a policewoman — who has suddenly appeared amidst the men — stands guard. They must think we have hidden something vital in amongst the bath lotion and cotton earbuds and that Emma and I are on a mission to conceal it. I try my best to distract Emma from the fact that her room is being ransacked, by pointing down the stairs.

'How about we go for breakfast at the cafe this morning, Emma?'

Her bottom lip is jutting out. Mine too. I can't believe my life has turned into a scene from a bad spy movie.

'Sophie,' says Elliot urgently from the doorway. His face is puce and he's flanked by two men. 'It's okay, but will you do something for me? Phone my work and tell them what is happening.'

'Why can't you?' I ask helplessly, while Emma starts to sniffle behind me.

'Because I'm under arrest.'

50

PAST

We were going on holiday, a camping trip to the Lake District. I wasn't really looking forward to it, being cold and wet and in such close confines with everyone. But James said it was about time we started holidaying in our own country and making the most of what it has to offer. He said the voters would love it, especially as the Tory politicians all liked to go abroad whenever they could. Barney was being sent off to the kennels. I was surprised that he didn't want to use the dog for photo opportunities.

'We should be spending our money here,' he said. 'In Great Britain. We'll have a great time. Lots of walks in the countryside and pub lunches. And we can do boating too, and maybe even fishing if you fancy it?'

He'd told us that we had limited luggage space if we were to fit it all in the car. Great. I had my trainers, a couple of pairs of jeans and some shorts and T-shirts in case the weather was nice. Julie had been quiet the last couple of days. She'd been in her room mostly, organising her drawers and packing and listening to music.

Gabrielle's '*Dreams*', Take That's '*Pray*' and Whitney Houston's '*I Will Always Love You*' seemed to be playing on a constant loop. When I went into her room she was sitting on her beanbag staring out the window as Whitney belted out the track. I caught her wiping away the tears from her eyes.

'Julie,' I said, running to her and hugging her. 'What's the matter?'

She shrugged. 'I'm fine,' she said, trying to brush me off. 'Really I'm okay. Maybe it's just my hormones.'

'Maybe,' I said. Oh, *please* let her be okay. 'Though are you sure there's nothing else the matter?'

She shook her head and looked away, then looked like she was going to say something. But she stopped herself.

'At least we have this fantastic, exotic holiday to look forward to,' I said. That made her smile. Then I stretched out beside her on the floor. 'Julie. Do you ever think about Dad?'

'What do you mean?'

'I mean our real dad.'

'Not really,' she said with a shrug. 'I mean, I was a baby when he died so I never knew him. And I guess I think of James as my dad as he's the only one I've ever known.'

'Do you like him though?' I asked, turning my head to the side to look at her.

'Yes. What isn't there to like? Everyone loves James.'

What could I say? He fools people, he's a magician. It's all an act.

'Matthew and I aren't going out anymore,' she said.

'Oh . . . Why's that?'

Julie shrugged. 'It just didn't work out.'

'Are you okay with that?'

She nodded and I wondered if I should say anything

about James. I wondered if I should tell her to be careful. Then I noticed the tears falling down Julie's cheeks.

'What's the matter?' I handed her a tissue. 'You're not okay, are you, Julie?' I *knew* it. This was my fault. It was too late. It had happened. I should never have been sent away, I should have been here to look after her.

51

PRESENT

I watch, numbly, while Elliot is marched down the stairs.

'Phone my work, Sophie and tell them what is happening.' He is trying his best to stay calm. 'It will be fine. I haven't done anything wrong. It's all a mix-up.'

I stand holding a now sobbing Emma in my arms as strangers invade every room in our home. 'Mummy, I want Daddy,' wails Emma. 'I want Daddy.'

'I know, it's okay though, love. He'll be back soon. He's just away on an adventure.' I pause, looking for the man in the suit who has shut the front door. 'Look I have no idea what this is about but we've only been in the country for a couple of months.' Thumping down each stair, I continue, 'We're from Sydney, we don't even live here normally.'

He scratches his chin. 'Just following my orders,' he says with a shrug.

'You are upsetting my daughter. How long will this take?'

He twitches his nose. 'As long as it takes.'

I feel Emma's soft, shuddering body burrow into me. 'Come on, sweetie. Let's go for a nice breakfast. 'I look at the policeman standing beside the kitchen. 'I need to get my daughter out of here.'

'Okay.'

I help Emma into her jacket and pull on my coat.

The policeman moves closer. 'Though I need to have a quick look in your bags before you take off.'

I stare at him as he looks through my handbag and then Emma's little blue rucksack.

'Will someone please tell me what is going on?' I ask him.

'Just following orders, love,' he says.

'Orders?'

He glances around, making sure the man in the suit is out of earshot, and whispers, 'Your husband is suspected of phone-hacking. We need to look for evidence.'

I am at a loss for words. What the hell is he going on about? 'Phone-hacking? What the hell is that?'

He looks at me and raises an eyebrow. 'Do you not read the news, love? The Leveson Inquiry?'

I shake my head and he laughs. 'Your husband is a journalist and you don't read the news. Classic.'

Smiling icily at him I walk out of my front door tightly gripping Emma's hand, and we walk up the road towards the cafe which we pass every day on the way to school. I am aware of curtains twitching and people lingering just a moment too long as they unlock their cars. Nobody makes any attempt to speak to me or check that everything is okay.

When we arrive at the cafe I make sure Emma is happy with her hot chocolate and croissant, then step away from the table to call Elliot's work and tell them what has happened. My hands are shaking as I punch in the numbers.

'Jeez,' says Rod, the desk editor, when I tell him what has

happened. 'Bloody plods and their dawn raids. Elliot's only been here five minutes.'

I don't know what to say.

'This happened to my mate a few weeks ago. They got a door-knock at five a.m. and his missus was forced out of bed so they could search the bedroom. Didn't matter that she's got cancer. Bastards weren't interested. I'll get onto the lawyer.' He pauses. 'Oh shit. You've got the little one as well. Is she okay? Did she see what happened?'

'She saw it all,' I say, smiling over at her as she pops a flaky piece of pastry in her mouth and looks up at me.

'Right. I'll call you back in a jiffy. Shall I send someone over to be with you?'

'I'm fine,' I say. 'I'll just get Emma to school and head back to the house and wait to hear from you.'

As I walk back from drop-off I can feel people staring at me, can hear their whispers. Though maybe I'm just paranoid. Maybe I'm imagining it? As I walk down our tree-lined street — which I always thought was so idyllic — I feel so alone. But I'm not. I know I'm being watched. I stand and stare as the police carry out Elliot's laptop and a box of papers which he keeps in his study. Now I feel sick and guilty and ashamed. Is this level of heavy-handedness really appropriate or necessary?

'What are you doing with our stuff?' I march over to the officer putting the box into his boot.

'Taking it in for examination.' He gestures that I should go back towards the house.

'Looks like you don't have a lot of the stuff in the house,' says the cop, the one who bothered to tell me what was going on, as I reach my front door.

'I've already told you we've only been in London a couple of months. Most of our stuff is in storage back home.'

'So you say.'

'Do you have a laptop?' he asks.

I cross my fingers behind my back and thank my stars I finally got round to taking my laptop in to the repair shop yesterday.

'No,' I say. 'I use my husband's.'

'Okay, well, we'll be out of here soon.'

I peer over his shoulder into my home. 'Can I go into my house?'

He smiles. 'Of course. I'd love a coffee if you're making one.'

Instead of punching him I smile back. 'Of course. Coming right up.'

'Thanks, love. Milk and two sugars.' He shrugs again. 'Just following orders from above. You know how it is.'

I fill the kettle and flick it on. I watch the birds hopping around the garden and flying onto the dilapidated coal shed and I turn away to spoon coffee into the pot. My mobile starts to buzz and I see Lucinda's name flash up on it. I haven't replied yet to the text she sent. I pause for a moment and almost reject her call, but decide to take it. 'Hello.'

'Sophie, it's Lucinda. How are you are doing?

'Oh God, were we supposed to be having a coffee?'

'No, that's on Monday, don't worry. That's not why I was calling. I just wanted to check that everything is okay. I saw the police cars. Is there a problem? Do you want me to come over?'

I look in horror at the policemen wandering through our house. 'Nope, it's fine. In fact, let's go for a coffee now. Today. Erm, maybe just give me half an hour or so. Is that okay?'

'No problem,' she says, her voice hesitant. 'Though — are you sure you want to?'

'Absolutely,' I say, trying to sound airy.

'Okay — well, how about we meet in the Gilded Balloon on the high street? I'll just see you in there.'

'Perfect,' I say and hang up. Why the hell have I just agreed to that? I'm so, so stupid. I should have cancelled. Maybe I am going mad.

'Right love, that's us off,' calls one policeman waving to me cheerily as if he's just been in to read my meter.

His colleague brings his coffee mug over to the sink. 'Lovely coffee, darling. Best I've had in ages.'

It is all so surreal that I have to stop myself from laughing aloud. When they leave and I'm alone in the house I suddenly realise that I don't want to be there, and I'm glad that I've got somewhere else to go. I will have to clean the whole house from top to bottom as they've touched *everything,* and I just can't face it yet. Just sitting here waiting to hear from Elliot is not an option either.

I walk quickly to the high street and into the café, which is crammed full of Bugaboos and women dressed in workout gear.

'Sophie, over here.' Lucinda beckons me over to a small corner table that she's managed to find.

I look at the bunting and the pine chairs and think how cosy it feels. There's an aroma of coffee and burnt sugar in the air and then I think about my husband who is currently either still in the back of a police car or in a police interview room. What the hell am I doing?

'Don't know about you,' she says sinking into the seat with a groan. 'But I could murder a coffee.'

'Me too,' I mutter. The waitress approaches and we order two strong Americanos.

Lucinda adds, 'Can I have an almond croissant too, please?'

At that point my stomach grumbles. 'Me too,' I say.

'I never eat breakfast. It's always too manic in our house in the morning.'

Not as manic as it was in my house this morning, I think. But for now, I keep that thought to myself.

'Is everything okay?' she says, leaning in towards me.

Should I say something?

'Tell me to mind my own business if you want, Sophie. But equally, please do talk to me if you think it will help.'

I nod and smile politely but I have to admit that I'm really not that focused, and the noise of the coffee machine and the babies crying is starting to hurt my head.

'You're not okay, love, are you?' she says, kindly.

'Sorry. It was just all a bit crazy this morning.'

She sits back and smiles at the waitress who has brought our order. 'Do you want to talk about it?'

I take a big gulp of coffee, which immediately burns my tongue. I shake my head and smile feebly, wondering if I should tell her about Elliot's arrest. Will she run a mile?

But all of a sudden, I feel I need a friend, an unfamiliar feeling. So I take a deep breath and say, 'Yes, if you don't mind Lucinda, I do.' So, I tell her what has happened to Elliot.

52

PAST

The day on the lake was warm and beautiful, with no clouds in the sky. Perfect really, despite my worries that it would rain all the time. James suggested taking a boat out on the lake with me and Julie. Mum said she was happy to sit and read her book on the shore and watch. It was sometimes hard to try and remember what happened. It was baking hot. Julie was wearing the T-shirt I got her for her birthday, which had the numbers 1984 across the front. That was the year she was born. When I spotted it at Top Shop I knew she would love it. It was bright pink with the numbers picked out in white. Mum told us we should wear our hats as it was so hot and would be even warmer out on the water with no shade.

Julie had been quiet all morning but she wouldn't talk to me, wouldn't tell me what was wrong. She barely ate any of her Rice Krispies when we were having breakfast outside the tent. She got annoyed when I pressed her, so I thought it best to leave things alone. Mum had shrugged and said just to give her some space. 'It's probably her hormones,' she said. 'Fourteen can be a tricky age.' She looked at me knowingly.

I watched Julie in the mirror as she stood with her purple cartoon toothbrush carefully cleaning every single tooth. Her face was pale, her eyes flat. She said something about feeling queasy, then she promptly vomited up the cereal. Bits of it stuck to the sink, while I tried to wash it all away. She said she felt better after being sick and insisted she was fine to go on the lake.

We weren't going to go too far. We had only hired the boat for an hour. I have gone over this time and time again in my head. James was at the front rowing, and Julie and I had an oar each behind him. All you could hear was the swish of the oars through the deep, turquoise water. Everything seemed so still and peaceful. We went out into the middle of the lake, further than we should have, I think. I did say to James that we could barely see Mum. She looked like a tiny dot on the shore. Julie had started to bite her lower lip. She only ever did that when something was troubling her, when something was on her mind. That's when I knew for certain that something had changed. Julie had changed. She whispered something to me. I gasped. I needed to hear her say it again. I tried to stand up to reach her and James shouted at me to sit down. I stood wobbling for a moment and then fell onto my bottom just as he stood up and toppled towards me. Then the boat turned over. Julie screamed and I heard a plop, a huge splash and then I was in the water too. I gasped; it was freezing and the shock of falling in seemed to have winded me. I could see Julie's arms flailing around in the water, her T-shirt clinging to her, her long blonde hair blooming around her like seaweed. I reached out for her and that's when she grabbed my hair. I was trying to tread water, go to a safe place in my head where I could cope with the pain. My scalp felt as though it was being ripped off. *Julie, hold on*, I tried to say. *It'll all be okay*. I wished my hair was lengths of thick, hairy rope. It just looked like fine, brown thread around me. Julie looked at me, terrified. The water was splashing and slopping over us. *Help, someone please help*. Then out of the corner of my eye I saw James desperately grab at Julie. Then everything stopped and I felt light, felt myself floating again. I tried my best to help Julie. I just wanted her to be safe.

53

PRESENT

'I just don't get it,' says Elliot, shaking his head. His eyes are red-rimmed and his face white. 'Back in Sydney I used to accompany the police on their PR-boosting dawn raids on gangsters and drug dealers. Now here, they're hammering on journalists' doors.' He sighs and falls back into the cushions of the sofa. 'I haven't done anything wrong, Sophie. I promise you. I have *never* hacked anyone's phone. I wouldn't even know how to.'

I pull him to me. 'I know you haven't. I *know* you haven't done anything wrong. They must just have mixed you up with someone else. Made a mistake.'

'It was awful, Sophie. I felt so guilty and ashamed as they drove me away.' He sighs.

What can I say? I know those feelings so very, very well.

'They took my fingerprints, made me remove my wedding band and take off my shoes. Then I had to sit in a cell until the lawyer arrived.'

My blood is boiling, especially as I know exactly why this has happened. But I can't tell him yet. He'll think I'm losing the plot. Elliot has been held and questioned for five hours at Kingston police station. He wasn't allowed to call me and it was only when I checked my smartphone that I realised the details of his arrest had been splashed across the news websites.

Somehow, we manage to get through the rest of the weekend, though Elliot spends most of his time drinking coffee and smoking.

'Why is Daddy smoking?' Emma keeps asking. 'Won't he get cancer and die?'

'He won't do it for much longer,' I promise her.

Elliot says he would rather just get on with things and go back into work as usual on Monday — and I agree it's probably best. I know this will blow over soon and someone else will become the gossip of the day. It just makes me even more determined to up my game and work out the next stage of my plan. I know *exactly* what James is doing. He won't come to the house again, he's too smart for that. He's trying to go after the person I love most, after Emma. He's trying to warn me to back off, and I am incredibly annoyed with myself for being so stupid that day when I let slip that I'm married and who my husband is. He's such a bastard — of course he will have looked into it and, let's face it, Elliot's not exactly difficult to find. You just have to Google his name to see his by-line at the paper appear. I can remember overhearing James talking to Mum when I was small and telling her about the relationship some M.Ps had with the police. Corruption was rife at Westminster, he said, and there were lots of favours being done. You scratch my back and I'll scratch yours, I think was the phrase he used. It seems now he has definitely become the back-scratching kind of politician, despite everything. I really thought he would have turned over a new leaf after the last scandal. Clearly not. This just makes me all the more determined to get him. It's time to play.

When I walk Emma to school this morning we both blow puffs of air into the cold autumn air. It's a beautiful, crisp morning, more like a spring day, but the trees are starting to lose their leaves and the shrubs in the garden starting to wither, a few cut back to stumps. Emma grasps my hand tightly. Her hat, a pink *Hello Kitty* one, is pulled down firmly over her ears and she trots to keep up with me as we head towards the school gate. A mother from our street overtakes us, but ignores me when I say good morning. I don't want to let go of Emma's hand. I just want to keep walking. As we near the door of her classroom she wriggles free from my grasp. 'Want to go and line up with others, Mummy,' she says.

'Okay.' I am trying to stop my bottom lip from wobbling. I force myself to smile and hand over her purple butterfly lunch box and her little book bag. She gives me a quick cuddle and then skips over to join her friends. I hover at the edge, just to make sure she's okay, and then I feel a presence beside me.

'Hellooo.' I look round and see Davina giving me a tight smile.

'Good morning,' I say. 'How are you?'

'Oh fine, fine thanks. Lots to get through. My cleaner has called in sick, though, so I'm rushed off my feet.'

I try to think of something suitable to say, but she doesn't pause for breath.

'I know we pencilled in a date for that coffee morning.'

'Did we?'

She raises her eyebrows and looks at her clipboard. 'Anyway, just want to say that, given recent events, we feel it's better if someone else hosts it.'

'Recent events?' I am totally perplexed.

'The dawn raid? At your house?'

I stare at her in disbelief, and she looks away looking a tiny bit embarrassed.

'What about it?'

'I just think it might be better if we do it elsewhere,' she says, wrinkling her nose.

I want to disappear and get away from this awful woman, but my feet feel like they are glued to the spot. I am so relieved to see Lucinda appear at her shoulder.

'Fortunately, Lucinda has stepped in and offered us her place,' says Davina.

Lucinda sticks her tongue out at Davina behind her back. 'Have I?' she says, and winks at me. 'I didn't realise I had. And the thought of you lot descending on my house after drop-off makes me want to break out in a cold sweat. I say we keep it simple, keep it relaxed. Let's just meet in Starbucks. Okay?'

It's not really a question, more of a directive, and I watch as Davina nods and scurries away.

'Silly cow,' says Lucinda dismissively. 'Now tell me, how are you? How is your hubby? How are things?'

'Okay, thanks.' I do feel a bit embarrassed for breaking down and confiding in her. But as I look at her face, earnest and focused on just me, I think maybe she is genuine and she really does care. 'He's a bit stressed, to be honest. Completely puzzled as to why it happened, given we've only really just arrived in London.'

She tuts. 'Hopefully it will all blow over and soon be forgotten about. They'll move onto something else next. They do love their dawn raids at the moment, the Met, don't they? Anyway, you just focus on keeping calm and it will all blow over. What we need is another scandal to get folk talking. Last year it was Jimmy Savile. No doubt there will be plenty of other stories like that emerging. Or an M.P. will be photographed with hookers in the Houses of Parliament.' She giggles, which should tell me it's just a joke — but it spooks me nonetheless.

I feel my breath quicken and I tell myself to keep calm. What is she talking about? Does she know something about me? Does she know about MacIntyre? I think it's the paranoia starting again. But how *could* she know that about MacIntyre?

'Sophie, are you okay?' She touches my arm.

'What?' I am touching my cheek which feels clammy. 'Yes . . . I haven't eaten. Just feeling a bit light-headed.'

She rummages in her bag and hands me a cereal bar. 'Have this.' She presses it into my hand.

'Thanks, Lucinda. I'd better get back to Elliot and check he's okay.'

She gives me a hug. 'Let me know if I can do anything at all to help.'

I smile and wonder if she really means it, or is it just one of those things that people say. What would she say if just asked her to fix it all?

54

PAST

A*ugust 2, 1997*

My little sister is dead. It doesn't matter how many times I say it aloud. It just doesn't make sense. I sit crossed-legged on Julie's bed. On the little white dressing-table, next to her bed, is a heart-shaped frame with a picture of me, her and Mum in it. We were in Paris last Easter. At the top of the Eiffel Tower. Mum was in the middle and Julie and I were either side of her. We were giggling. It was spring. Happy times. Julie was squinting slightly at the camera, the sunshine in her eyes. James was behind the camera, capturing us that day. His little family of ladies, as he used to call us. I looked at myself in the picture. My eyes don't sparkle like Julie's. Even back then I looked sad, despite the smile on my face.

. . .

I LAY BACK and rested my head on Julie's pillow. I could still smell her. Her Julie smell. Like honey mixed with lavender, and it was a scent I never wanted to forget. How could I make sure I always remembered her smell? I turned my cheek towards the pillowcase and looked at the tiny daisy pattern which was dotted all over, as if a handful of them had been scattered across the bed. I traced the little stems with my finger, then reached under the pillow and pulled out her teddy. She always left him there if we were away for the day and said he would look after her room for her. She didn't want to risk losing him either. He was her most prized possession. I clutched his fluffy body to me, wishing he was Julie.

55

PRESENT

I have been sitting in the chair in the front room for nearly two hours. When I try to stand up, my limbs are stiff and I have to grip the back of the sofa. I glance at the clock. Elliot should be home any minute. He decided to go back into work today as normal. Said it was important for him to show his face and get on with business as usual. I am waiting to find out if it has all gone smoothly. Hearing his key in the lock, I freeze in my spot and when he walks in through the door he smiles at me but I look at him indifferently. Perhaps he'll wish we'd never met when I tell him. He might think I should have let him go rather than pull him into this mess.

'Hiya, hun.' He shrugs off his coat and walks over to me. He hugs me close to him and kisses the top of my head. 'Jeez. I'm as tired as. How has your day been? How is Emma?'

'Fine.' I look up at him. 'Fast asleep.'

'I know it's rubbish that I keep getting in so late. I miss her. Miss reading her bedtime stories.'

'You can do it at the weekend.'

He moves away from me to go into the kitchen and I follow.

'How was your day?'

'Yeah. Okay.' He takes a bottle of wine out the fridge and pours himself a glass. 'Do you want some?"

I'd love to swallow the bottle in one, but decline. 'No thanks. Have you eaten?'

'I had a big lunch out with the team, so I'm good, thanks.' He perches on the kitchen stool, his hands curled around the stem of the glass. 'What did you do today?'

I shrug. 'The usual. Took Emma to school, went for a run and tried to avoid the mad mums. Not that it's hard, of course, as they're avoiding me. Can't be seen to be mixing with the wife of a potential criminal.' The words are out of my mouth before I can stop myself but Elliot has the grace to chuckle.

'I saw that woman, is it Davina or something, at the station this morning. She walked straight past me. Had time to throw me a glare though.'

I smile. 'That definitely sounds like Davina. What did you do?'

'Gave her a wink and a huge smile, of course.' He takes another sip of wine. 'You look so worried, Sophie.' He puts down his glass and walks towards me. 'Are you okay? Is it worth going to see the doctor?'

I feel myself tensing in his arms. 'What about?'

'May be worth getting yourself checked out and explaining that you are tired and — you know . . .' his voice trails away.

I breathe slowly for a few moments and smile reassuringly at him. This is so typical of my husband, life and plans go on as normal regardless of what's going on around us.

'Elliot, it's fine. It will all happen when it's supposed to do. It's not exactly the main thing on my mind right now.' I see his face crumple and quickly say, 'It will happen when it's meant to. Anyway, the more we practice the more likely it is to happen.'

He picks up the mail from the kitchen table and has a quick look through it. 'Oh — I know what I was going to tell you. I got an email from Mum. She sends her love. Says she's missing us.'

'Is she having a good time with her friends?'

'Yes,' he says. 'She seems to be. Doing lots of sightseeing and shopping by the sounds of things.'

Smiling, I nod. 'When is she coming back?'

'Mmm, next week I think.'

I nod. 'Does she know?'

'No — she didn't say anything and I thought I'd leave it and tell her when she's back.'

'What about at work? Has anything else been mentioned about your arrest?'

He frowns. 'Nothing. It's just hanging there. The charges remain outstanding and I'm still on bail pending further enquiries. But work is fine about it. Said I just need to get on with it in the meantime.' He puts his glass by the sink and stretches his arms above his head. 'I'll be so pissed though if it gets in the way. I want to do well while I'm here.'

I don't really know how to respond to that because he's not going to do well here. I know that MacIntyre will put a stop his ambitious plans. I know he's behind all of this and I'm about to blurt out my suspicions to Elliot. Yet something stops me. Why spoil it for him now? Instead, I walk to the cupboard, take out a glass and pour myself a large measure of wine.

'I didn't think you wanted one.'

'I changed my mind,' I say, taking a large gulp and swallowing. He watches me as I drink and I *think* — though I may be imagining it — that a glimmer of disapproval crosses his face.

56

PAST

August 5, 1997

Mum hasn't been able to look at me properly since it happened. I can't help wondering if she'd rather it was me who had perished instead of Julie. Mind you, I can't really blame her. Julie was perfect. She was beautiful, like a porcelain doll. Me, I'm gangly and awkward and horrid. And bad.

I HEARD Mum crying at night. It was usually always at the same time, in the small hours of the morning when the house was black, and I woke up to hear the sounds of her muffled sobs. I wanted to go to her and cuddle her, but I was stuck in bed, scared of the heavy darkness which felt like it was pressing down on me like a shroud. And I knew James was there for her. He would make her feel better, I hoped. Even though their bedroom was right down the hall I could hear him saying 'shhhh' to her and trying to calm her down.

Nobody comforted *me*. The gaping hole that I had in my heart felt ragged and raw and I didn't see how it could ever possibly heal. I needed to wee and as I reached for the door handle to open the bathroom I heard a gentle banging. At first, I wondered whether it was a window banging in the wind. I paused for a moment and then heard a scream. My blood ran cold. It was a sound I had heard before. A low, deep noise coming from the back of James' throat and muffled crying from my mother. Then the banging stopped. I tiptoed into the bathroom, quickly peed and closed the lid. There was no point in flushing, I didn't want them to know I was up. Then I ran as lightly as I could back to my bed and shut the door. My heart was thudding and I felt a whole flood of different feelings take over. Anxiety, disgust, guilt and sadness. And loneliness. I felt truly alone.

57

PRESENT

Things are still at a standstill while we wait to hear from the police and the CPS. In the meantime, we are trying to get on with life as best as we can. Joan has arrived back and is staying with us, which has actually been good. She wasn't as shocked as I thought she would be when Elliot and I filled her in on what had been happening since she'd been away. That puzzled me slightly, as I thought she would be horrified at the thought of her precious son being targeted by the police. However, she seems quite relaxed about it and hasn't mentioned it since. Instead, she seems to be trying her hardest to help around the house. She has even offered to babysit for us. However, I won't leave her alone with Emma again, not just now. Maybe not ever. I know if I stay focused on my everyday life, on what really matters, I can get through this. I even allow myself to brush away the niggling fear I have that Elliot doesn't approve of my decision to prosecute MacIntyre.

This morning, Joan is sitting in the kitchen when I arrive back home after dropping Emma at school. I go to pour myself some water.

'I'm so sorry, sweetie?' she says.

'What for?'

'Elliot told me what happened.'

I freeze. 'Which part?' I manage to ask.

'About his arrest. And about your step-father and his arrest.'

I turn and look at her. 'Never a dull moment, eh?'

Joan just looks at me sadly. 'I'm just so sorry about what you've been through.'

I bite my tongue to stop the tears, which are starting to gather.

'How about we go out for a coffee this morning? Would you like that?'

'That sounds like a good idea, Joan. Let me just get a quick shower.' I grab the excuse to run upstairs and compose myself. It's nice of her to say something to acknowledge that she knows. But I don't want to get into the details just now with her. There hasn't been much time to hear about exactly what she did on her trip away, so maybe we can talk about that. Now I know why she pulled me towards her and just hugged me for a while yesterday. How I wished my own mum had hugged me like that. Even just once would have been enough.

We walk to the cafe by the park and take our coffees to sit outside, as it's still warm despite the time of year.

'I think you're incredibly brave, dear,' she starts. 'This isn't easy for you.'

I look at the table, feeling my cheeks flush red. 'No. But I have to do it, Joan. Even though I think Elliot's annoyed with me . . .'

'Why do you say that?'

'He's just become distant.'

She's about to take a drink from her cup, then stops. 'You

know, Sophie, I think he's probably just worried about what happens next. You know he covered a lot of these cases back home. They had an effect on him. He's a sensitive sort, you know. He used to say how amazed he was that the accused could get away with things because they had clever lawyers. I think he's just worried for you.'

'Yes,' I say, starting to panic. The thought of standing up in front of a court and telling people what *he* did to me suddenly hits me and I feel exposed.

'But don't you worry, my lovely. We'll get through this together, okay?' She looks at me for a moment. 'Can I trust you with a secret?'

More secrets? *No, no more,* I want to scream, but say, 'Of course.'

'Elliot doesn't know this. So please don't tell him.'

More secrets.

'My husband, Elliot's father, well . . .' She drops her head in her hands.

What bombshell is she about to drop? I don't know much about Elliot's dad, other than that he died of a heart attack. Reaching out, I pat her arm. 'Are you okay?'

She looks up. 'Yes, sorry.'

'You were about to tell me something?'

She looks at me. 'It doesn't matter.'

'Are you sure?'

She nods.

Taking a sip of coffee, I don't speak for a minute, in case she wants to continue. However, she just looks beyond me at the trees. For a moment or two we both sit there, listening to the sound of the leaves in the breeze.

'You're never really free, are you?' she says, shrugging.

'What do you mean?'

She looks away. 'The memories are always there.'

I shudder, wrapping my cardigan tighter around my shoulders. *Why* does she keep going off at tangents? 'I guess so.'

'It's good that I am here, isn't it?'

'Tell me about your trip.' I think the best tactic here is to try and distract her.

'It was great,' she says, her eyes shining. 'I saw so many places that I had wanted to visit for such a long time. I visited the village near Swansea that my grandmother was born in.'

'You mean near Cardiff?' I say.

She looks at me quizzically. 'Yes, that's what I said.'

Did she? Am I the one who is imagining things now?

'I heard you met someone that I know. Or used to know?'

'When?'

'When you were in Wales, Elliot said.'

'Did I?'

'Yes,' I say. 'Elliot said you met someone I used to go to school with.'

'Yes. That's right. A boy you were at school with. I recognised the accent and I happened to say that my daughter-in-law is from Glasgow and did he know you. It was a long shot but he said yes.'

'Did he say much?'

'Not really. He was quite vague. He recognized your name. Then he had to go. Said he had a train to catch.'

'Oh,' I say, picturing him making his excuses and leaving. I wonder where he lives now and what he's doing. I've tried searching for him online but he doesn't appear to have a profile. But it's such a common name, perhaps I couldn't find him amongst all the people with the identical name.

Joan is smiling at me and I decide to tell her about Julie. 'Actually,' I say. 'I want to tell you something, Joan.'

'What is it dear?' She tilts her head.

'Well,' I say, seeing yet another secret in the corner of my mind, popping up from the past. 'Well, actually, Joan. That's another thing I need to tell you. I used to have a sister.'

'Oh.' She looks blankly at me and I feel another wave of guilt that I have lied to Joan too. 'Did I know that?'

'No, I didn't tell you.' Now I am getting worried about her memory. 'I'm sorry, Joan . . . I just didn't want to talk about her.'

'Does Elliot know?'

'He does now. But I only told him recently.'

'And what was her name? What happened to her?'

'She was called Julie. And she died. In an accident. And it broke my heart.'

58

PAST

I sat on the floor in my bedroom, squishing my bare toes into the fluffy rug, feeling the wool tufts tickle the soles of my feet. I kept thinking the door would fly open at any minute and thump off the wall and she'd come running in. Even when I shut my eyes really tightly, until I saw gold stars, then snapped them open . . . well, nothing had changed. It was just me. Here and alone.

The phone had been ringing constantly, the doorbell chiming. There were flowers everywhere. Bunches of roses and fat lilies which had burst open. The orange pollen just hung there and I knew it would stain the carpet when it fell, but I didn't care. I just wanted to stuff the poisonous pollen into James' mouth and for him to die a slow and painful death.

Mum had taken to her bed. In fact I think she must have gone to bed almost immediately after it happened, since I didn't know when I last saw her. I remembered that after the accident she stood there, waist-deep in the water, screaming Julie's name. She barely looked at me and James when the rescuers brought us in. I was shivering and someone wrapped a blanket around my shoulders. I looked up and saw that James had placed his arm around my shoulder, and I was so upset, so shattered, I really didn't mind. It was comforting and Mum wasn't going to do it. My teeth chattered and my knees trembled.

'She's in shock,' he said to someone, I have no idea who.

It was strangely quiet there at the water's edge. Then Mum's sobs broke the silence and her body spasmed quite violently. I ran to her, desperate to bury myself in her bosom and make her feel better. She was muddy and wet and shaking. A paramedic in a fluorescent vest was trying to calm her down. His voice was soothing and he was rubbing her back. I remember looking up at the sky, seeing the tall trees with heavy branches, and for a moment I felt peace, as though Julie was trying to whisper through the breeze that she was okay. Then Mum's gasps started again.

'Julie,' she said. 'I want Julie.'

'Come on, love,' said James in his gentle voice. 'Leave your mum be. She's in shock.'

Like I wasn't? Julie was my *sister,* but nobody seemed to remember that, or care. Anyway they had to sedate her and in the end, she was now in bed refusing to talk to anyone, refusing to eat anything. I had no idea how she expected to make it through the funeral.

James had tried to comfort me. He kept pulling me to him and stroking my hair. I felt nothing. Just empty.

'It'll all be okay, Sophie. It will all be okay,' he said over and over until my ears felt as though they were bleeding. I knew I should nod and agree but nothing would ever be the same again and it was his fault. I blamed him for what happened. My mum didn't want me. Even now I was her only surviving daughter, she couldn't care less about me. She looked at me with cold, dead eyes. I just wished I could have done something else. I lay on my back and fell asleep staring at the stars on my ceiling. Then I woke to find him lying beside me and I froze. Please, I prayed. I don't want this. I just wanted my Julie.

It was my sixteenth birthday. I would have done anything to rewind time and still be fifteen and have a little sister.

59

PRESENT

Emma's teacher has just called to ask me if I can come in and have a word with her. There is nothing to panic about, she says, she just wants to make sure that Emma is happy as she's been a bit unsettled lately. But of course I am now utterly panicking. My daughter is unhappy at school and I haven't even noticed because I've been so wrapped up in my own grief and self-pity. I really need to get a hold of myself and sort my head out. These feelings can't go on. This situation can't go on. I don't want to become like my mother.

I walk round to the school after lunch and tell the stern-looking receptionists that I have a meeting with the teacher from Elf class.

'You mean Ms Roberts?' she asks.

'Yes.' I am trying to smile, yet also chastising myself for being unable to remember the name of my only child's class teacher. God — there is just too much stuff swirling around in my brain right now.

'Take a seat.' She points to the royal blue chairs which have been arranged to face each other in a square. Sitting down, I study the kids' art on the walls, so impressive I'm thinking it could be hanging in an art gallery. It wasn't like the hastily crayoned pictures we did in my day.

I hear a door swoosh open behind me and a voice. 'Mrs Lewis?

Turning, I see a small woman dressed in a red-spotted wrap dress, her hair piled in a bun on the top of her head. She smiles at me and extends her hand, which I take, and she firmly shakes it. 'I'm Ms Roberts,' she says. 'Shall we just pop through here?' She points at a small office which I haven't noticed.

'Of course.' I stand and picking up my bag. I suddenly feel under-dressed in my jeans and old trainers and sweater. Why didn't I make more of an effort?

'Please do sit down,' says Ms Roberts. She has a kind face and her eyes crinkle at the corners when she smiles.

'Now, please, there is nothing to worry about. I just thought it might be an idea to get you in so we can have a little chat about Emma.'

'Okay,' I say feeling very much like the child in front of the teacher.

'She's a lovely little girl,' says Ms Roberts. 'Very helpful and generally quite happy. She seemed to have settled into the class quite well which is sometimes hard at that age, particularly with you having just moved from Australia. But she has been doing well.'

She shuffles some papers around on her desk. 'Ah yes here it is. This is what I wanted to show you.'

She hands me a picture which has been drawn by Emma, and it's of a little girl with her daddy and mummy. Nothing really out of the ordinary except the daddy has a u-shaped frown and the mummy has tears on her face. Big, fat, child-like tears which have been drawn on to my face by my little girl. In the corner of the picture is a baby.

'This seems to have become a bit of a recurrent theme with her pictures,' says Ms Roberts looking across the desk at me. 'She says her mummy is sad and Daddy is sad too and that makes her sad.' She pauses. 'As I said on the phone, it's nothing major to worry about, but I thought I should talk to you about it now so you are aware of what she is saying in class.'

I brace my foot against the floor, leaning across the table to have a closer look at Emma's picture. Pointing at it, I say, 'What about the baby? Does she normally draw pictures of babies?'

'Ah no, this is a new thing,' she says. 'But quite normal. A lot of the children have younger siblings and there is quite a lot of role-play going on. Emma loves playing with the babies in class.'

'I see.' Shifting in my seat, I'm not sure what else to say to the teacher. I wonder how she will react if I tell her that Emma has captured our family life very well. Yes, I am sad. Daddy is sad too. She looks at me expectantly and tucks a tendril of hair behind her ear.

'Well, thank you for calling me,' I hear myself saying. 'It's reassuring to know that you are keeping a close eye on Emma. Life has been a bit stressful these last few weeks what with the move, and then we've had some sad family news which we wanted to protect Emma from, but obviously she is picking up on the mood at home.'

Ms Roberts is now sitting back in her chair, her fingers forming a steeple, and I wonder if she has ambitions to become head teacher. She certainly has the body language for it. 'I'm sorry to hear that,' she says. 'Is there anything I can help with?'

I shake my head. I don't want to tell her any more. 'Thank you for everything you have done. I will talk to my husband, and of course to Emma, and reassure her that everything is okay. I'm sorry that I haven't noticed. I feel awful.'

She shakes her head. 'No, no. It's quite common for parents not to notice anything is amiss, especially during periods of stress at home. I know what it's like when you're trying to keep everything together and put on a brave face. You are just trying to cope and get on with it.'

I smile and nod, wondering if she knows. Has she worked out who I am? 'Yes, well, things have certainly changed since my school days when the teachers didn't notice whether you were happy or sad — or even there.' A memory of Miss Bell, my English teacher, flits through my head. Suddenly I am back in her classroom and I can see her nails — she always had lovely nails — and they are painted a delicate pink. She is worried and asking if everything is okay at home. 'Everything is fine,' I say. 'I'm okay. Yes. I am fine.' Then I feel a hand on my arm and I flinch.

But it's Ms Roberts who's sitting next to me, not Miss Bell. For a moment I'm disorientated.

'Are you okay, Mrs Lewis?' she says, her brow creased with concern.

'Sorry. Yes, I am. I was just reminded of something there. Thank you.'

'Not at all. It's much better now that we are all switched on to what can happen at home. When you think what used to happen in our day behind closed doors,' she says, and shudders.

'Oh I know,' I say. 'It doesn't even bear thinking about.'

Well — don't hesitate to contact me if you have any

concerns, or if there is anything I can do to help support Emma through this sticky patch.'

Rising from my seat, I say, 'Thank you very much for taking the time to call me in. I appreciate your concern.'

She smiles again. 'No problem at all. I always tell the kids that a problem shared is a problem halved.'

'Thanks again.' I turn to leave.

'Oh, something else I wanted to ask you,' says Ms Roberts, walking me to the door. 'Emma has started talking about someone called Julie. I wondered if it was her gran, as I know she has been staying.'

'Oh,' I say. 'No, her gran is called Joan.'

'Maybe it's just a name she likes. She usually calls the doll Auntie Julie.'

I manage to thank the teacher and bid her a polite goodbye, but a shiver is running down my spine.

60

PAST

August 24, 1997

Julie's funeral was today. I kept expecting her to appear and ask everyone what they were doing. I shuffled into the packed church next to Mum and James. Mum stared ahead, a white, gaunt shell of herself. James's eyes were red-rimmed and he kept dabbing them with his handkerchief. The one Julie gave him for Christmas. I sat back in the pew and tried to focus and listen to the minister who was telling the congregation what an amazing girl Julie was. How she was an angel and would be safe in her new home in heaven. I felt myself nod in agreement.

He said she was loved by everyone. He said she was popular at school, a devoted daughter and a beloved sister.

WAS. WAS. WAS. WAS. I didn't want her to be described in the past. Everyone should have been saying how wonderful and amazing she is. IS. IS. IS. Why were we only talking about her positive qualities in the past tense? Why don't we tell people how much we love them and how amazing they are when they are here and alive to hear it all?

I sat on my hands and stared at my feet for the rest of the service, hauling myself up only for the hymns. 'All Things Bright and Beautiful' was her favourite. I thought she would have giggled if she'd heard the croaking voices behind. She would have wrinkled up her nose if she'd smelt the musty scent from the man's suit in front. Clearly it had been a while since he'd taken it from his wardrobe. Then I flicked my eyes over towards the coffin. Mahogany with shiny brass handles. That's when it struck me again that my sister was lying inside that box. Dead. I gripped the pew in front as my legs wobbled, and James caught me before I collapsed. He pulled me close and uttered a few soothing words. Was I bad because I felt grateful to be held and cuddled? Even though I hated myself even more for doing it, I inched further into his embrace and stayed there until the service ended.

61

PRESENT

I meet Lucinda this morning, after drop-off, and the plan is to go for a jog through the park. I'd suggested that it might be a good idea for her to do some exercise after she told me the other day that she was having trouble sleeping and was feeling a bit chubby and unfit.

'Let's try the natural methods first,' I said. 'Let's get some fresh air and see if it makes a difference to your mood and your energy levels. I'm sure it will.'

Standing there in her tracksuit and trainers, she looks worried. 'You must promise to take things easy and don't go sprinting off like Jessica Ennis,' she says as we start walking to the park gates.

'We'll just start walking, then do a bit of gentle jogging, then walk again. We'll just build it up that way,' I say, as gently as I can. We do exactly that, and after half an hour she has a lovely glow on her face.

'Do you know, that wasn't actually that bad,' she says as we walk towards the park's cafe. 'Though I am absolutely gasping for a coffee.'

'Me too.'

'Shall we sit outside?' she says, pointing at a table. 'You sit down and I'll' go and get the drinks.'

I sit for a moment enjoying a quiet moment and watch Lucinda walk over with the coffees.

'So when did you take up running?'

'A long time ago. When I was a teenager, in fact. I just found it helped with my hormones. Whenever I'm feeling groggy I always find it helps me clear my head.'

'Well, I certainly didn't think it was easy. But I do feel better after that,' she says, sitting back.

'I just think medication should be the last resort.' I take a sip of coffee. 'Sleeping tablets are not the solution, honestly. I've seen people get so they can't do without them.'

'Round here medication seems to be the first resort, not the last. One of the mums at school has told me that most of the women around here are taking happy pills.' She leans in further towards me and lowers her voice. 'Some are on speed too, just to keep them awake during the day.'

'Good God,' I say. 'That is really quite awful isn't it?'

Lucinda looks away again. 'I'll let you into a secret, Sophie. And I've never told anyone this before. But my mother had terrible post-natal depression, which wasn't properly recognised at the time.' She shakes her head and sits back in her seat. 'She even tried to kill herself.'

'Oh,' I say. 'I'm sorry to hear that.' And I am. I don't want anything bad to have happened to Lucinda.

'Sometimes I still can't believe it. It was only years afterwards that a forward-thinking doctor recognised the signs and did something about it. But my brother and I just thought we had the grumpiest bitch of a mother in the world. She was always sleeping and when she wasn't in bed she was screaming at us.'

'Oh dear.' I think of my own mum. And my dad. 'Depression is a really tricky thing to live with for everyone.'

'It got better. She got better and got happier. Then of course she developed breast cancer.' She pauses. 'I often wonder what her life would have been like if she hadn't become a mother or had the depression. And it made me a bit paranoid about what I would be like when I had kids.'

I nod. 'That's not surprising. I think it is so common for us to hope that we either do or don't turn out like our parents.'

'What was your mum like?'

I'm quite stunned by her question. I don't think anyone has ever asked me that before. 'Mmm. She was a bit difficult.' I shake my head. 'I'll save that for another day. Maybe over a glass of wine.' But I'm not sure that I'm ready to share that memory with anyone else yet. She might think I'm making it all up.

'Fair enough,' she says. 'So are you all up to speed on Grey's? Can I tell you about the latest episode?'

'Yes,' I say, giggling. 'I saw McDreamy in action, so go ahead. You're not spoiling anything for me.' I don't see any point in telling her about my link to MacIntyre, the court case, or lack of, and my plans to return to Sydney early. I don't want to load my emotional baggage onto her lap — she must have problems of her own to deal with.

Joan's meeting friends up in town, and so Emma and I are home alone tonight. As I sit with her at my feet, she makes a sudden high-pitched squeal of pain. I didn't mean to hurt her. I was being gentle and handling her as delicately as I could. But the tears are streaming down her face and her small shoulders are shuddering and heaving up and down.

'I don't like it, Mummy,' she says.

'I know you don't. But I just have to get it done Emma,' I say, pausing for a moment and stroking her head. 'It's just one of these things that we have to go through when we're little.'

Her head slumps forward as she sobs again, gulping in air and wheezing.

'Come on sweetheart,' I say as soothingly as I can. 'We're nearly there. Not long to go.' I'm lying, actually, as I've been saying that since we started all of this close to an hour ago. Up and down I go trying to be tender with her, though I am close to screaming as the frustration surges through me. How hard can this be?

'Please, please Mummy. Stop it.'

'Sssh. It's okay Emma. It's okay. My mummy used to do this to me too.'

That momentarily distracts her. 'Oh,' she says. 'To Julie too?'

Did she just say what I thought she said? 'What was that, sweetie?"

'To Julie too?'

I stop combing. 'How do you know about Julie?' I ask, keeping my voice soft.

'Granny told me,' she says.

Of course. Though I feel a flash of irritation that Joan took it upon herself to say anything about my dead sister — who would have been Emma's Auntie Julie if she'd lived — to her without first checking with me. (But then, if I'd still had Julie, would I ever have gone to Australia and met Elliot?)

'I want a sister,' says Julie.

'I know you do, darling.' Despite my better judgement, I start to wonder what Joan is playing at. I trusted her, I really did, otherwise I wouldn't have shared my memories of Julie with her. What is she up to?

'Can I have one?' says Emma.

'What's that?'

'A sister.'

'Maybe one day,' I say, stretching my toes out and flicking the remote control so the *Frozen* DVD comes back on. '*Do you wanna build a snowman*' blasts out from the TV, Emma's breathing steadies and she starts to suck her thumb as she watches the animated princesses twirl around. I don't have the heart to tell her to take her thumb from her mouth. It's the only thing giving her much comfort these days. I hear Elliot coming in but Emma is so transfixed that she doesn't even notice when he pops his head around the door. I lift my finger to my mouth to quieten him and shake my head, narrowing my eyes at him. He raises his eyebrows at me and then backs out the room quietly.

Bloody nits. I scratch my head viciously. This is the tipping point for me with everything else that has happened in the past six months. Every other week someone in Emma's class seems to infest the rest of the kids with it. We've been lucky until now, but tonight, as I sit painstakingly combing the little fuckers from my daughter's, long, golden hair and wiping the silver-toothed comb against a damp cotton wool pad, leaving a trail of tiny black dots, I am completely resolved. There is no point in feigning indecision any longer. Maybe we should just go back to Sydney. Maybe it's time to leave this all behind and head home.

62

PAST

August 24, 1997

Afterwards, at the hotel where the wake was being held, I lost count of the clammy kisses forced on my cheek, the squeezes of my hand, the mutterings of 'I'm sorry' before people walked away. A couple of the teachers from school were there, though there was no sign of Miss Bell. How I would have loved to have seen her that day.

Then I saw Matthew standing in the corner, his hands stuffed deep in his pockets, his head down. It was the first time I'd seen him in a suit. His mum stood beside him and she looked over at me and gave me a small wave. Then she elbowed Matthew and pointed over at me. He looked up, his cheeks flooded crimson and he slowly walked towards me.

'Hi, Matthew,' I said.

'Hello, Sophie.'

Then we were both silent. He dropped his head again, his hands fiddling with his striped tie.

Eventually he spoke. 'I'm sorry, Sophie.'

I nodded. 'I know.'

'I miss her.'

'Me too,' I said.

I looked at him, the boy who had been my best friend for years and who now seemed a stranger. I would have given anything to go back to the way it was before. I wouldn't have been jealous of his crush on Julie or her crush on him. I would have risen above it and been happy for them. I waited, wondering if he might say something else. But he just shuffled from one foot to the other.

'Well, I guess I will see you at school,' I said, catching a glimpse of Mum out of the corner of my eye. She was sitting at a table deep in conversation with the minister.

'The thing is, Sophie . . . the thing is I'm sorry. This is all my fault.' Huge tears started to slide down his face.

'What do you mean?' I said.

'Julie. It was my fault that she was so down and so unhappy.'

'What do you mean?' I could feel a knot of tension start to form in my stomach.

'She was really down, you know. When you were away well . . .' his voice trailed off to a whisper.

'What,' I said, urgently.

'It all happened when you were away.'

'What did?' I was grasping the sides of my itchy black wool dress.

'She said it was our fault that you'd been sent away. Said you'd been so down in the dumps since we started . . . well, you know. Since we started hanging out.'

I saw the pattern on the carpet swirl in front of me, my vision started to blur.

'She was really down when I got back,' I said staring at him. 'Like something had happened.'

'I loved her,' he whispered. 'I didn't mean for things . . .' He was now crying. 'Her period was late . . .'

The atmosphere in the room suddenly became charged with emotion and I felt my chest constrict. '*What*?' Did he really just say that? 'You slept with my sister?'

He stared at me and shrugged. I stood there, rooted to the spot while waves of shock swept over me. 'It was you?' I said, horrified. I'd got it all wrong and now it was too late. That was when the guilt came crashing down around me and I fainted.

63

PRESENT

This afternoon I find Joan on her hands and knees in the living room, looking under the sofa for one of Princess Elsa's missing stilettos. I don't have the heart to tell her that there is an extremely good chance I have hoovered it up. She is completely undeterred, though, and decides she will just make a new one for Elsa, using a little piece of modelling clay which she will then bake in the oven to harden. I mean, who knows how to do these things? She hasn't even brought up girls either. She says it's amazing the tips she picks up from her friends when they are talking about their grand-daughters at their bridge nights.

'Um, Joan . . . have you got a minute?' I've not yet had a chance to approach the subject of Julie and Emma with her, and it's not really the kind of thing to drop into conversation over breakfast. Elliot said she probably wasn't thinking when she mentioned it to Emma.

'Yes sweetie,' she says, leaning back on her heels. 'What is it?'

I sit on the sofa, patting her to come and sit next to me. 'The thing is, Emma has been talking about babies at school. And . . .' I'm unable to finish the sentence. How on earth do I bring this up casually? 'Look. Emma has been calling the doll at school Auntie Julie. She said you had told her about Mummy's sister Julie and that she would have been her auntie if she was still around.'

Joan looks utterly confused. 'I don't think so, dear.'

As I stare at her, sitting there with her perfectly coiffed hair and her carefully applied make-up, I wonder if she's having a senior moment. Surely, she wouldn't lie to me?

Leaning towards me, she says, 'Are you sure it was Auntie Julie she said?'

'Yes,' I say, biting my tongue and focusing on remaining calm. 'Her teacher said she had called the baby Auntie Julie. And when I asked Emma about it she said you had told her about Julie.'

'But why would I do that?' asks Joan, her face etched with concern.

'I don't know, Joan. That's why I'm asking you,' I say patiently.

'You know what kids are like,' she says. 'They have such vivid imaginations.'

'Are you saying that she is lying?' I say, feeling a heat spread across my chest. I know my voice is shaking, but is that what she is suggesting? I'm a liar and my daughter is a liar too?

'No, sweetie.' Her gaze never wavers from me. 'I'm not saying that at all. Maybe I did tell her and it just slipped my mind.'

Now I am feeling totally overwhelmed. How can it have slipped her mind? The room feels as though it is closing in on me, I need to get out of here. I need to get away. 'Okay. Sure. It must be some kind of misunderstanding.' I don't want to apologise to her, though. Right now, I dislike her intensely. I think she is lying to me, just like everyone else.

'You're under a lot of pressure right now, Sophie. Understandably. There is so much going on and I worry about the stress you are all under.'

Her voice sounds tinny, though, and when I look at her, her smile looks twisted and distorted. My breath is ragged, I clutch at my chest, desperate to gasp in some air.

'Sophie, are you okay? You are looking at me very strangely.' Her voice is echoing around the room. 'Do you want me to call Elliot? Shall I call Elliot?'

Is this some sort of out of body experience that I am having? I can't breathe, I need to sit down again. My legs are wobbling and I sink back into the cushions unable to move. I feel as though I am stuck in time. Joan is stroking my head, and making soothing noises. She tells me to breathe in and out very slowly. 'It's okay Sophie,' she says. 'It's okay.' But her voice is muffled, it feels as though she is talking to me underwater. Then she helps me upright and gets me to lean forward to drop my head between my knees. She gently rubs my back, over and over. My breathing starts to slow down and the walls have stopped moving towards me. My vision isn't as blurred and my heart has stopped thudding quite so fast. Her stroking movement is helping. The edges of the room are no longer pressing in on my head, and slowly I start to feel okay again. I begin to breathe normally and I can hear what Joan is saying.

'You're okay lovely. I am here with you, and you are okay,' she says, over and over.

Eventually my arms stop trembling and I am able to sit forward on the chair and look at her properly. 'Thank you, Joan. Thanks for helping me.'

'Oh, sweetie,' she says, soothingly. 'It's okay. It is just

horrible for you. I remember that happened to me a lot. You know . . . well, before with . . .' She can't say his name.

I nod, waiting for her to say more, but she doesn't.

'Has that happened to you before?' she says suddenly.

I shake my head and tell her no, but I'm lying. It has happened. Lots of times. It just hasn't struck me for quite some time. Not since it all began. The panic attacks I had regularly as a teenager have come back to visit me now. To remind me of what happened before. To remind me about my vivid imagination and my accusations and my lies. It's my fault this is happening, I tell myself. I should have let sleeping dogs lie, I shouldn't have started to rake up the past. This is a sign, I tell myself. This is a sign, that I have brought all of this on myself.

64

PAST

I desperately wanted to talk to someone about Julie. Someone who knew her before when she was little and we were happy. I couldn't tell anyone about what Matthew has said. It would have destroyed Mum and James would probably have killed him.

I decided to take myself back to Dudley Drive in Hyndland, where we used to live, to find our old neighbour Agnes. She wasn't at the funeral. I thought she might have come. But then maybe she wasn't told about it.

I thought if I visited her that would help. Maybe I could talk to her about everything that had happened. Well, maybe not everything. I needed someone I could trust. Maybe I was trying to recapture happier memories. I knocked on Agnes' door and as I rapped the brass knocker on the thick green door, which I could have sworn used to be red, I realised there was a different name on the disc by the letterbox. The door swung open just as I realised my mistake. A boy— he looked like a student — dressed in black, with long hair and a pale face peered out at me.

'That was quick,' he said.

I must have look confused, because he asked me if I was delivering the pizza he'd just ordered. I shook my head and said no, that I was looking for Agnes but I thought I'd got the wrong door. 'Agnes,' he said. 'Old dear that lived here before?'

'Yes,' I said, feeling hopeful. 'Has she moved. Do you know where she has gone?"

'Nah. She died.' He yawned.

'What? What do you mean?'

He frowned. 'She's dead. She carked it. She's over and out.'

'When?'

'Dunno. Couple months back.'

'Are you sure? I just saw her at the start of the year.' I thought about seeing her in McDonald's. She'd looked fine then. I hadn't noticed anything untoward about her.

'Aye. Well it's October now isn't it? The landlord here said there was an old lady who used to live here. The place was pure mingin' so it was, and he put in new carpets and painted it all magnolia.'

'It was definitely Agnes?'

'Aye because we keep getting letters in the post for her.'

'Oh.'

'See ya,' he said, shutting the door in my face.

I sat on the step, too stunned to do anything else. I could feel the cold stone underneath my bottom, which was starting to feel raw and numb. Agnes was dead? And we didn't even know. It felt like another part of me had just died. Eventually I stood up and walked towards the train station. I walked straight through the underpass, ignoring the splashes of colour on the walls. Agnes and I always took our time when we walked through there. We would look at the artwork from kids at the local school and try and work out what the shapes and patterns were supposed to be. I plodded up the stairs and stood waiting on the platform, gazing across at Gartnavel Royal, the hospital for patients with mental health problems. I looked at it and wondered if it was somewhere I might end up one day. A train was approaching the platform and for a moment or two I seriously thought about jumping.

65

PRESENT

'What's for breakfast, Mummy?' says Emma, running into the kitchen and throwing herself at me.

I sniff the top of her head and wish I could bottle that scent forever. She's dressed herself in a tutu with trainers, and I smile. She is so excited about our day in London. The last day with Granny Joan.

It has been a few days since my panic attack episode, and Joan announced yesterday that it's time for her to return home to Sydney.

'I've been here long enough,' she said, smiling across the dinner table.

'Granny going home?' says Emma.

As I look at her now, I can't say I'm upset that's she is leaving. It was nice having her here for a bit, but now I've had enough. Especially after what happened the other day. I now feel exposed and vulnerable around her, and a nugget of doubt has entered my head about what she said to Emma. Or what she said about children and their vivid imaginations. In my mind, I now think she believes I am a liar.

Watching her now, spooning some muesli into her mouth, I wonder what she's thinking privately. Does she wish her son had married someone else, anyone other than me? Of course, she would never say such a thing outright. But who would choose me for their son? Someone with a troubled past like me, with so much emotional baggage? Taking a sip of water, I think about Elliot and think how much I love him. I don't want to let him down. I don't want him to think he made a mistake in marrying me. I vow to try harder, to do whatever it takes to make my husband fall in love with me again, the girl he used to know.

'Where's Daddy?' she says, and climbs up onto one of the stools at the breakfast bar. 'Is he here? Is he still asleep?'

'Don't worry, my lovely,' says Joan. 'He's just popped out to get some milk for your Cheerios.'

'I'm hungry *now*, though.' She sticks out her bottom lip.

'Here — have a banana to keep you going.' I hand her one and pull out the stool beside her. 'Now, tell me — what do you want to do first? Hamleys or the London Eye?'

She squeals with excitement. 'Hamleys. Hamleys,' and claps her hands together.

'Hello, you three,' says Elliot walking into the kitchen. 'Look what I've got. Pain au chocolate from the baker's'.

'Yay.' Emma's eyes light up. 'I want one please.'

I watch her munch on the flaky pastry, trails of chocolate on the corner of her mouth, and I wish I could capture this moment forever. This is happiness. Being here together just like this.

A couple of hours later she's taking turns at being sandwiched in between me and Elliot, me and Joan, Elliot and Joan, clasping our hands as we wander down the South Bank taking in all the sights and smells. It's a crisp, bright morning and it's fairly quiet at the moment. I try to savour the moment, really everything and everyone. I stare at the slow-moving river, which looks blue and cold, and notice the boats gliding up and down. I look at the buildings overlooking the water, the tourists wandering around staring at the sky and the buskers who are juggling ahead of us.

'I've got a good idea,' I say suddenly.

'What, Mummy?'

'We should do that.' I point at the water. 'We should take one of the Clipper boats down to Greenwich.'

'Yes, I guess we could. Emma, do you want to go on a boat?'

'Yay,' she shouts. 'Now? Let's go *now*.'

We walk down towards the pier and Elliot buys tickets. We stand there waiting for the next ferry to stop and I smile. I feel content and am even looking forward to later on when I'm having a night out with Lucinda.

We have a lovely day in Greenwich wandering around the Maritime Museum, and then we buy a picnic lunch to take into the park. Emma runs ahead into the playground where she immediately plonks herself into the huge sandpit. Then she's climbing up and down the frame and sliding down the slides, as Joan waits for her at the bottom. Elliot slips his arm around me and I feel . . . *normal*. I feel like we are a happy family enjoying our Saturday and this is what it should always be like.

'Do you know what?'

'What?' he says kissing the top of my head. 'Careful, Emma,' he calls as she starts to gingerly make her way down the frame.'

We both stand watching for a moment until we know she is going to be okay, even though Joan is right there with her. I desperately want to reach out, scoop her up in my arms and lift her down. But I know I have to give her some space and let her take risks.

'Sorry, darling,' he says. 'No wonder I have grey hairs.'

I chuckle.

'What were you going to say?'

'I can't remember. If I do, I'll tell you later.' I squeeze my arm tighter around his waist. I was about to tell him that he's right. That we should have another baby, a sibling for Emma. But I just can't bring myself to say the words. Now the moment has slipped away.

'Come on — let's go and get an ice-cream,' says Joan, when Emma back runs back over to us. Elliot lifts her up and puts her on his shoulders and we walk towards the booth.

We are all shattered by the time we take the boat back to the South Bank, and I know we should really just go back to Waterloo and catch the train home. It's much busier now, the crowds of people milling about are irritating me and I can feel the throb of a headache beginning at the base of my neck.

'Look, Mummy, look, Granny.' Emma is pointing at the fairground rides which are lining the side of the river. The sound of the carousel makes me want to run in the opposite direction. Suddenly, I just want to get us all home. I'm not sure what is wrong with me but I want to get away from here.

'Okay, love. How about we just have one shot on the carousel,' says Elliot. 'Then it's straight for the train.'

'Okay, Daddy.'

'I'll stand at the side and watch,' I say, massaging the knot in my neck. I watch as they choose a pink unicorn for Emma, which Elliot lifts her onto it and stands beside her. Joan clambers onto a grey horse. Then they start to go round, slowly at first until they blur into a rainbow of colours along with everyone else. I look up to check on Emma and something catches my eye. Then my heart starts to race and I stand there trying to breathe slowly. But I can see him. He's there on the carousel, holding onto a little girl. I know it's him and I feel sick. I don't want to be anywhere near him. I don't want him to be anywhere near my daughter. My eyes flicker over to the man in charge of the ride, and I wonder if I can go over and ask him to stop it.

'Mummy.' Emma beams in delight as they pass me again.

I wave and smile, then look at the ground when he goes past. I can't let him see me. I'm appalled that he can even show his face in public. I glance up and I see him again and I turn around and he's behind me. I bang into someone and they steady me. But it's him and I shake him off in disgust. He's everywhere I look and my skin feels like it is crawling with ants.

The music starts to quieten down a bit as the ride slows down and I march my way to the other side waiting for him to come off. I am going to confront him. Right here and now. Bastard.

'Where is Mummy going?'

I can hear Emma in the background calling me, but I can't stop. Not now. I know Elliot is with her and she is safe. Then I hear Joan calling after me and I know I should stop — but I can't.

'Excuse me,' I say as he walks away from the ride. He has his back to me and is holding a girl's hand. 'Excuse me, Mr MacIntyre,' I say louder this time, my voice dripping with contempt.

I land my hand on his shoulder, my rage giving me

strength to force him to spin around. He looks at me in annoyance and brushes my hand away.

'Get off,' he says.

'Oh,' I say in a small voice. 'I'm sorry. I thought you were someone else.'

He looks at me pityingly — obviously written me off as a madwoman — and walks off, pulling the little girl closer to him.

I turn and see Elliot shaking his head at me and Emma looking on in confusion.

'Who is that man, Mummy?'

'I got the wrong person,' I say, quickly. 'Did you have fun, poppet?'

'Sophie, what on earth's the matter with you?' says Elliot, under his breath so Emma and his mother can't hear. 'Have you gone mad?'

I don't answer him, I just walk alongside him in silence. That's' exactly what my mother used to say. He sounds just like her. I'm starting to wonder if perhaps I am.

66

PAST

I sat pressing my bony knees together thinking this was it. James had left early to go back to Westminster and the smell of that cloying aftershave, mixed with the tea tree oil he dabs on shaving nicks still lingered on me. Surely Mum must have been able to smell it. I went into the kitchen where she sat reading the paper at the table, holding her coffee mug against her cheek as if trying to warm herself up. She barely glanced up to acknowledge me as I said good morning and headed straight to the toaster. Sitting down, I began to spread the honey onto my toast. Honey, thick, pale and fudge coloured. It never spread smoothly though, and my knife started snagging and ripping the toast. I gave up and put the knife down on my plate.

Even as I said the words to my mother they felt alien, as if they weren't really coming from my mouth. I spoke quietly as the tumble of jagged, ugly words fell out of my mouth like I was vomiting a mishmash of letters which swirled on to my lap and left me feeling soiled again.

My mother spoke softly to me. She asked, quite calmly,

why I would say such hateful and wicked things about my stepfather. She didn't shout or get angry or even reach for my hand in sympathy. It was then that *I* began to feel sorry for *her*. Maybe she was the deluded one, sitting there like an empty carcass devoid of emotion. Then she pushed her chair out from the kitchen table and took her mug to the sink to rinse it. Her leather slippers slapped against the tiles of the floor as she walked out of the kitchen. She hovered in the doorway for a moment and said, in a low gravelly voice, 'I do not ever want to hear you say such things again, Sophie. I don't know if you are doing this to get attention or some other warped reason. But for the love of God, and in memory of your sister, never mention this again.'

There it was. A double whammy of guilt was thrown at me. Think about God *and* Julie. I wasn't so bothered about the God part. There wasn't one in my world, otherwise these things wouldn't have happened. But the mention of Julie's memory was like being given an electric shock. Mum knew I would still do anything for Julie, even though she was no longer here. If my own mother didn't believe me then who else would? Who would believe the word of a grieving 16-year-old-girl against the word of a star politician whose constituents loved him? What chance did I have? Even my real dad couldn't even be bothered to keep his promise to me. I was unlovable.

'Sorry,' I whispered to the floor. Maybe she was right. I was warped. I wanted attention. I was mad. Nobody cared anyway. I was wicked.

67

PRESENT

Two days later, after waving Joan off in her taxi to the airport, I go back into the house and breathe a huge sigh of relief. The house is still and quiet and it feels good just to sit and try and gather my thoughts.

I think back to the morning we arrived in London, the plane taxiing down the runway and Emma fast asleep between me and Elliot. My arm had pins and needles and I didn't dare shake it in case I woke her up. Typically, she had only just fallen asleep about thirty minutes before landing. I had my face pressed up against the window, my hand on Emma's hair, and I stared out at the grey skies and early morning drizzle which left me with a feeling of resignation at what lay ahead. Perhaps I should have taken that as a sign. I shiver as I think of the blue skies and warm sunshine of Sydney, which now seem like a vibrant dream which has started to fade. Perhaps I should have tried harder to make things work here. But it just seems to have been one thing after another. I know I didn't ingratiate myself much with the other school mums over the whole coffee morning fiasco, but surely I couldn't be the only person in the world who found being in a large clique of women just far too overwhelming? I glance at the clock, glad that I am going out to meet Lucinda.

As I sit at our usual spot in the café, I think about secrets. What's the worst secret a person can have? I wonder about this quite a lot. My secrets? All of them? My secret about MacIntyre? About Julie? My secret about my mother? Joan's secret about Elliot's dad? Does Elliot have secrets too? He must have. Do I want to know what they are though? I look around the Gilded Balloon cafe and think about conducting a small survey. Would the people in here have secrets that would provoke outrage or surprise? I wonder about the elderly gentleman in the corner who is sipping a cappuccino. Is he happily married? Or has he been living a lie? Perhaps he is secretly gay? Then my eyes flicker to the young mum pushing the buggy through the door. Is that her husband's child? Or her lover's? I watch Lucinda, who is at the counter ordering coffee, and I wonder if she has a secret too. What's she like behind closed doors? What is *anyone* like when nobody is watching? It's a game I often play when I'm trying to tell myself that secrets are normal and that I'm not the only person in the world to have secrets. I wonder about Lucinda again and whether I can tell her about MacIntyre. I've never told any friends before. So how do I go about telling her that I am the woman at the centre of the MacIntyre scandal?

'Here you go,' she says, sitting back down beside me. 'Got a couple of pastries too,' she adds. 'I didn't eat breakfast this morning and I'm starving. I drink my coffee, wondering if she will still be my friend when I tell her. I wonder if she will want to drink coffee with me or introduce me to her friends. I look at her across the table, strong and confident and capable. I take a long sip of my coffee. 'How are you?'

'Much better thanks,' she says. 'You were right. The running has really helped. Thank you.'

'You're welcome,' I say, glancing around the cafe. Lowering my voice, I tell her that I need to tell her something. 'You've been so honest with me, Lucinda. It's only fair I'm upfront with you. Especially as you've been such a good friend to me.' I tell her about MacIntyre and the story that is currently splashed across the news.

Lucinda shrugs at me, tilting her shoulder towards me, and I know her sympathy is genuine. 'You don't have to explain,' she says. 'It's okay, Sophie. Nobody's perfect. We've all got histories.'

I exhale loudly, feeling massively relieved. 'Thank you,' I whisper. 'I've been so embarrassed. Though I'm not sure why. I know I haven't done anything wrong but I can't help feeling bad. I even tried to fudge where I was brought up. Remember that time with Davina? I was just so anxious and paranoid. I still am.'

Lucinda waves her hand dismissively. 'Don't worry about any of that, Sophie.' She takes a sip from her mug. 'And you don't need to worry. I won't tell a soul. Do you want to talk about it some more?'

I dip my head. 'No.'

'You sure?'

'Yes. But thank you. Though you don't seem that surprised,' I say, now feeling vulnerable and a bit exposed. Lucinda is smiling kindly at me and I wonder if she thinks I'm mad. I do feel a bit unhinged at the moment, and everything with Elliot has unsettled me.

'Nothing really surprises me, to be honest,' she says. 'Journalism kind of does that to you.'

'I don't know what to do,' I say eventually. 'I don't know what to do now.'

Lucinda leans in towards me. 'There's not a lot you can do right now. You've done everything you can. You just need to try and be patient and let the police do their job.'

I know she is right but it seems unfair. All of it. Elliot's arrest, MacIntyre's freedom to go on as before. I wonder if he is in turmoil right now. Do his feelings of guilt keep him awake at night? Lucinda obviously sense my fears and panic. She reaches over and pats my hand. 'Be patient, Sophie. With a case like this, the police need time to build the whole picture and gather evidence. If you try and push any aspect of it then it may collapse before it's even started.'

I want to say something but Lucinda keeps talking. 'Just give them a chance to do their job. Otherwise you will regret it.'

I can feel the tears welling up again. 'But how can you be so sure?' I ask. 'How do you know?'

Lucinda bites her bottom lip. 'Look, I've covered quite a few of cases like this when I worked for the paper, Sophie. And I saw lots of cases collapse because the Crown hadn't built a strong enough case. They need this to be rock solid before they proceed any further. And that means appealing for witnesses to come forward. Others who can corroborate your story.'

My eyes widen in shock. 'You mean other victims?' I whisper.

'Yes,' she says. 'Others who can testify that MacIntyre was an abuser.'

Until that moment I have managed to control everything: the tears, the sadness and the grief. But when Lucinda says that to me I can no longer hold it in. My tears come gushing like a tidal wave. Lucinda pats my hand again reassuringly and reaches down to root for a tissue in her bag. I know others in the cafe are staring at me, curious to know why I'm howling. But I am beyond caring. I no longer care about keeping up appearances.

'It will be okay, Sophie,' says Lucinda. 'I promise it will all work out.'

I say nothing for a moment, as I wipe away the snot and tears from my face. I take a deep breath. 'How *can* it be okay though?' I whisper.

'You just have to have some faith, Sophie. Trust that the police will do their job properly. With all the publicity about MacIntyre, you just have to hope that other victims will get in touch. I know it was a long time ago, but there may be other women out there like you who were victims.'

I know Lucinda does have a point, and that she is just trying to be helpful. But the hope I had is ebbing away now. Even if MacIntyre's reputation is now ruined by the publicity, he will surely bounce back again like before, unless he is convicted of his crimes?

'But Lucinda,' I say. 'How on earth am I supposed to find them?'

She just stares at me, her lips twisting together, but she says nothing. For she can't offer me an answer.

68

PAST

October 2, 1997

Sometimes I think Barney is the only one keeping me going. It was Julie's idea to call him that. He was a big, shaggy mongrel and I wanted to call him Shep or Dusty or Shadow. But Julie insisted that we call him Barney after the purple dinosaur, and I'm glad we let her have her way.

Mum is still spending most of the day in bed. Though sometimes she does get up briefly, wearing that mustard-coloured terry-towelling dressing gown. She smells musty and sour. I tried to suggest that she took a bath and she got up, but then she'd skulk back to bed. James has been away lots but came back today, and so there was a double cloud of darkness hanging over me. Usually I sit in the kitchen doing my homework, but I went outside into the garden in search of Barney. He's been a bit neglected since the accident. Poor thing. At first I walked him as much as I could, but he's an old dog, not so keen on walks and lately he has developed a preference for going into the garden to do his business and sniff around. I wondered if he thinks it strange that Julie is gone. The lawn was scattered with lumps of doggy mess in varying shapes and sizes, and I always have to make sure I don't step on it when I go out to hang out the washing on the line. There's nothing more horrible than having to scrape the dog muck out of the tiny grooves in my trainers. Sometimes, though, that is when James' toothbrush comes in handy.

Barney always makes me feel better, no matter how sad I am. He just lies there happy to have his ears scratched or his back rubbed. I must have been out there for a while tonight talking to him, oblivious to the flies buzzing around the crap beside us. I told Barney all about my day, how I am worried about Mum and that I hate James. As I chatted, though, I had the sense that something was different. Then I heard footsteps creeping across the grass.

It was him, wanting to know what I was doing. I looked at him

casting a shadow over Barney in the early evening sun. That's when he told me to sort things out to save him and mum any "hassle".

I bit my lip and stroked Barney's ears and ignored James. I just wanted him to leave me alone. I just wanted some more time with me. But he just looked at me and then marched back up the lawn. I was so pleased when he swore when he realised what he'd stepped in. He turned back and shouted at me to get a bin bag for Barney.

You see — Barney is dead. He died just a few days ago. But I just can't bring myself to accept that he too was gone.

69

PRESENT

I've been trying to think really hard about what Lucinda said. The police are looking for more witnesses who can help my case. People who can tell the police that what I say about MacIntyre did really happen. She called earlier to tell me she had spoken to some of her newspaper contacts, who have confirmed to her that MacIntyre has a reputation for being a sleaze. No surprises there. That's what Elliot's colleagues said too. It's just whether or not there will be enough evidence to nail him for abusing me. She admits that she can feel the buzz of the old days starting to come back, the surge of adrenaline as she starts to piece things together.

I go out into the garden shed and pull out my special box from behind the lawnmower. The one that has a few photographs, Julie's necklace and a couple of old diaries. I made sure the incriminating ones were inside the house just in case I needed them. Perhaps they can be used as evidence if we do finally get to court. But these other diaries that I brought over and hid in the shed contain my very private thoughts. Ones that I would never want anyone else to read.

I'm not sure they would be of any use in evidence anyway. But I flick through them and try and find anything I may have mentioned about anyone who can help me now. Though I'm not sure who can, as I didn't tell anyone. Then an image of Miss Bell, my old teacher, floats into my mind again. Miss Bell, the only person who ever paid me attention and made me feel I was clever. She invested her time in me and for a while I believed in myself. I believed I was worth it. Then suddenly she vanished. I reach for my laptop and flick it on. Typing in 'Miss Bell, teacher, Glasgow' reveals plenty of results. I click open a few of the school sites which have teachers of that name working at them. None of them are her. Sitting still thinking for a moment, I try and work out how old she must be now. She was young and pretty and I think she must have been in her first job. Not that I gave it much thought at the time. Hindsight is of course a wonderful thing. But I am wondering if my school was her first. That was why she was so full of enthusiasm. Life hadn't yet knocked it out of her. I tried to remember her first name but there was nothing. I could only remember Miss Bell in her lovely dresses, with her kind smile and her flowery scent, which wasn't much use.

As I sit there desperately trying to remember anything else, my phone starts buzzing. I see Lucinda's name flash up on the screen.

'Hello,' she says, her voice breathless.

'Are you okay?'

'Yes. The thing is,' she's talking quickly, 'The thing is, I checked out Facebook to find out if there was anything of interest there. But nothing. Then I looked at his Twitter account and checked what he was tweeting and who he was tweeting to.'

'Oh,' I say.

'Yes,' she almost squeals. 'And I found something, Sophie,' she says. 'I found a pattern.'

'Okay, what do you mean?'

'He has been messaging someone called Rhona. Looks like she's a party worker, a campaigner. And very pretty. Young, too. I mean what an absolute idiot.'

My heart is racing.

'You know, I always wonder how men in high positions can be so stupid. Especially someone like him with his track record. He obviously just can't help himself. I mean, there is definitely a flirty narrative going on between them.

'Oh,' I say, trying to sound surprised. 'That sounds interesting.'

'Yes. I mean in the old days the hacks would have been all over this but because everywhere is so short-staffed now, things aren't investigated the way they used to be. Never mind the fear of offending anyone in a position of power, thanks to all these enquiries.'

'What does this mean?'

'Well. If we can find out who the Rhona person is, then we may just have some more incriminating evidence against him.'

'Right, but that won't help my case, will it?'

'Well, no. Not directly,' she says. 'But it's all about building a picture.'

'I see. Well, thanks Lucinda. I really do appreciate you doing this for me.'

'Not at all, Sophie. I know you would do exactly the same for me.'

But would I? I'd like to think that I would. But sometimes I worry that Lucinda would think I was crazy if I told her everything.

'Did you think about the other thing I said? Thinking about anyone from the past who can help?'

'Yes, I did.

'And?'

'Well the only person I can think of who may have noticed something was a teacher.'

'Uh-huh,' says Lucinda. 'That could be helpful.'

'Well not really. All I remember is her name, and then only part of it.'

'Which was?'

'Miss Bell. That's all I can remember.'

'Don't worry,' she says. 'Tell me the name of your school and the years you were there, and I will see what I can do.'

70

PAST

Life limped along for a while until it emerged that James had been cheating on Mum. It wasn't just a discreet affair with one woman. It was several and it was splashed across the press. Mum didn't even need to kick him out. He left of his own free will.

For a while Mum actually got better. She seemed energised and started talking to me and treating me like her daughter. We never spoke about James or what he did to either of us. But we managed to go shopping and go out for lunch together and talk in an edgy, polite sort of way. Not affectionately — it's too late for that — but at least she isn't criticising me at every turn and looking at me like she used to. She even helped me fill in my application form for college. I'd decided to do nursing. Partly because that was what Mum had done but mainly because I realised it could be my ticket out of here. I could go anywhere in the world with it and get a job. Being a nurse would help me to run away.

Eventually we had to sell the house, and bought a small flat in the Shawlands, in the south-side, which was nearer to college anyway. But her depression came back and just got worse. Then the doctors confirmed that she had cancer. It was the final straw.

One afternoon I brought Mum a cup of tea and I watched her lying propped up on the pillows. That was the day that things began to click into place. Her mouth moved and words I never ever wanted to hear came out of her mouth. I couldn't hear and I couldn't breathe.

She told me I deserved to know the truth. I didn't think I did because it really hurt. I wanted to hold onto the hazy memories of my dad rather than these things that I could make no sense of. She said she'd told me my dad had died because that was kinder than the real truth. She said she could never have told me, when I was little, about his awful mood swings, his addiction to alcohol and the way he'd treated her. But I didn't believe her. The man I saw that day didn't seem like that, but she said he was. She said she'd read all the letters he sent and knew he would try and contact me. When she found his number on the paper in my room that day, she rang him and told him never to contact me again. She said James would cause trouble for him if he came anywhere near us. It seemed that that was the final straw for him, for instead of meeting me at the station that day, he killed himself. He threw himself in front of a train.

She said she just wanted me to hear the truth but I didn't want to hear any of it. I wandered out of the room in a daze, desperate for a breath of fresh air. I pulled my coat over my shoulders and went out into the garden where I sat on the patch of damp grass under the tree. It wasn't a quiet spot, but at least the wall hid me from people walking past. I sat with my head in my hands trying to compose myself. My whole body tightened and I started to wring my hands.

When I stepped back into the house I headed straight to the kitchen and poured myself a glass of red wine which I quickly glugged down. Wiping my mouth, I went back into Mum's room and stared at her. She was asleep. It had all been a lie.

71

PRESENT

Some days I do wish I hadn't started all of this stuff with MacIntyre. I find myself longing again for the excitement I'd felt when I decided to go to Sydney and leave everything behind. I wonder if I could do it all again. Could I run away leaving everything behind and start again? I've done it before so, surely, I could do it again?

Elliot keeps telling me to eat more but I just don't have an appetite. Food turns to a dry mess in my mouth and I want to spit it out. Today I am going to see the counsellor Elliot suggested. Well, at least that is what he thinks I'm doing. She's based in Kingston and so I tell him I have an appointment with her after drop-off and will catch the train straight there. He's got a meeting in town and so I know he won't check up on me. He can't even call the counsellor to check that I've been, thanks to client-patient confidentiality.

I stand on the platform waiting and wondering and watching as the yellow speck of the train's headlamps appear in the distance. How easy it would be just to take a few steps forward and end it all and find some peace. I completely understand why people jump in front of trains.

They're in such a desperate place and, in a few seconds, they could be somewhere happier. They're not thinking about the inconvenience they're going to cause to everyone else. I step onto the train, though, rather than in front of it, and spend the morning in Kingston browsing the shops around the market square and drinking coffee in Caffè Nero, where I pick on a chocolate muffin and flick through a magazine.

Later, I'm preparing dinner when I hear Elliot's key in the door.

'Daddy,' yells Emma, and she drops her crayon on the table where she's been sitting drawing happily.

'Princess. How are you?'

I hear him drop his bag on the floor, and his keys in the box by the door and then him lifting her up. I manage a smile when I hear her giggle and squeal.

'Dinner won't be long,' I say, when he walks into the kitchen, Emma following closely behind. 'It's lasagne.'

'Okay,' he says.

'How was your day?'

'Fine,' he says, though he's not quite meeting my gaze.

'What's wrong?' I say.

'Work's just a bit stressful right now.'

'Oh. Any reason in particular?'

'I've been side-lined. Asked to step away from the editing role. The boss said it's not working out the way he thought it would.'

'Oh,' I say again, desperately trying to think of something else to add. 'I'm sorry, Elliot. That wasn't the plan, was it?'

'No,' he said, walking to the fridge. He yanks it open and pulls out a beer. Opening it, he takes a swig and walks into the front room without saying another word.

I sit back down at the kitchen table. He's just stressed, I

tell myself. It's his job and it's not working out the way he planned. No wonder he's upset. He's a man, it's a pride thing. Rationalise, rationalise, rationalise. Then I slap my hand across my mouth. This is what I do. This is what victims do. Try and reason. Is this what Joan did? Is this the start of it? I sit there, my eyes heavy, my mind fuzzy and I think. I think too much until the timer on the oven starts to beep, dragging me back into the here and now. 'Dinner's ready. Elliot. Emma. Wash your hands and come on through,' I shout. I catch my reflection in the window and I try a positive affirmation. I try to tell myself that I am safe and I am secure and that I will be okay. But it's no use, it doesn't work. I'm never going to be okay.

72

PAST

I did everything for Mum, looked after patients in the hospital and then came home and nursed her. And I was now fantasising about what it must be like to live on my own. Or with friends. I listened to the girls at work talk about their nights out or dates with their boyfriends and I felt so jealous that I had never been able to lead a normal life. I longed to have a little place of my own with just myself to worry about. I'd paint everything pale blue, have scatter cushions on my bed, fresh flowers in the lounge and keep my kitchen so clean. I hated the flat that we lived in. It was old and grotty and there was a constant smell of stale air which probably wasn't helped by the fact we never had the windows open. Sometimes the doctor or nurse would call to find out how Mum was but really, she was under everyone's radar as they thought she had me to look after her. As far as the system was concerned, she had a carer and so she wasn't classed as being at risk or alone.

I didn't think too much about it at the time. It just happened. She'd been ill for so long and, really, what kind of life did she have? Mum had been lying in bed for days like a delicate shell. The doctors had prescribed antidepressants years ago. Said the breakdown of her marriage to James following so quickly after Julie's death had obviously triggered severe depression. Manic depression. The irony of that was not lost on me.

I'd tried my best to be a good daughter and look after her, but really I wasn't quite sure what else I could do. Life had become exhausting with racing to and from the hospital to work my shifts and then get back to make sure Mum was okay. When she died, it was meant to be. Part of me was angry at her for those final days when she told me about Dad — so I felt relieved. But I also felt immense sadness. I think she was the one with depression and she felt guilty about failing in her role as mother and failing to protect us from James. I think it was just easier for her to blame Dad rather than admit to what was going on underneath the surface, here in her own home. I wondered why she had even bothered to tell me about Dad. Was it to spite me? Or to hurt me? Why couldn't she just leave me with my own memories of my father rather than the ones I was now left with?

She lay there, peaceful and still. My mum. The doctors said it would just be a matter of time and they were right.

73

PRESENT

Lucinda still hasn't had any luck in tracing Miss Bell, and the latest from the police is that the Crown Prosecution Service are still considering whether there is sufficient evidence to proceed with a trial. Obviously, it is my word against his and they don't have Mum or Julie to offer corroborating evidence. I need to keep us busy and organise some fun.

I sit down with my laptop and look into booking tickets for the Eurostar. We had discussed visiting Paris while we are over here, and I think we should. Rooting around in my handbag for my purse, I pull out my phone which has been on silent. I notice there are several missed calls on my phone from Elliot. I click on his name to call him back just as I log onto the BBC news website and see a breaking news story. The air is completely knocked out of me.

The Crown Prosecution Service says it will not proceed with claims against James MacIntyre M.P.

Then I hear Elliot come through the door just as I am listening to the rings on my phone.

'Sophie, I'm here. I tried to get back as quickly as I could.

I've only just found out.' Elliot's jaw flexes and tightens as he walks towards me.

'No,' I whisper. 'No, no, no.'

'I'm so sorry, Soph. I'm so sorry. They should have told you first. You shouldn't have had to find out like this.'

'Why didn't anyone tell me?' This is completely surreal, I just can't believe this is happening. 'Why did nobody tell me?'

'I bet they were going to call first thing,' he says and draws me to his chest. 'But the story has obviously been leaked.'

'I thought things like this weren't meant to happen anymore. I thought that if police officers and officials leaked stories that they were breaking the law?' I pause. 'I just don't understand it.'

Elliot shakes his head. 'It's all crap, Sophie. There are rules for some and rules for others and they're all bent to suit.'

It feels like ages before either of us speak and when I finally do my words just hang in the air. 'What do we do now?'

What was the point of it all? Why did I even bother? I look at my purse, and am reminded of the trip I was planning to Paris. I throw it back in my bag in disgust.

The next day the papers are full of MacIntyre's lucky escape.

DAILY NEWS

. . .

James MacIntyre said he had been the victim of false and malicious claims after learning that he will not be prosecuted for allegations of historic sexual offences.

The M.P. said he has been through 'unimaginable stress' since his arrest several months ago. The Crown Prosecution Service ruled there is no case to answer.

Speaking at an impromptu press conference today he said the last few months of his life had been horrendous and said: "It has just been the worse time you can image for myself and my family. I was completely innocent and there was absolutely no truth in any of these false and nasty claims. Yet police officers ransacked my office and my home and took away many of my personal possessions including my wife's laptop."

He added: "I'm just so relieved that these allegations can be laid to rest and that I can get on with my life. What I have been through has been a nightmare. I'm angry that people are allowed to make these claims anonymously and then all of a sudden my reputation is ruined and my picture is plastered all over the newspaper. That has angered me most. That I was arrested and held up to a blaze of publicity while the person or persons making the allegations can remain anonymous. I now just want to get on with my life and do the best job that I can for my constituents. I would like to thank my family and friends for their ongoing support. I hope the person making the allegations now gets the mental health support they so clearly require.'

In a statement issued today, the CPS confirmed that a decision had been made to drop the case against MacIntyre following an inquiry, by the Metropolitan Police, into historic sexual abuse. The Crown Prosecution Service said there was "insufficient evidence" to prosecute the politician.

. . .

As I CRUMPLE the paper up and throw it against the wall I am angry that he is making himself out to be the victim in all of this. He's twisting everything and is blaming me, again and again. *I* am the victim. *I* am the one whose life has been ruined. Yet all I feel is guilt. And shame.

D.I. Wells comes to see us first thing and apologises for the way in which we found out. I'm not sure if I'm most angry about that or the fact that MacIntyre is the one who is in the limelight. 'It's the lack of corroborating evidence,' she says. 'If your mum was still alive then maybe she could have been used as credible witness.' She looks resigned and shrugs. 'Between you and me, it's all down to the collapse of the last couple of high-profile trials. They know they need to have a water-tight case before they can pursue these things.'

Elliot nods. 'There's a lot of public anger at the money being spent on these historic abuse cases. I just don't think the appetite is there for it, especially with the collapse of the last two.'

'So he just gets away with it?' I say, my voice rising. 'What about if I go public?' I blurt out, trying to contain the hysteria I can feel rising from the pit of my stomach. Elliot and D.I. Wells exchange a look.

'Sophie,' he says gently. 'Are you sure that would be a good idea? He pauses. 'Think about what that would mean.'

'Your husband is right, Sophie,' says D.I. Wells. 'It would be a huge gamble.'

'Think about the effect it would have on Emma.'

My cheeks flush and I don't know whether to punch him or D.I. Wells. 'I'm *always* thinking of Emma. Why do you think I'm doing this?'

He frowns.

'It would be a nightmare for you all. The whispers, the

press intrusion . . . your life would never be your own again.' She pauses. 'You would always be known as *that* woman.'

'It just feels so unfair, though, that he gets away with it all.'

'He's not, though. This is not the end of it for him. His face has been splashed all over the paper. His reputation has been tarnished and it's also given the press the chance to rehash the stories from the last sex scandal he was embroiled in. So please don't think he's getting away with it.'

'But he is,' I wail. 'He's getting away with it and making out he is the victim.'

'Look, I completely understand how angry you must feel about this. I am too. I hate it when the perpetrator of a crime walks away without being punished for something.' She rubs her brow and sighs. 'Believe you me, I take it as a personal failure whenever one of these cases I have built collapses.' She pauses. 'There will always be question marks hanging over his innocence. There will always be people who doubt him.'

So, as quickly as that, the case I have built against MacIntyre and all my careful planning comes tumbling down around me.

Later, I force myself out of the house and sit in Caffè Nero in the high street, tucked in a corner, nursing a large latte. The chatter around me seems to be getting louder and louder. Across from me, a woman is typing on her laptop, occasionally nudging the little dog sitting curled at her feet. I feel so jealous of her. I wish I was her. I wish I was normal. The whir of the coffee grinder and milk steamer are all I can focus on, yet part of me would like to stand on the table and scream at them all, 'Do you know who I am?' I doubt they would bat an eyelid.

Maybe it's a sign that it is now time to move on. Perhaps

Elliot is right. I could keep pushing and fighting against MacIntyre but I just don't think I have any fight left. I look around at these women in the café, thinking how horrified they would be if they knew who I am. What would they say? What would they do? Who would they think is the victim? Who would they think was to blame? Then, out of the blue, I remember Miss Bell's name. It was Rebecca.

74

PAST

After my mum died, I scattered her ashes on the shore at Loch Lomond as she had wanted. It was a grey morning, with that thick, heavy sky which seemed quite oppressive just hanging there above me ready to burst at any minute. As I drove out to Luss the drizzle started, the light smirry of rain falling on the windscreen. I shivered and turned on the heating even though it was June. Mum was in the casket in the passenger seat beside me and I chatted to her while I drove, occasionally reaching over to adjust her position in the seat after we went round a bend in the road.

When we arrived in Luss it was quiet. The village was pretty and quaint in a chocolate-box kind of way, so the tourists flocked there in their droves. I had decided that if I wanted some peace and quiet to finally lay Mum to rest, then it would be better to come early. It was just after seven when I pulled into the car park. I carefully lifted Mum from the seat and gently eased her into my shoulder bag and then walked towards the path which led to the pebbled shore. I could feel the stones jabbing at the soles of my feet, pushing through my canvas trainers. Trying to focus on the gentle lapping of the waves, I was distracted briefly from what I was about to do. Mum used to love coming here as a child and it was where she and my dad had married. It was so peaceful apart from a few birds chirping. The water was navy blue that day and there were just a few ripples of waves which barely licked the shore. I clutched the urn closely to my chest as I knew once I had done this my link to Mum would be gone. There would be nothing left. I'm not quite sure how long I stood there on the beach looking out across the water. I can scarcely remember the actual act of scattering the ashes either. They didn't really scatter. It was more of a dumping.

Afterwards I sat on the beach for some time, I have no idea how long, and then eventually after my trousers started to feel damp and my legs numb I gingerly stood up. I turned and walked back towards the car park which had now started to fill up. I must have been crying because a lady walking her dog crunched over the stones towards me and handed me a tissue. I took it gratefully, though I just had to try and wave my thanks at her as I knew I would break down if I tried to speak.

I opened the car door and got in, sitting there silently for a while. Then I rummaged in my bag for a bottle of water which had rolled to the bottom and was underneath the urn. What should I do with that now? Keep it? Or bin it? I think that's when the pain of what had happened really hit me. I could feel my insides twisting with pain and the nugget of grief that had been burrowing away seemed to explode.

An hour or two must have passed while I sat there crying. Yet as I wiped away the tears and tried to start the car, I realised I was now truly on my own. An orphan. It was just me. Mum was now out there blowing in the wind and free. I did sometimes think it would be easier to join her.

Mum had a younger brother who lived in the States. He had flown back for the funeral but he could have been anyone. He looked nothing like Mum. I accepted his condolences and he pressed his business card into my hand. But he was a stranger. Mum's parents had died when she was a teenager and so there were no ties to keep me there in Glasgow anymore. I'd always wanted to travel, it was a bit like running. I thought if I left everything behind me I could make a fresh start. I hoped that new sights and cities would be enough for me to move on from the past.

Finally, it was then, sitting in that car park in Luss, that I decided I needed to do something to fill the void. It was time for me to think about my next step. I needed to do something radical.

75

PRESENT

We've now been back home in Sydney for three months and it just so good to be back. I've missed the sunshine, the blue skies and the warm air which seems to wrap itself around me like a comfort blanket. Even walking to the grocery store for milk in the morning is enjoyable. I love the smell of jasmine which fills the air and the gentle lap of the ocean and the birdsong. Life just feels so much more vivid and vibrant.

Emma is happy to be back and no longer at school, though she has settled in to a lovely kindergarten around the corner from our house. She doesn't have to wear a uniform and seems to be enjoying having the freedom to choose which dress she'll wear each day and skips happily in. It's such a liberating change from being at school in London. Less pressure, more focus on play and having fun, plus the extra shots of vitamin D are helping us all. Life feels better although I do miss Lucinda. She has emailed me a few times since we left. I think she's still trying to track down Miss Bell, but hasn't mentioned anything recently so I just have to assume that she hasn't had much luck. That's the thing. Who knows where she is? She could be anywhere.

WE'RE LIVING BACK in Manly and I feel as though I am looking at it through rose-tinted spectacles. Everything is bigger, spread out with wide sweeping streets and parks, and being just a few moments from the beach is just amazing. I never realised before how lucky we are to have all of this on our doorstep.

I've been spending time sorting out all our things and having a good old clear-out, which has been cathartic. I found the box of my old diaries and so have been flicking through them before I consign them to the bin for the very last time. I just want to remind myself of what I used to be like and what went on before meeting Elliot and moving on with my life.

Elliot is pleased to be back too, and takes the ferry to work rather than the train. He says he is glad we spent the time in London, but I know he is happier to be back in his own territory. He says we need to move on with our life now.

Joan is delighted to have us back, too, and seems to have curbed her social life slightly so that she can spend more time with Emma. I am still holding her at a distance, still unsure over what happened with Emma and the Auntie Julie story, despite it obviously being my fault. Sometimes I have flashbacks which unsettle me slightly, although on the whole I am okay. I couldn't sleep last night and lay awake listening to Elliot's gentle snore. For some reason, I remembered a young girl who I treated when I worked in the hospital in Glasgow. She stumbled into the A and E department in a daze and was assigned to my section. She was filthy and covered in sores and very drunk. I reckon she must have been about fifteen. She told me that her stepdad had started touching her when she was eight and she thought it was her fault. He'd told her they were his special tickles and that they should keep it a secret. He's my dad, she told me, so there can't be anything wrong with it, can there? He'd said to her that if she didn't like it then she should tell him and he would stop. She hadn't said anything and now years later he was still doing it. I sometimes wonder what happened to that girl. It's times like these that remind me that I failed, as I didn't get justice or closure for what I went through with MacIntyre.

I know his career is now in tatters. Well, kind of. He is still an M.P., still being paid a salary and gets to go to work every day. But I know there will always be doubters. D.I. Wells was right about that huge question mark which will follow him around wherever he goes. I'm just glad that we live on opposite sides of the world. I never want to see him again.

Tonight, Elliot waits until Emma is in bed and fast asleep until he tells me the latest gossip from his London colleagues who continue to email him. He obviously left a good impression and was more popular than he thought — though I reckon his arrest must have elevated his status in the office.

'Not sure whether to tell you this or not, Soph,' he says, as I fill a vase with water to arrange the flowers he's brought in for me.

Twirling the stems in between my fingers, enjoying the slight nip from the thorns, I wait for him to continue.

'You would have thought MacIntyre had learned his lesson with everything that went on, and would have known to keep a low profile.'

I feel the sickness lurch in my stomach and wait.

'You'll never guess what he's done?'

Child abuse, hookers, take your pick, really. 'What?'

'The stupid twat has only just gone and sent some flirty and inappropriate chat to a party activist,' he says.

I plunge the flowers into the vase and slam the vase down on the kitchen worktop. 'What do you mean?'

'Just that. He's obviously learned nothing from his party colleagues.' Elliot shakes his head. 'He's only gone and sent some DMs to someone he thought was a 25-year-old Labour party activist.'

I feel a surge of excitement ripple through me. Good old Twitter. My gamble to have a back-up plan has worked. I feel awful about lying to Lucinda about it, especially when she has been doing so much to help. But I didn't want to take any chances. I will do anything to pay him back for what he did. I need to make sure we have as strong a case as possible. So you see, I'm the one who has been conducting flirty banter on Twitter with my step-father. I am Rhona, the party activist. And Rhona has come good. She did, of course, always post admiring and complimentary tweets praising his intelligence and charm.

WITTY SPEECH by lovely @jamesMacIntyremp

brilliant debate @jamesMacIntyremp

I SOMETIMES SPICED them up a bit describing him as "hot to trot" and "handsome". I targeted a few other MPs just to spread myself out a bit and make it less obvious that he was my target, but they responded with polite comments, as did MacIntyre to begin with. There was a bit of flirtatious banter to begin with and then I increased the pressure and MacIntyre responded. I decided to pass this onto Lucinda, anonymously of course, in her role as a freelancer to get her to use her press contacts to do a bit of digging.

'So what is happening now?' I compose myself before turning to look at Elliot.

'Well, I'm not sure that the story will actually go to print . . . apparently the party worker sent screenshots of the messages onto the paper anonymously but suggested they may want to speak to the researcher that MacIntyre was involved with years ago. Anyway, in the light of everything that has happened, the likelihood is that he will resign his post, sooner rather than later. Mud sticks and he is now dripping in it.'

What Elliot means is that the newspapers will be too nervous to print anything potentially libellous about MacIntyre in the wake of my allegations. 'Have they managed to track down the party worker?'

'No, so it may not even be real. It could be a hoax but on the back of it, I heard someone had gone and interviewed that woman. You know — the researcher from before?'

'The woman in Spain?' I whisper. 'Well, seems like it wasn't as straight-forward as just an affair. She's never spoken before and apparently has quite a lot to say about it.' He grimaced.

I put my hands up to my ears, not wanting to hear any more details about that. Although I'm glad that she has finally broken her years of silence. Do I feel relief and a sense of closure? I'm not sure that I ever will. Isn't revenge supposed to be bittersweet? I mean it's quite astonishing how easy it was to get MacIntyre to fall for the bait. However, I needed it just to make sure there was never any doubt about what kind of man he is. Lucinda had contacted Rhona, and I struck up a rapport with her, never letting on that Rhona was me. Eventually I sent her the messages in the hope she could do something with it. I sent it to another newspaper too. Although they never ran it, it was enough to feed the rumours and stories that were circulating about him being a sex pest. But that's the thing with rumours and stories and newspaper articles. Who is telling the truth? Only those involved can really know.

76

PAST

After I scattered Mum's ashes, I decided I needed to leave. I'd had enough of colleagues at the hospital tiptoeing around me and whispering when I came into the room. Some people did try and make an effort. But it felt like they were just being polite and going through the motions. Some of my colleagues from the hospital had come to Mum's funeral. Perhaps I didn't help myself as I really didn't want to let anyone near me emotionally. I felt that I would just have to be self-sufficient and accept the swirling thoughts in my head. Yet as the weeks and then months went by, I began to emerge from being on auto-pilot and started to grow increasingly restless, until one day I decided I had had enough. I started to look at recruitment agencies in Australia. I'd always wanted to live somewhere hot and far away. I knew they needed nurses in Australia and that I would easily be able to find a job out there. I was nervous though and in need of some reassurance that I was doing the right thing. But there was nobody to give that to me anymore. I was in charge of my own destiny, which gradually became a liberating thought rather than a frightening one. Starting afresh, as far away as possible, was the answer.

'What is this?' asked my boss, Shirley, when I handed her my letter of resignation.

'I'm leaving, Shirley. It's time for me to move on,' I said. 'There's nothing holding me here anymore. It's time for me to go.' I paused then and thought I should add something. 'I will miss you.'

She looked relieved. I'm sure it couldn't have been easy having me on her team. I tended to lend a sense of heaviness to things, as I wasn't the type of person to skip through life brimming over with joy. I never brought any happy news to the workplace. No news about a new boyfriend or an engagement or a wedding like my colleagues did. They seemed to bubble over with enthusiasm at the smallest thing which brought them joy in their lives. A holiday, a new car — even a new pair of shoes. I often wondered about my sister Julie and what life would be like if things had been different. Then a twinge of regret and sadness would start to gnaw away at me and I would push the memories back down into the depths of my soul where I thought they should remain.

As I began to make plans for my adventure and fresh start I did begin to feel some little stirrings of excitement which gave me hope and made me smile. It had been so long since I'd felt anything like that I had become used to feeling numb and dead inside and bereaved.

When I told my colleagues about my plans they did seem to be genuinely excited for me. There were squeals and gasps of pleasures. They offered me travel tips, suggested places to stay and contacts to look up. I gratefully accepted all the pieces of paper filled with scribblings which were pressed into my hand.

'How long will you go for?'

'Will you move there permanently?'

'Maybe you'll find yourself an Aussie hunk?'

I didn't know the answers to any of their questions. But I knew now was the time to take a leap of faith and try and find some answers and some peace for myself. Shirley insisted she would write me a glowing reference in case I decided to stay there for good, in which case I would need to try and find work. She hugged me tight on my last day, the way Mum used to when I was small. I could feel the tears starting to well up and I had to focus hard on pushing them away. She held me away from her and gave me a fierce look.

'Sophie, my darlin'. I wish you every happiness with your new life. You deserve to be happy, ducky. It's about time life treated you a bit kinder.'

She smiled and handed me a card. I put it in my handbag along with all the other good luck cards and presents. When I took my uniform off for the last time at the end of that shift I felt a huge weight lift off my shoulders. I walked along Byres Road looking at everything in a new light. The tenement buildings looked brighter, as if all their stonework had had a good scrub, the shops inviting with their twinkling lights. I stopped off at the delicatessen, which I had always admired from afar and thought it was too posh for me to go into, and bought myself some dinner. A piece of quiche, a salad and some garlic bread with a large slice of chocolate cake for afters. My last supper.

Back at the flat I finished packing my bags, tidied up and put the last of the rubbish into the black bag before taking it down the stairs to the bin store in the lane behind. As I opened the front door I suddenly remembered the contents of my handbag. I picked it up from the floor and took out my purse and lipstick. Then I tipped everything else into the black bag. The cards and chocolates from work, my mobile phone, my diary and address book. I paused for a moment, wondering if I would regret it and end up fishing about in the bag trying to rescue the last items from amongst the remnants of my dinner and the last remnants from the fridge. But there was no regret. This was about moving on. I didn't need any reminders of my past.

77

PRESENT

Elliot thinks I'm continuing with my counselling sessions now we're back in Sydney. I told him having someone to talk to has been incredibly helpful and really helped me sort things out in my head.

He doesn't need to know that I go to coffee shops and sit and talk to Julie in my head or write her letters that will never be read or posted. It's just so incredibly cleansing to be able to offload onto someone who will never judge me.

Emma is thriving at her old kindergarten and happy to be back home near Granny Joan, who is now finally playing the role of the doting grandparent. She has cut down on her bridge games and travels less, saying she wants to be around for Emma as much as possible. She has offered to teach me how to quilt. I've been collecting lots of Emma's old clothes since she was a baby, and I want to make them into a memory quilt for her to spread on her bed and be reminded of her happy childhood and how very much she is loved. Joan pops in a couple of times a week without it feeling overbearing, and she brings me flowers or cakes.

Today we make a start and she shows me one of the first

quilts that she made, and threads the needles as we chat. I watch her hands gently touching the fabric, and as we sit there she asks me about my parents and whether or not I remember them. I'm able to brush her questions off quite easily and I ask her about herself and what it was like growing up in Sydney. She was a late child for her parents, who thought they would never have children, and she said they doted on her as she was an unexpected gift they had been given. She smiles as she talks fondly about them, and about the smell of baking in the kitchen and the weekends with her dad at the sea, where he taught her to swim. She smiles and looks happy and content and safe, and I feel a surge of envy, because this is a feeling that I will never have when I talk of my parents. It makes me even more determined for Emma to have happy memories and to be able to wrap herself in this cocoon of love. I want her to know how loved she is.

'Would you have liked a sister or a brother?' I ask Joan as she deftly stitches a piece of an old cream babygro with tinny teddies on it onto a square. 'Hell, yes, I think I probably would have — but then my parents doted on me so much and spoiled me so that I never thought that I was missing out on anything. I mean it would maybe have been nice to have an older brother or a younger sister . . .' her voice trailed away as she bit the thread. 'But I never thought too much about it if I'm perfectly honest with you.' After a bit, she asks, 'What about you?'

'Oh, I did have a sister long ago,' I say, and my eyes flicker towards hers.

She gasps. 'Really? I didn't know that.'

What is she talking about? 'I told you, Joan. In London.'

'No,' she says. 'You didn't, dear.' Joan says nothing for a moment and I watch her as she clasps her hands together.

I lean forward. 'It's okay, Joan. I must have thought I did.' Although I know I definitely did.

'What was her name?'

'Her name was Julie.'

'What happened?' Joan is now clutching at the pearls hanging loosely around her neck.

'She died in a boating accident . . . we were teenagers. I don't really like to talk about it.' I take a sharp breath in. 'It's too painful. But I think about her every single day.'

She nods at me. 'I'm so sorry, my dear.'

For a moment, we both tilt our heads as we concentrate on the quilt and the memories we are pulling together for Emma. After a little while, Joan starts talking about Emma and what a lovely little girl she is.

'Do you think you might have a brother or sister for Emma?' she says. This feels like deja-vu, as we had this conversation several times in London when she visited.

'I would love to, Joan. But you know, I think it will happen when it's meant to.' Smiling at her I continue, 'All good things come to those who wait. That's what my mum always used to say to me.'

'Wise words,' says Joan and she puts the quilt aside for a moment. 'Where is your mum?''

I'm now concerned about Joan. A thought has been niggling at the back of my head for a while now, but I didn't want to alarm Elliot.

'She died too, Joan.'

'You poor thing. You'll have another baby soon, I'm sure,' she says.

I smile, for she is right. I am a few weeks pregnant but I think it's only fair to tell Elliot the good news first.

78

PAST

When I first arrived in Sydney, with all my worldly belongings stuffed into a backpack, there was no need for me to fake my jollity. It was completely real. This was a new start for me and I couldn't wait. I felt as though I had left all my tension behind on the plane. For years I had felt like the weird outsider. Now I was free to be who I wanted to be. There was nobody to answer to, nobody to look after and nobody to be afraid of anymore. I felt free.

Of course, the blue skies and sunshine helped massively. I couldn't believe how much of a difference the good weather made to my mood and frame of mind. Being thousands of miles away from my old life felt amazing too. Although it took me a while to stop constantly looking over my shoulder.

To begin with, I shared a flat with five other girls and we slept in our sleeping bags rolled out on the floor. I'd spotted an advert for it in the youth hostel I had stayed in for a few nights when I arrived. The girls were great and said I could move in immediately, so I did. Two of the girls were French, two were from New Zealand and one was from New York. That was in Bondi Beach. I spent most of my days strolling around the local neighbourhood, hanging out on the beach, and learning what it meant to be young, independent and free.

After a couple of months, I moved to Manly and found another flat share, this time with a proper bed and a Spanish girl who was rarely there, but when she was we had great fun and although I didn't always understand what she was saying her infectious laugh always had me in stitches. Then she left to backpack around Australia. After that I had to find another place and this time I was lucky enough to find an apartment nearer to where I'd started working. I had enough money to keep me going for a couple of months, which had been great and gave me the chance for a much needed rest. But I missed the routine of work and I needed the money. I only liked sharing with certain nationalities and never with Brits. It was just too much of a reminder of what I'd left behind. I now shared a small terraced house with a Japanese girl in Darlinghurst. It used to have a reputation as a red-light district but now it was quite upmarket and advertised by estate agents as being trendily cosmopolitan. We lived on the corner of Crown and Burton streets, so near to lots of restaurants and bars; and what I loved too was that in a few minutes I could find some peace and quiet if I needed it in Hyde Park. It was noisy but I didn't mind. I liked it. The hustle and bustle reminded me that there were people around. Aika had limited English and kept herself to herself, so apart from coinciding with her occasionally in the kitchen I really didn't see much of her. I tended to socialise mostly with other nurses from work. But I was also keen to make myself available to work extra shifts should the opportunity arise. It kept me busy and I wanted to stockpile as much money as I could, just in case things went wrong. My rent was cheap and I lived quite a minimal existence, so it was easy to do. If I did go out with work it tended to be for drinks at a club which gave us free entry on Thursdays for Nurses' Night, and even then I really never liked the taste of alcohol, so it didn't cost a lot. Two drinks was my limit and after that I was happy with tap water. I usually watched everyone else get legless and then I'd see them couple off and I'd be on my own again. At which point I would wander home and tuck myself in with a large mug of tea, and read a book or whichever newspaper I had managed to pick up at the hospital that day from the waiting room.

Sometimes I would get hit on by guys and girls at the club and sometimes I'd reciprocate. It just depended on how lonely I felt. My Scottish accent had softened in time and was now a blurred hybrid, the result of living in two continents. I could be from either depending on my circumstances and where I wanted to be from. Sometimes I would be Jane from Canberra and other times Gillian from Aberdeen. It didn't really matter as it was always no-strings attached sex which usually turned out to be a bit of a grope and a fumble. I always took charge of undoing the buckle and pulling off their jeans or skirt. It surprised some of them, but mostly they liked to be taken charge of. Then it would be a quick fuck, a few thrusts or pokes and a release for both of us lonely souls. It was the only way I could forget things for a very short while and become someone else who wasn't me. It was the only way in which I could forget how much my heart ached inside for all that I had lost. I never slept over with anyone and didn't encourage them to linger at mine. After the release of sex I didn't want to be held, or have my hair stroked or to chat. I wanted to be by myself again. That's when I would ask them to go or if I was at their place, I would just get up and leave. I had reinvented myself with this new life which I loved. Yet at the very heart of it all, I still felt alone.

79

PRESENT

I wake up and immediately need to run to the toilet to be sick. Gripping the edges, I watch the white, foamy vomit splash down the bowl and decide I am going to tell Elliot about the baby tonight. The thought of becoming a mother again excites me but scares me, even though I've already been through it with Emma and everything was okay then. But what if it doesn't go smoothly the second time? I'm scared that I won't love another child as much as I love my daughter. What if I don't have any love left to give? It makes me think about my own mum again and why she made the decisions and the choices she did. I no longer blame my mother for the way things turned out. I just feel sad. A tiny part of me doesn't understand and can't forgive her for not being there for me and keeping me safe. Every night when I tuck Emma into bed, I hold her tighter to me when I think of Mum's last lost days where she would fail to get up or in the morning, despite my pleas. I tried as best as I could to keep going for her sake, to try and motivate and cheer her up. But I could see that there was nothing inside. Not even a tiny sliver of zest for life. Everything had been extinguished. That continues to break my heart. My mum didn't fight for me. The thing is, I know I would do anything for my daughter's sake. *Anything*. I would even die for her if it would save her. I know now why Mum could never love me the way she loved Julie. It was because I was my father's daughter. It's true. I now understand why she hated me, why she didn't believe me and why I was sent away to that residential centre. I think about the notes I saw. The notes about my dad and the notes about me. And I think about Patricia and the way she told me my mother was worried I had inherited a condition from my biological father. I had to pretend I had no idea what she was talking about, that I hadn't discovered that when I was sneaking a look at her folder.

'I don't know what you mean,' I said.

'She says some of your behaviour traits remind her of your father. The mood swings, the volatile behaviour.'

I didn't reply. For a minute, in fact I thought she was referring to James. But then I realised she wasn't.

'I was too young to remember him. And — no. My mother has not discussed any of that with me,' I said. Or had she? Maybe I'd chosen not to listen?

'What is the condition?' I asked.

'Well it used to be called manic depression. Nowadays, though, it is known as bipolar disorder,' she said, maintaining eye contact with me.

'Oh,' I said. 'What does that mean?'

'It can cause your mood to swing from an extreme high to an extreme low. People affected might experience depression and feel very low and lethargic but can experience episodes of mania where they feel overactive and high. These episodes can go on for several weeks at a time.'

. . .

THIS DIDN'T REALLY SEEM relevant to me, unless there were other symptoms. 'Does it mean you imagine things? Or get confused about what has really happened?' I suddenly asked her.

'Well …' she began. 'The psychotic symptoms of someone with bipolar disorder could be delusions and hallucinations. This would be with someone who was having an acute manic episode.'

For years I have managed to bury her words, but since London and what happened with MacIntyre, her words have been chipping away inside my head. Maybe my life has been one big manic episode since it all began. Or since I *think* it all began. Maybe I really was my dad's daughter and had his condition. Perhaps I was deluded and the things I thought happened with James were hallucinations. Yet they felt so real. Was I deluded about everything?

If only those doctors had given me some *time*, rather than forcing medication on me that clearly made me feel worse. I wonder if MacIntyre told them to give it to me. I know my treatment was another thing he was complicit in. If only my *mother* had given me some time and had cared for me, instead of looking at me as an extension of my dad. Instead of being paralysed with the overwhelming fear that I was something she didn't want to deal with again.

I can't remember ever having rapid mood swings or negative thoughts when I was younger, other than the panic and anxiety I felt whenever James came near me. Did I feel inadequate and useless and hopeless? Yes — I probably did. But wouldn't you, if you were the victim of abuse? Yes — I had problems getting to sleep, but that was probably more to do with fear rather than manic depression. I never felt overly happy or excited or full of energy other than when I was running, I certainly didn't spend excessively as I stayed well within my monthly allowance, and I didn't talk quickly. I hardly talked at all. Teachers at school always described me as being quiet and thoughtful.

Now I realise my mother must have thought I had imagined the abuse from James. That I had hallucinated it. Apparently that is quite a normal trait for people with manic depression, or bipolar as it is now called. They can hear and feel things that aren't there, but I can assure you there was nothing imaginary about what James was doing to me. I can understand that she was worried that I had inherited the condition from my dad, as it does run in families, but apparently the risk of inheriting it is just ten percent, so she completely over-reacted. I used to wonder if she was just waiting and watching for me to start showing signs, anything at all, and then she would grasp at straws trying her best to protect me from getting into a downward spiral like Dad. But if my poor mum had researched the illness properly, then she would have learned that, although we may have been genetically predisposed to inheriting it from Dad, it might never have surfaced unless it was triggered by a specific life event. And here's the thing. The doctors now think that a stressful event is usually needed to trigger the onset of bipolar symptoms. Such as a bereavement or a breakdown of a relationship — *or physical or sexual abuse*. It's now all starting to make sense, isn't it? So maybe you can understand why I have only admitted to what went on before at this stage in my story. Because as soon as you are labelled with a condition or an illness, then it's so easy for people to make assumptions and judgements and call you a liar.

I have made a special dinner for tonight, a Thai curry — one of Elliot's favourites — even though the spices are playing havoc with my senses right now. I put Emma to bed sharp; she is shattered by the end of the day and sleeping so much better now we are at home. Then I go downstairs to set the kitchen. I light some candles, make sure the fizz is in the fridge and I sit down for a moment and wait, feeling flutterings in my stomach. Elliot comes into the kitchen, but his face is chalky white.

'What's the matter, love?' I say, standing up in a panic.

He sighs. 'Sophie, I just popped into see Mum on the way back. She said she needed to talk to me urgently.'

'And?' I say, thinking that whatever it is must be serious for Elliot looks as though he has been slapped.

'She told me my dad wasn't my real dad. But then she shut down the conversation and refused to say anymore.'

I gasp as another secret from the past surfaces to join us in the present.

80

PAST

The very first time I saw him I'd just clocked on for the early nursing shift at St Vincent's Hospital and was in the middle of pulling my hair up from my hot and sticky neck and twisting it into a ponytail when he came limping out of the ward and towards the nursing station. Technically I still had a few minutes before I officially started work but nobody else was around so I gave him my most welcoming smile.

'Hello. Are you okay there?' By this time, I'd had a chance to look at him properly. He was tall, I would say six feet, though he looked quite vulnerable, which was perhaps down to the way he was gripping onto his crutches. His hair was very short, almost shaved to his head but his features were soft, his lips plump and pink and he looked apologetic when he started to talk.

'I'm really sorry to bother you. I know how busy you girls all are. I'm just so desperate to get out of here and get home and let you use this bed for someone else who really needs it.'

I stood listening, more astonished at myself for not

flinching when he referred to me and my colleagues as girls. It didn't come across as patronising though. He did seem quite genuine. I reached over behind the reception area and pulled over a clipboard. 'Let me just check for you,' I said. 'What's your name?'

'Elliot Lewis,' he said.

The name sounded familiar though I wasn't sure why. I scanned the list and saw that he was due for discharge later that morning when he'd been signed off by the consultant. 'Torn ligaments and concussion.' I winced. 'Oh dear. What happened?'

He smiled sheepishly. 'Footy tournament. And yes, before you say it the doctor has already told me that I'm not twenty-one anymore.'

I laughed. 'Dr Smith? The Irish fellow?'

He nodded.

'Yes, he's got a thing about football injuries in the older man . . .' I blushed. 'Not that I think you are older of course . . .' I began and then ploughed on as he raised his eyebrows at me. 'It's just that he seems to treat a lot of men in their thirties and forties for broken ankles, snapped achilles' tendons, concussion, knackered kneecaps . . . the list goes on.' I paused for a moment studying Elliot's face. I liked his eyes. They were kind eyes. 'Mostly done by playing football at the weekends. Dads at school football tournaments are the worst. They seem to be notorious for the most brutal injuries. I think they all get a bit competitive.'

He shook his head. 'Not me. I don't have kids. I just like to act like one. This was just an old-fashioned kick about with colleagues from work. We've got a league which has been going all season. It's as fun as.'

I raised an eyebrow. 'What kind of business are you in for your colleagues to give you these kinds of injuries?'

'Ah,' he said. 'One of the oldest professions.'

I laughed.

'I work for a newspaper.'

'You're a journalist?'

'Afraid so. I'll start to hobble away now before you hit me.'

'Depends on what paper you write for.'

'*Daily Herald*,' he said.

'That's okay. You don't have to run away. I read that one. That will be why I thought I recognised your name.'

'Morning, Sophie,' said Nicola the sister in charge who bustled past me. 'Are you just gonna stand there chatting all day? We've got other patients you know.'

'Sorry,' mouthed Elliot and he turned to limp back to the ward.

I paused for a moment to watch him until I became aware of Nicola's heavy breathing beside me.

'Can you check ward three please Sophie,' she said. 'Now.'

I didn't see him again that morning. I was so busy that it was later on after lunch when I stopped to have a quick cup of tea that I realised he must have been discharged. Oh well, never mind. At least he had brightened up my day. There was something very alluring about Elliot which made me feel curious and also a little bit hopefully that maybe there was a slight chance of brighter times out there waiting for me. I was so glad that I'd reinvented myself.

81

PRESENT

I still haven't told Elliot about the baby. He was left reeling by Joan's confession the other night, and it wasn't the right moment to stun him all over again with another shocking announcement. Even though I know he'll be delighted, I need to allow him time to process what Joan said. Of course, she is now denying she ever said such a thing. In some ways I am feeling very sorry for her right now. But that isn't helping Elliot. He's quiet, thoughtful and become quite introverted, taking himself off to his study in the evening.

Things take a slight twist tonight when Lucinda sends me a WhatsApp.

Sophie, let me know when you're free to talk and I'll Facetime you.

Glancing at my watch, I work out that it's just after 9am in the UK. She sent the message after midnight. I call her straight-away. Lucinda normally always emails me because of the time difference. Does this mean that she has news?

'Aw, Sophie, it's so good to see your face,' she says. 'I miss you. It's just not the same.'

'I know. I guess you've just taken Daisy to school?'

She nods. 'Yes. And I wanted to talk to you. How are you?'

'I'm okay,' I say.

'I miss you. It's not the same without you.

I want to tell her that I miss her too, but I can't. If I get sentimental I'll start to cry and then the tears won't stop.

'Anyway, you won't believe what happened last night.'

I hold my breath.

'I found her.'

'Who?'

'Your teacher. Rebecca Bell.'

'But how? What do you mean? How did you find her?'

'Well I couldn't find any trace of her anywhere as you know. . . but I was going through local press cuttings from that time.'

'And?'

'And there were reports of a woman's body being found in the woods near Drymen.'

My mouth is dry. 'That's not far away from where we lived.'

'I know. And the body was never identified . . .'

82

PAST

After that first meeting at the hospital, I knew I had to see Elliot again. I worked out his offices were in Surry Hills, an area I happened to know fairly well as I'd lived there briefly when I first arrived in Sydney fresh from backpacking through Asia. I had no idea whether he was married, engaged or seeing someone and so I knew this had the potential to be disastrous — but I couldn't get him out of my head. I decided I would need some help and so broached the subject from a sneaky oblique angle during a coffee break in the staff room one morning.

'Listen,' I said. 'Does anyone know any decent pubs in Surry Hills?'

Susan looked up from the magazine she was flicking through. 'Yes, a few, why?'

'Um,' I muttered. 'It's just . . .' At that point Sister Nicola strode in and everyone fell quiet.

'Don't stop on my account,' she said, walking to the water dispenser.

I bumbled on. 'Um I just thought it would make a change from the usual places.'

Susan sat back in her seat and steepled her fingers together. 'Mmmmm, that doesn't sound very convincing.'

'It's about that handsome hunk that was in the other day isn't it, Sophie?' Nicola stared over at me and everyone turned to look at her in surprise. 'You haven't been the same since. You've been wandering around in a daze and I would like my hardworking Sophie back. Why don't you let me make this nice and easy for you?' She leaned against the sink and took a sip of water.

Nobody dared to say a word and I held my breath.

'He's a journalist, works in Surry Hills and I happen to know that every Friday night they all head over to the Tipple wine bar across the street from their office. They're usually there from around eight and I am told, on good authority, that he never misses it.'

I managed to mutter thanks.

'Okay everyone, can we get back to work now? We're meant to be helping the sick, not reading up about the latest fashions.' She was looking directly at Susan. Then she disappeared out the door.

'How on earth did she know that?' I said.

Susan laughed. 'Her brother is a sub there. She must have done a bit of digging on your behalf. Must like you after all.'

'Tomorrow night then? Are you on for a few drinks at the Tipple?'

Susan was always up for a night out and always on the lookout for a man — especially since she'd recently been dumped by a rather handsome consultant in A and E. 'Deffo. Let me rally up some more of the troops and we'll make sure we are there to hold your hand.'

Approximately thirty-six hours later there we were, a bunch of nurses, six of us in the end, in our finest outfits trying to look casual in the corner of the bar. We'd managed to bag a large table with a few stylishly placed plants which could come in handy later on if I needed camouflage. Susan and I had been to the bar and our wine in coolers was being rapidly depleted. I offered to take the kitty up and replenish supplies, so I walked over and leaned against the polished wooden bar and tried to catch the barman's eye — and then yelped when I felt a foot slam down on my heel.

'Oh, I am so sorry,' said a voice behind. I turned round and there he was standing right behind me. How *easy* was that?

'You,' I said, and laughed.

His brow creased as he tried to place me.

'Don't worry you haven't bedded me. You just borrowed one of my beds for a bit the other week.' I smiled.

I could see the cogs turning slowly. He brought his hand to his head. 'You're the nurse? Florence Nightingale. I tried to come and say good bye and thanks but every time I tried you were busy.'

I rolled my eyes. 'Sure.'

'Yes, I did, I swear.'

'And how's the ligaments and the head?'

'Good thanks. All better.' His eyes snaked lazily over my dress. 'You look very non-nurse like tonight.'

'Yes. I don't tend to wear my uniform when I'm off duty.'

'Well it's lovely to see you . . . I'm assuming you didn't get any of my messages?'

I frowned. 'What do you mean?'

'I called the hospital and asked for you.'

'Nobody told me.' I shrugged. 'Happy coincidence that we bumped into each other then.'

He nodded. 'Indeed. Let me buy you and your friends a drink. It's the very least I can do after everything you've done for me,' he said as the barman handed over another cooler with wine. 'It is Sophie, isn't it?'

'Yes, that's right,' I said. 'Sophie MacIntyre.'

'It's lovely to meet you properly, Sophie,' he said and grasped my hand in his. It was firm and warm and I liked it. 'That would explain why you never returned my calls. I left messages for Sophie *Murphy*.'

I giggled.

'And where are you from, Sophie?'

'Oh, here and there. What do you want to know?'

He put his hand on mine. 'Whatever you want to tell me.'

83

PRESENT

'But it's not what you're thinking . . . Miss Bell is still alive. The body wasn't hers.'

'Lucinda, please can you just get to the point. I don't understand what you're telling me,' I say.

'I got in touch with the reporter who still works at the local paper and who wrote that article. He was really helpful and managed to go back through the cuts and check the weddings for the summer of 1997. And guess what?'

'You found her?' I whisper.

'Yes. Rebecca Bell. She was the *only* Bell to get married in the parish that summer to a Dylan Williams.'

'Wow.'

'I've spent the last few weeks scouring social media sites for Rebecca and Becky Williams who may fit the profile.'

'And?'

'And, bingo,' says Lucinda, triumphantly. 'I found her on Facebook and messaged her. She took a while to get back to me. Turns out she has been abroad and not checking her messages regularly.'

'Why didn't you say anything before?' I say, looking at Lucinda's smiling face.

'I didn't want to get your hopes up . . . not until I had something solid to tell you. I wanted to wait until I knew it was definitely her and for her to get back to me.'

'And?'

'I explained I was a friend of yours. And that is when she said she would talk to me.'

'What did she say?' I hold my breath, waiting and wondering what Lucinda is going to say next.

'She said she would talk to the police.'

THE NEXT DAY it's D.I. Kaszuba who calls me and says she wants to update me on an interesting development in my case.

'We have another witness,' she says.

'Another witness?'

'Yes.'

'Who?'

'A former teacher of yours has come forward.'

I can't speak.

'Miss Bell?' I whisper, hopefully.

'Yes. Rebecca Bell, though she is now Rebecca Williams. She didn't know anything about the charges as she was away travelling when it was all over the press. Then somebody persuaded her to come forward and speak to us.'

I SIT DOWN, trying hard to focus on what she is saying.

'She said she remembers you from school and that she always worried about you. She says she spoke to the headmaster at the time and mentioned her concerns. She said that unbeknown to her, he was a close friend of your step-father's. She was young and naive at the time, and was called into the Head's office for a meeting with MacIntyre.' Then she pauses. 'The Head left her alone with MacIntyre to have a chat. She reckons they were alone for maybe ten minutes or so. He threatened her . . . and he also sexually assaulted her, Sophie.'

'Oh,' I say, feeling a dull thud in my belly.

'Then she quickly found herself out of a job. Her contract wasn't renewed and she was advised not to stir up trouble or she would find herself without a career. The old boys' network . . .' Her voice trails off.

'Where has she been since then?'

'She says she was so shaken by it all that she went away to China and ended up teaching there for several years. She lives in Manchester now.'

'Oh,' is all I can manage. I am too choked to speak. 'So why did she choose to come forward now?'

'She says she has often thought of you over the years. And she wished she had done more at the time to help. She said coming forward seemed like the right thing to do.'

I am silent for what seems like an age.

'Are you still there, Sophie?'

'Yes,' I manage to croak.

'She's happy to give a witness statement. However, we're still not quite sure whether the CPS will proceed yet.' She pauses. 'There are a couple of other women who have come forward and we're just in the process of interviewing them. But it may take some time. It will then be up to the CPS whether they think the cases are strong enough to take to trial. But we'll keep you posted on all of that.'

'Thank you. Thank you for letting me know.' I hang up

the phone and stand there for several minutes. Finally. *Finally,* it's not just my word against his.

I can't be inside right now. I need to get out and breathe. I pull on my trainers and follow the usual path that I take every day down to the beach. I need to smell the salty air and hear the sound of the waves lapping the shore. That soothing sound of the water pulling in and out on the beach, dragging the grains of sand back with it, soothes my mind as I think about what Miss Bell went through. I rub my stomach as I think about the growing bump inside of me. My hormones feel as though they are swooshing all over the place at different tangents. One moment I feel like the happiest woman alive, then within the same hour I can be sobbing. Though perhaps that has more to do with the case, which I thought was dead and buried before we'd even started. I walk along, pushing my feet into the sand, and think about what this could mean. A court case? Justice? The end? I reach the community toilets, a little red-brick building at the side of the car park, and realise I need to pee again. The block is always immaculate and every day I see the same woman there cleaning. I've named her Samantha. She always arrives in the same small white van. The polythene-covered seats intrigue me as I wonder what she is keeping on the seats other than her bucket and mops. Her lemon polo shirt has a council logo on it and she always wears the same baggy combats, but she also takes the time to apply a pale pink lipstick. Her hair is always groomed and pulled into a tight, high pony-tail. Her trainers are black with bright orange laces and I can tell she takes pride in her appearance and her job. I've smiled at her a few times and complemented her on the immaculate condition of her toilets and the beautiful flowers she puts in an old juice bottle every morning. She always smiles back and says thank you but doesn't engage any further. So I can't help speculating on what her story is. Maybe she's escaped an abusive marriage? Or has been in prison for murder? Perhaps she's been a victim of sexual abuse too? But you just can't tell with people, can you? Clearly she wants to be invisible and focus on her work and just lead a quiet, anonymous life. Part of me envies her. Having the freedom to come and go as I please. Just me on my own. Sometimes I think I would love that solitude, but then I know I could never ever leave Emma behind. I would absolutely need to take her with me.

Walking gives me time and space to think and to air some of the thoughts that I've kept tucked away. I have sometimes wondered why I didn't join Julie. I often wished that I could. But I didn't feel I could leave Mum. It was bad enough that she had lost Dad and then Julie. Losing me would have been the final straw — or so I thought. But that's why I hung onto life. To protect her. She was still my mum, even after everything that we'd been through. Even though she was never a good mum to me, she was still my mother. Despite everything I suppose it's built in, isn't it, to love your mother. I always knew things were strained between her and James. If they were happy together then he wouldn't have come for visits to me at night, would he? I had a feeling that things would begin to crumble with James after Julie died, and I was right for both me and Mum. I mean Mum had lost all sense of purpose and interest in herself and her appearance. Whenever she did make an effort to put on some make-up she looked like a china doll or a small child who had got hold of her mother's make-up bag. There was too much blusher on her cheeks and her lipstick was always smudged against her teeth. She lost lots of weight, leaving her clothes hanging from her bony frame. It didn't matter that she was grieving, James turned away from her instead of comforting her in her hour of need. So much for 'for better or for worse'. I was left to pick up the pieces and wipe away the tears and the snot that dribbled from her nose and eventually the saliva that dribbled from her mouth. Now, as the thoughts churn around inside my head, I am once again going through my mental check-list working out how many boxes I am ticking and wondering if the condition I am genetically predisposed to might rear its head now I am pregnant again. I don't think I have had any extreme moods other than the usual overwhelming tiredness that can sometimes overcome me. I feel quite positive about being back in Australia, not necessarily full of energy. I do admit there are some days when I wish I was working even part-time as it doesn't seem enough to be a full-time mother. Sometimes the weight of social expectations press down heavily on me but then if you did a quick survey of the local young mums I would imagine they would say the same. Does that mean they are mentally unhinged? I would say I am fairly balanced and level-headed and, yes, I have good and bad days but don't we all? Is it normal to be happy and full of energy all of the time? Isn't it more normal to have a mixture of moods? But that's all down to my interpretation, isn't it? Would a doctor think differently if he or she knew my family background?

I sit down on a bench and stare at the different shades of blue of the ocean and the sky. Staring at the horizon I think about what the future holds. I allow myself to smile as I feel the sensation of sun on my face, and I think about Miss Bell. For years I'd thought she didn't care about me. But now I know she was just like me. A young woman, threatened by MacIntyre. A victim, just like me.

84

PAST

Elliot was the first man I allowed to sleep over and the first one to hold me all night without that dreaded weight of claustrophobia and panic pressing down on me. That first morning I woke up and, realising how soundly I had slept I did panic. I worried he would open his eyes, see me and regret everything. I lay there not daring to move, even though I was desperate to pee, making the most of the moment I didn't want to come to an end. But when he opened his eyes he kissed me gently on the nose, then the lips and then moved his kisses down my body. As I lay there I couldn't work out what felt so strange about it all. Then I knew. I felt safe and I was smiling. That had never happened to me before. After that night Elliot and I were inseparable and spent every moment together that we could. He was single after his fiancée had broken off their engagement a couple of years before. Since then he hadn't dated anyone seriously, he said he couldn't face it. Finally, something seemed to feel right for me. I think fate played its part in bringing us together. When

Elliot proposed to me I didn't hesitate to say yes. Should I have told him everything before I married him? Some would say yes, honesty is the best policy. But I would disagree. Telling the truth isn't always the right thing to do. Is it?

85

PRESENT

'Have you painted in here? It looks different,' says Joan, pushing her way past me as I stand at the door. I watch Joan's eyes snaking greedily around the hallway and longingly up the stairs. Then her gaze flickers towards the lounge door and she steps towards it.

'Why don't you come through to the kitchen?' I say, placing my hand on Joan's cashmere waterfall cardigan and firmly steering her down the hallway. 'Aren't you too hot?' I add, looking down at my own cut-offs and T-shirt.

'Well,' says Joan, still examining her surroundings, as though she has never been here before. 'I am a bit hot, now you mention it.' She focuses her gaze on the shiny coffee machine on the workshop. 'Oh, I'd love a coffee if you don't mind.'

'Of course not,' I say, shuddering at the empty breakfast bowl which is in the sink. A few Rice Krispies bob around the dirty water and my stomach churns.

Joan sits herself on a stool at the kitchen island. Slipping her cardigan off her shoulders, she leaves it hanging untidily around her waist.

'Here,' I say, 'Shall I take that from you?'

'Ooh, yes please.' Joan stifles a yawn. 'A flat white would be great, please,' she says.

I reach for the milk and start to ask how she is, but she's unable to hear anything else due to the noise of the hissing steam. Joan glances at the clock.

'Are you okay?' I hand Joan her coffee.

'Oh, thanks,' she says, taking a sip. 'It's quite milky, but never mind.'

I take a large breath and rest my back against the sink. 'Elliot was upset when he saw you the other day, Joan.'

Her eyes wide and she almost spits out her coffee. 'Really? Why was that?'

'Because of what you said about his dad.'

'His dad?' She looks confused.

'Yes, Joan,' I say, gently. 'Elliot said that you told him his father wasn't his real dad.'

'Oh,' says Joan. 'Did I?' She is now staring at the window shutters. Her cheeks colour up and she shakes her head. 'No, no. I wouldn't have told him that. Why would I say such a thing?'

'He just seemed upset about it, Joan. I thought I would just check with you if everything is okay?'

'Yes dear. I think so. Everything is fine.'

A phone starts to buzz, a high-pitched ringtone which is coming from her bag. She roots around and pulls it out. 'Hello,' she says, brightly. 'Oh, I am so sorry. I must have got the days mixed up. Yes, yes that is fine. So sorry.' She puts the phone on the worktop and takes a sip of coffee.

'Everything okay?'

'Yes. Just one of the bridge ladies checking if I can play.' Joan's cheeks are still flushed. 'I must have written down the wrong dates in my diary. They said I should have been playing last night.' She shakes her head in frustration. 'I don't know what is wrong with me.'

I decide not to push any further for the moment.

Later on that night, Elliot gently shakes me on the sofa.

'I fell asleep,' I say. 'I'm sorry. I was waiting for you to come in.'

He looks at me quizzically, loosens his tie from his shirt and stifles a yawn. He is home just in time to read Emma her bed-time story, except she doesn't want to go to bed now that her beloved daddy is back. She launches herself into his arms.

'Emma,' he says, putting her down. 'Come on now. It's time to go to bed. I need to talk to Mummy.'

'Don't want you to. Want you to read my story.'

I watch as my husband tries to negotiate a deal with our daughter. 'I'll come up in five, okay sweetheart?' Emma remains standing there in the kitchen, in her pink nightie, her cheeks flushed red in excitement.

'Come on now, Emma,' he says sharply.

I watch as her bottom lip quivers, but she doesn't cry. She looks up adoringly at her dad and says, 'Okay, Daddy. See you in five.'

'So how was your day? What did you get up to?'

'Busy, I guess,' I say with a sigh. 'Your mum came round for a coffee this morning.'

His raises an eyebrow. 'Did she say anything else?'

I shake my head. 'No.' I decide not to tell him that she denied saying anything to Elliot about his dad. 'But I'm a bit worried about her. She seems to be getting quite forgetful.'

Elliot just shrugs. 'What else?' he says. 'Anything else from the cops?'

'No.' I reach for my glass of water, which is sitting beside the sofa, and take a sip. 'I saw the doctor today though.'

Elliot's flicking through his phone now, checking his unread emails. 'Mmm.'

'And I went to the moon.'

'Right,' he says, still scrolling.

'And George Michael was there and we had lunch.'

'What was that?'

I laugh at him. 'Elliot, you are not listening to a word I am saying.'

'Daddy,' calls Emma. 'Want my story.'

I smile. 'You'd better go. I'll get dinner sorted.'

Thanks, love. He walks over and kisses the top of my head. 'You're a gem.'

'Elliot . . .' I smile at him again. 'I have some news.'

AFTERWARDS

Eight months later

Two weeks ago, Elliot and I became parents for the second time when I gave birth to baby Samuel Ross Lewis. Emma is delighted to have a little brother, Joan is excited to be a granny again and Elliot is overjoyed that he has a little boy as well as a precious daughter. Me? I am not quite sure how I feel. A bit numb, I think, and confused and dazed. But I am starting to fall in love with the little squiggly bundle in my arms.

The birth couldn't have been more different to Emma's, which was all very graceful and calm. This time there were complications. My birth-plan went out the window and I was rushed into theatre for an emergency C-section which I can't remember much about. Yet I can still see Elliot's face turning white as he watched all my blood slop off the operating table onto the floor. I focused on his green scrubs and vaguely wondered what my life would have been like if we hadn't met? It was like being underwater, as I watched things happen through blurred vision. Everything sounded muffled, then I began to drift in and out of consciousness. When I woke up I saw Elliot sitting anxiously next to me, holding a baby wrapped in a blanket.

'Is everything okay?'

'It's a boy,' Elliot said, a huge grin spread across his face.

But my first reaction was that I just wanted to turn away and sleep. A boy? The bundle in his arms was a boy? But I wanted another girl. Even though we opted not to be told the sex of the baby at the scan, I was so sure this baby was a girl. I didn't want a boy. Everything felt sore and raw and the stitches across my abdomen throbbed. I felt as though my insides had been mangled and I could feel a surge of panic start to rise from the pit of my mutilated belly. This felt completely different to having Emma. Then Samuel refused to latch on and wouldn't feed so the midwives suggested we put him onto formula. So then of course the feelings of hopelessness and inadequacy started to surge and threatened to overwhelm me. Samuel wouldn't sleep, had terrible colic, and just cried constantly. His cry was a sore, terrible wail that made me want to run away. Those horrible feelings, of never wanting to come back, washed over me like a tidal wave. I wanted to put my hand over his mouth to quieten him and that is when I realised that it was time to talk to the GP and ask for some help.

And Joan? Well, fortunately Elliot wasn't too shocked when we worked out what was wrong with her. I was so absorbed in my own problems that it took me a while to pick up on all the warning signs when we were in London. I mean — when I think about it they were all there. Her confusion, her forgetfulness, her strange behaviour. Every case is unique and there is no linear progression in terms of what happens next. I do sometimes wonder what she was going to tell me that day in the park when she started talking about Elliot's father. Was it something bad? She never mentioned it again. I wonder if she will in time. Apparently, it's not unusual for dementia patients to make false accusations against others. Isn't it strange how memories and secrets can pop up at any time? Even when you think it's all safely buried in the past. I feel for Elliot watching his mum deteriorate. He now knows not to challenge her mum when she starts to ramble incoherently. He has since learned it is part of the condition and he has to be patient and go with it. These are just yet more fractured fairytales in our lives.

I have been trying to write in my diary and get my innermost private thoughts onto paper for the future. I want to have a record of what has happened now in case I need it again later. I wonder if that would help me to try and contextualise my feelings around Samuel's traumatic birth. It's always helped in the past but since his arrival I just can't write. Not like I used to. Of course nobody was supposed to read my diary entries at the time. It was just a place for me to write down my feelings and thoughts. Little did I know what a wise thing I was doing. I'm so glad I took them with me to London. That was a stroke of good luck. It made everything else a bit easier. We are still waiting for official confirmation but it looks like the CPS will proceed with a case against him now I am no longer the only victim.

TWO YEARS LATER

Shamed politician James MacIntyre arrived today at the Old Bailey for sentencing. The former Labour M.P. was found guilty of three counts of indecent assault against a teenager during a two-year period from 1995 to 1997 and a sexual assault against a woman in 1997 and three women in 1998. He smirked at the cameras as he said: 'I stand by everything that I have previously said. These women are fantasists. They are making it all up.' He wouldn't make any further comment and refused to apologise to his victims.

It doesn't matter how many times I read it, or watch the TV footage of him speaking outside the court. I don't feel any better. I only feel guilt. I'm not blameless in all of this mess.

If Mum was alive, I wonder what she would make of it all. Now, when I think of her I remember her funeral. Because at this moment it's the only happy memory I have. There was something quite peaceful about it. I can remember the soft green slopes, flanked by a road, stretching beyond the modern built crematorium in a part of Glasgow I'd never been to before. There was a tired waiting room with a sofa and toilets that didn't flush. I remember the hugs from nameless faces, the slightly musty smelling suits mixed with cloying perfumes and aftershaves. The cool, hard pews. The flow of lines on the wooden floor. The white flowers on top of the dark mahogany coffin with brass handles. Shiny brass handles. And watching the coffin as it squeakily rolled behind the thick velvet curtains. It felt almost liberating to know she was finally at peace. I still think of finding my own peace.

And so, it is now time for me to speak to someone about everything that happened. Today, finally, I *am* going to see a counsellor. No more lying to Elliot, who thinks I've been seeing her for some time. But in order to move forward with my life I need to off-load and speak to someone who won't judge or blame me.

As Joan and I can both testify, memories are such delicate things. Time can distort perceptions, details fade or are interspersed or replaced with others. Rewriting the past is not so hard to do. Interpretations vary. Mum always said I had a vivid imagination. Maybe she was right. Does anyone *really* know who I am?

I sit comfortably in my chair and look at my counsellor.

'What would you like to talk about today, Sophie?' she says, giving me an encouraging smile.

And so, I begin. I explain that Julie and I had different fathers. It was just another detail that Mum decided to tell me on her death bed. She told me that she and James had been having an affair and she fell pregnant with Julie. Mum having an affair was shocking enough. In fact, it was the very final straw for my dad, who was exposed and vulnerable. Her infidelity tipped him over the edge and drove him to drink. That's what made him leave. That's why he never mentioned Julie when he saw me that day. He *knew* he only had one daughter.

Mum said she couldn't cope with his mood swings and his weeks of depression. She said she knew she was weak but she had fallen for James's charm. I could understand that, as I'd seen women fall at his feet throughout my life. Mum said it was easier to pretend Julie was my real dad's daughter too. It was less embarrassing and scandalous for James. He didn't want people to think he'd had an affair with a married woman. Typical. Knowing the truth, well, it explains a lot, doesn't it? If truth be told I did always wonder if we were really sisters. I mean, we looked nothing alike. She was beautiful and bright. I was awkward and ugly. But she was still my sister and we had a bond.

And so, it seems a good time to come back to the beginning of my story and tell you more about the day I confronted MacIntyre at Westminster. The thing is that I didn't want to disclose everything that happened that day that I went to see him. I didn't want to be judged or have my version of events doubted, as I know what it is like never to be believed.

The last thing he said to me when I saw him that day, just before I left his office and saw Joy ordering her groceries, took me by surprise.

'I know the truth, Sophie. I *know* about you and Julie.'

His candour stopped me briefly in my tracks but, with a determination I didn't know I had, I swung back to face him. Standing there I could feel the sweat pooling at the base of my spine. I was about to talk but then he put a finger to his lips, something he used to do after he'd been in my room. I needed to get out of there because I could see images I didn't want to and hear voices screaming in my head.

He shook his head, leant closer and he whispered, 'I know what you did.'

Or did he? That's where things all get a bit hazy in my mind and I get slightly confused. I *should* have asked him to repeat what he'd just said. I *could* have challenged him on what I *thought* he said. But I was gripped by fear and panic once again. That's when I left his office and ran and never looked back. Until now.

You see, I thought I had saved my sister. Who else would have looked after her and kept her from her disgusting ways? It's true. That day on the lake I had to make a decision. And when *he* made a comment about how lovely she looked in her new bathing suit, I knew that it was time. I needed to save her from him.

She was struggling to hold onto me, her eyes wild and her face chalky in the water. But she was dragging me down with her, and I knew it was the kindest thing to do. I clawed off her fingers which gripped the knots of my hair and desperately pulled away from her. My scalp was burning as she held on, violently clutching at my hair to stay afloat. I shrugged her off, pushing her away and then dived underneath to get away from her. My eyes were stinging as I opened them and watched her sink. Down, down through the icy water she fell. Her hair blooming out around her, her skin so very pale, almost tinged blue, then her body falling limp. That was how much I loved my little sister. It was the kindest thing I could have done for her. Letting her go in the water meant I was freeing her from what was waiting ahead. I just wanted her to be safe and away from James. That's why I unclasped her grip from my hair and let her float away. Perhaps James saw what I did. I'll never know.

Sometimes in my less lucid moments I did wonder if I imagined it all. I fantasised that I was an only child and there was never a Julie other than the imaginary friend in my head. I didn't really think about the effect it would have on Mum. I was thinking so much about Julie and making sure she was safe. But I think it was the final straw for Mum — and for that I feel bad.

That is why I decided I would help her find peace, too, and reunite her with Dad and Julie. Her death was a blessing too, and so much less harrowing than Julie's. At least she didn't struggle. Maybe that's because she was ready to go. Mum's death didn't give me nightmares. She slipped easily over to the other side and didn't fight me in the same way that Julie had.

It was so different though with Julie's death. I've tried to rationalize it, over the years. When I realised it was Matthew who she'd been sleeping with, I wanted to die. I'd got it so wrong. So I tried to justify what I'd done. There was no guarantee that James wouldn't have touched her. I was just trying to keep her safe.

I had one of my chats earlier with Julie about this. I said that I hope by talking about all of this, it will help me make sense of things. And I hope that one day we can become close again. I know we will be together again one day. I miss her so much. I loved Julie as much as anyone could love their little sister. Except I would say that I loved her even more.

You could say that Sophie MacIntyre was the girl I left behind and that Sophie Lewis is who I have become. But for me it has always been about Julie. She's the significant piece in all of this. *She* was the girl I left behind. Julie was my sister and I loved her to death. Does that make me bad?

AUTHOR'S NOTE

Thank you for choosing to read *The Girl I Left Behind.*

I wrote this book in 2014 and since then, on its long journey to publication, it has grown and developed in ways I didn't expect.

Over the years I have worked closely with survivors of abuse and those affected by gender violence and the decisions I have made in writing this fictional book sadly reflect reality. As a writer, raising awareness of abuse is something that I will always strive to do. The importance of sharing stories, no matter how difficult they are, is something that will always be at the heart of my work.

If you enjoyed this book, I'd be grateful if you would write a review. If you want to keep up to date with my books news, just sign up at www.lornaehill.co.uk. Your email address will never be shared and you can unsubscribe at any time.

ACKNOWLEDGMENTS

This book wouldn't have been possible without the encouragement and support of many people.

Thanks to Eleonor, Fiona, Elaine, Lynne and Laura for reading it in advance. Thanks to Heather and her lovely reading group: Siobhan, Kate, Morven, Suzy and Fiona and to Andrew, Karen, Mark, Jeanette, Tricia, Alex, Zoë, Laura, Euan, Lindsey, Neill, Sue, Sandra, Lorna, Frankie, Karen, Senga, Claudia, Grace, Alasdair, Dougie, Mum and Eleanor for cover advice and feedback.

Thanks to Emmet MacIntyre for designing an amazing cover; to Brenda Copeland for general advice and encouragement; and to Janine Mitchell for her website help and encouragement; Miriam Owen, Frances Sessford, Claire Squires and Tricia Golledge who I was lucky enough to meet during the research years.

I have been fortunate to learn from some amazing writers over the years who have been generous with their time and encouragement and would like to say a huge thanks to them. They include Liam Bell, Lin Anderson, Elizabeth Haynes, Louise Voss, Kate Harrison, Hanif Kureishi, Elif Shafak, Val McDermid, Andrea Stuart, Kati Hiekkapelto, Ann Cleeves, Louise Welsh, Alison Belsham, Alexandra Sokoloff, Magi Gibson, Alexander Masters, Denise Mina, Heleen Kist and Gwyn GB.

I'm also indebted to the agents and publishers who have given me feedback over the years. Their advice has undoubtedly made this a better book.

Thanks to my family for support, patience and encouragement during what has been a bit of a roller-coaster. Alasdair, thanks for encouraging me to keep going. And to Dougie - I couldn't have done this without your unwavering enthusiasm. This is for you.

ABOUT THE AUTHOR

LE Hill is a writer, researcher and creative writing facilitator. Her background is in journalism and communications and she now runs a small social enterprise, Sharing A Story CIC. When she's not reading or writing books, she likes walking, strong coffee and eating cake - in no particular order.

Twitter: @lornaehill

Facebook: @lehillbooks

Website: www.lornaehill.co.uk

COMING SOON . . .

Don't miss *The Invisible Chains*, the next novel from LE Hill.

When the body of a young Nigerian girl is pulled from the River Clyde in Glasgow, journalist Megan Ross is certain there is more to the girl's death than meets the eye.

Then when she is tipped off about another body in the city's Botanics, her investigations into the two murders leads her to uncover an international trafficking ring. But in the race to report it she starts to fight for her own life and reputation. Who is trying to conceal the story and why?

Printed in Great Britain
by Amazon

44241774R00213